THE SHADY ELDERS OF ZION

BOB GILBERT

CALUMET EDITIONS
Minneapolis

CALUMET EDITIONS

Minneapolis

SECOND EDITION December 2022
THE SHADY ELDERS OF ZION Copyright © 2016 by
BOB GILBERT. All rights reserved.

This is a work of fiction. Names, characters, places and incidents either are the product of the author's imagination or are used fictitiously. Any resemblance to actual persons living or dead, events, or locales are entirely coincidental.

Cover and interior design by Gary Lindberg

10 9 8 7 6 5 4 3 2

ISBN: 978-1-960250-16-2

For Leslie

Also by Bob Gilbert

Mintwood Place

ACKNOWLEDGEMENTS

I began writing *The Shady Elders of Zion* in 1996. In the twenty years since, it has evolved the way I have evolved as a man. What began as a macrocosmic, polemical rage against anti-Semitism has softened into a comedy filled with insights into the human and spiritual condition. The narrative emerged with the help of many individuals and many books. Homer's *Iliad* and *Odyssey*, channeled books from the Kryon series, and the many translations of the I Ching honed my understanding of how the spirit and mortal worlds interact. Susan Anderson, Susan Douglas, and Alicia Gordon were psychic mediums who opened me up to my own spiritual possibilities. Men like Ian Graham Leask, Bruce Ackerman and the late Thomas Angelo Dougherty taught me volumes about manhood. Best of all was Leslie Sue Bonk, who shared her Jewish values and her family, many of whom were Holocaust survivors, and deepened my understanding of my own Hebraic roots. Here, in final form, it's become a story about relationships and forbearance. It's also a Valentine to my Jewish brethren.

THE SHADY ELDERS OF ZION

BOB GILBERT

CHAPTER ONE

It's a great day to be dead. On this March afternoon in Hibbing, Minnesota, the air is cold, a mere nineteen degrees beneath a bright blue sky. The wind blows strong. But here inside, it is warm.

I'm at a funeral home for this great wake. And it's all for me. The people I knew on this frozen prairie, the iron men and women of the Mesabi Range have turned out en masse to celebrate my life, and the mood is joyous. If you didn't know better you'd mistake me for an Irishman.

The corpse, all stark and somber and stretched out straight, is me. For a guy who lived past his hundredth birthday I look pretty good. An Italian homosexual designed that three-piece sharkskin suit I'm wearing. I hesitate to sound bourgeois, but I keep waiting for someone to recognize it from the pages of *Gentleman's Quarterly*. It's double-breasted, the way I liked my women. On my feet, wing tip shoes, the key to success. Of course, the tie is red. The white shirt is well starched. Not exactly my choice, and thank God I'm not alive to feel it around my neck, because by now I'd have broken out in a rash.

My white hair has been cut short. The makeup and rouge that covers my face was applied with great discretion. They even gave me a manicure for the occasion, not to mention a little clip job for my nose hairs and those annoying wiry ones inside my ears that sprang out like spider legs.

As a stiff I cut a pretty good figure. Strong Semitic nose, delicate ears, a chin that could always take a punch, blue eyes, and you'd never know it now but I once had hair as black as a Gypsy. With the ladies I was quite the rake, yet a man's man to the core. Competent with both genders… that to me is the consummate individual.

Of course, my body broke down over the years in a woeful progression of stages, and so I am now gleeful to be a spirit free from the laws of physics and no longer a mortal tied to that ancient container of flesh and bones.

It's not easy growing old. Without a hearing aid I was deaf… without eye drops my cataracts ached, and my teeth… oy vay— three root canals in the past five years. The ability to take a solid crap constituted a good day. But all that is now in the past.

Check out the casket. It's mahogany with a red velvet interior. Not bad, huh? The United Brotherhood of Steelworkers paid for it. The casket handles they'll carry me to my grave with are made from real brass and, from my vantage point, glint the same color as the buttons on my jacket.

The party's tone is correct—somber enough to honor my widow but festive nonetheless. After all, we get lonesome up here on the Iron Range in winter. People haven't been out and about for several months and any excuse for a get-together is welcomed. The man who said 'no good comes from a corpse' was mistaken.

It's an impressive turnout that exceeds my expectation. Not to sound smug mind you, but I deserve all this. Old men have a moral obligation to accept such tribute from younger men. So if I gloat, please don't think poorly of me.

Men are at their best when bragging. I've seen ninety-eight-pound weaklings transformed into Homeric heroes while reciting some daring-do they say they actually did. Even if it's only brag, who cares? A good story is better than the truth and, let's be honest, nobody brags better than a Jew.

My comrades contributed much of the food and it's quite a spread. The buffet table must be thirty feet long. Fine meats like Fraboni sausage, made right here on the Iron Range, and porketta—easy on the fennel, the way I like it—is plentiful. There's roast beef and turkey and three roasted pheasants that my wife's nephew Ollie Koskinnen shot last fall. Hearty bread and pastry recipes from old Europe make for one fine feast, all of which is laid out upon white doilies that look like snowflakes.

The pickled vegetables were canned by red-haired Rosie Meyerhoff. In her early years, Rosie was a charity girl to local iron miners but later became treasurer of the American Communist Party. The red veggies came from her garden and have spent the past two years in Mason jars in her basement. The tomatoes, peppers, radishes, and beets add great color to the display.

Up here on the Iron Range we drink like fish—mostly Canadian whiskey and American beer. There's plenty of both. But in my honor there is also vodka. For the kids, there's Pepsi Cola.

An old newspaper photo of me is taped to the door. Nobody can enter this chapel without noticing it. It's from a *Mesabi Daily News* someone found down at the union hall. They took it to Kinko's and had it enlarged and then mounted. It's a flattering portrait of me, standing at a podium, addressing a throng of steelworkers during the great strike of 1968, which I engineered so brilliantly as head of the strike committee. The headline reads: "Vukovich Fires Up Striking Steelworkers."

Leaning forward with all the choreography of Lenin, hand in a fist, face contorted with anger, I harangued the crowd from a makeshift podium surrounded by my favorite goon squad. You can see from my breath it was a cold afternoon. If you didn't know better, you'd think I was breathing fire. I rumbled, I railed, giving that crowd passion like they had never seen before, and just when they were about to bow down to those capitalist dogs of the Hanna Mining Company, I put lead in their pencil with that speech... I can tell you that. The old timers still speak of it. Offered my preference, it's exactly how I want to be remembered—a firebrand.

I look back on those glory days of class struggle proudly. Contract negotiations with management were pitched. True, I was only holding out for an extra two cents an hour. But jerking the chain of those hen-pecked Babbits was the closest thing to revolution I'd enjoyed since leaving Mother Russia. Plus, I wasn't getting laid that year, and delaying the settlement was like putting off an orgasm when you're inside a woman and you just want that excitement to last a little longer.

I've had my share of kibitzing this afternoon. The phrase 'oh to be a fly on the wall' has a deeper meaning now. I'm invisible and buzz around unafraid of sticky yellow ribbon, fly swatters, or insecticide.

I've looked down ladies' dresses. I've looked up ladies' dresses. Unfortunately, peeping at tits and ass is about the most harm I can do. After all... I'm dead.

I've divided my time between Rosie's pickled beets on the buffet where the old folks are gathered and the back door where the young people are smoking cigarettes. I still love the smell of tobacco smoke and even in death can catch a buzz. Hmmm, nicotine... I love it.

Eavesdropping on conversation has proved interesting and I am privy to many new secrets. For instance, Mae Dahl's daughter took a trip to Minneapolis, not for a job interview but for an abortion. Should the mother ever find out there would be hell to pay. Mrs. Albert Jenson is making sexual advances to Mrs. Dorothy Bidwell while their husbands discuss Vikings football. Duane Simonson is selling nickel bags of marijuana in the bathroom. Little Susie Perich is in love with Peter Popovich but is afraid to announce her feelings because one is a Croat and the other a Serb, and the two families still hold a grudge against each other from the old country.

But, by far, my favorite thing is to sit on my casket and watch people as they come forward to pay their last respects. Little Sammy Nord, still in kindergarten, slipped a cherry lollipop up my sleeve as a bribe that I might say hello to his grandfather, Dick, who died last October.

"Sammy, no problem, I'll even tell him you're no longer wetting your bed."

Mary Graziano came up to the casket, said a few kind words, winked at my dead face and actually touched my groin. She was surprised to find me hard. Honey, the whole body is hard. What do you expect from rigor mortis? That was the most beautiful tribute of the day. No one saw her do this of course, except maybe her husband, Buster.

Buster took some black pepper from a shaker and sprinkled it in his palm. When it was his turn at the casket he put the pepper to his nose, inhaled deeply, and sneezed all over my suit. He whispered, "Fuck you, Vukovich, you little prick. Were you alive now I'd a smack that smile right off your face."

Okay, I can look past that. He's never forgiven me for screwing his wife. It was the annual May Day picnic, we were drunk, and those things happen. Were it not for the mosquito bites on her tushie he'd never have found out. God, I miss the sixties. But when she got pregnant, nine months of anguish ensued. Fortunately, the child had Graziano's ears and not my nose, and it was apparent the first day—a blessing for the family.

But Buster has a point. In truth, I am a little disappointed with the way the mortician, Tim O'Shea, shaped my mouth. It suggests a serenity I never knew in life. And if Buster noticed, the others probably noticed as well, even though they're too polite to mention it.

Now, Tim O'Shea was a good friend to me in this life, and I trusted him so much that he is also the executor of my will. O'Shea, the middle class mortician with the blonde wife, the big boat, the twelve kids, and the thirty-one grandchildren. O'Shea, the affable Irishman who never met a man he didn't like, the devout Catholic who never knew alienation, a man who had prepared thousands of old, beaten, and battered bodies for the grave.

I was staring over his shoulder in the embalming room, which is in the basement of his funeral home. With such panache did he cut into my arteries to suck the blood out of my body. It's a hell of a way to make a living, I'll tell you that. But this O'Shea is quite the artist. The man can cut hair and apply makeup as well as anybody in Hollywood.

I was watching when he smeared Krazy Glue in a long swath across my bottom lip and carelessly pushed my jaw up with his thumb. He was in a hurry. His wife Mona hates it when he's late for dinner. So there it was, that fucking smile! Goddamn it. I want to look like that fire-breathing dragon in the old newspaper photo hanging on the door. That's who I really was... an angry, Jewish rabble-rouser. Now the last glance people have of me is looking like a dandy.

I wanted to tell O'Shea that the smile he glued on my face really stunk, so I marched up to the chapel door. I found him standing there with a red carnation in the lapel of his crisp blue suit. It's kind of his trademark, this flower in his lapel. Usually it's white, but for me, today, he chose red. He stole it from one of my bouquets. He too is an old man and recently gave his mortuary business to his youngest son, Tim Jr. However, for old timers like me, he comes out of retirement to prepare old friends for the grave.

"O'Shea, it's a good thing that I like you or I'd get you for that silly smile," I shouted, my index finger wagging in his face. "And don't think I don't keep score either. I'm willing to look past that goofy smile, which my body will wear until it rots away in its casket, and that other insult as well—the satisfaction you took shoving a cork up my ass so I didn't foul my good suit during this wake. I've known you for forty years, even liked you, you Philistine, but don't ever make light at my expense again or you'll get it in the neck."

O'Shea couldn't hear any of my rant, but nonetheless I felt a little better.

And why shouldn't I feel better? At least I don't have to be Joseph Vukovich anymore. That wasn't my real name. Of course, if I do say so myself, I performed my role as Joseph Vukovich with aplomb. Yes, aplomb I tell you, aplomb.

Poise, self-assurance, confidence... yes, that was me. Okay, so not all at once. You try playing the role of a second-stringer for half a lifetime while waiting for the revolution. My God, I tell you, no agent provocateur ever did it better. But now it's over. You see, Vukovich was one of my assumed names. With that alias I led a secret life here in Minnesota.

My own passage through the twentieth century was no picnic. During my boyhood, in a dreary Ukrainian village near Kiev, before I repudiated my family, my name was Gerson Broverman. I grew up in a girl house—Jewish mother and three sisters. My father was murdered in a pogrom following the Russo-Japanese War. I was later adopted by a rabbi named Moses Yedwab, who married my widowed mother.

But a passion for adventure ran through my veins and propelled me beyond the narrow confines of my little shtetl. I was inspired by stories of my mother's first cousin, a political radical named Lev Davidovich Bronstein who changed his name to Leon Trotsky and went on to lead the Bolshevik Revolution. I ran away from home at the age of fourteen, pledged my life to the Communist Party, steeped myself in the dogma of Karl Marx, and changed my name to Ivan Kalinsky.

I worked as Trotsky's personal secretary for ten years. My reputation was that of a man who could make problems disappear. I was at Trotsky's side when he negotiated power with Lenin after we brought down the Czar. I was Trotsky's captain when, as Commissar of the Red Army, he defeated an international army of counter-revolutionaries and saved the Bolshevik Revolution in 1919. I marched in step with the dictatorship of the proletariat and socialized with great men like Gorky, Zinoviev, Kamenev, Kirov, and Stalin.

As a Soviet cultural attaché, I accompanied Ambassador Maxim Litvinov to Washington, DC, attended state dinners with President Franklin Delano Roosevelt, and ran a spy operation out of the Russian embassy during the 1930s.

Following the assassination of Trotsky in Mexico in 1936, I was recalled to Moscow for a special briefing. I knew it was a trap. Stalin was kissing Hitler's ass and purging the entire

Communist Party of Jews in those days. The writing was on the wall—a bullet awaited me. So I secretly hopped a flight from Washington, DC to Minnesota and went into hiding.

I accepted the protection of Gus Hall, head of the American Communist Party, whom I had worked closely with in Washington. He was from Cherry, Minnesota, and I was brought here to the Iron Range under his aegis. Only a small coterie of dedicated party members knew my real identity, and in those days we ruled northern Minnesota.

I settled into this small community so quietly that people didn't notice. They had no idea they were harboring a famous fugitive. When two Stalinist agents pursued me, Gus visited their room at the Kahler Hotel in downtown Hibbing with a few hired hands, beat the hell out of them, escorted them to the Hibbing Airport, put them on a plane, and told them never to come back. I didn't know it then but I was safe. Unfortunately, within the next five years, Stalin extirpated the Yiddish flower of Communist revolution.

I spent most of my life here in obscurity, more afraid of Communist assassins than the FBI. It was Gus Hall who changed my name from Kalinsky to Joseph Vukovich because the man had just died. Gus gave me his driver's license. It allowed me to drive, open a bank account, and join the union.

I worked as a janitor in the Hibbing library. Overnight, I went from a big shot to a nobody. My fall from grace caused great anguish, not to mention the culture shock of living here in this American Siberia. I nearly drank myself to death.

But you might say, Kalinsky, at least you were alive. But I am going to tell you the truth—life without revolution is no life at all, especially so far away from everything I loved. During those years, my list of complaints about life in Minnesota could have filled the Torah.

While World War Two raged for control of the collective European soul and my former brothers in the Red Army were toe-to-toe against the Fascist Wehrmacht, I sat it out in a quiet Minnesota backwater, a man battle-ready with the scars and kills to prove it. But I could not contribute to the cause. Me, the great Kalinsky, Bolshevik Jew, one of the founding fathers of the Communist movement, was now persona non grata, alone, unwanted, and anonymous.

So I drank some more and cursed my fate. I took to the notion that if I only hated myself sufficiently then God might be appeased. Yes, I know what you must be thinking: *Kalinsky, you're a Communist and Communists don't believe in God*. But no, I did believe in God, despite the anti-Semitism, the war, and the heartache He let happen. It was religion I hated, that ridiculous opiate of the masses. God held a special place for me. I wasn't about to let that bastard hate me more than I hated myself.

It was my idea that incredible self-loathing would relieve Him of the obligation to thwart my intentions; that seeing me suffer, He might be satisfied, take pity on me, and end this damned isolation. So I hated myself mightily. But nothing in my life changed. Over time I learned something very important—a man should hate himself less and hate God more.

Slowly, I made a life here. I went from janitor to union organizer for the steelworker's union. That's how I met my wife, Hilda Rukavina. Hilda worked down at the union hall. She didn't have much money, education, or culture. But she had a great set of knockers that entered a room one full second before the rest of her torso.

Hilda liked to garden, watch soap operas, and hang out at the hair salon. Unfortunately, she was unable to conceive children. But she was a dutiful wife.

Of course, as a man of the world, I dallied. It's like they say, a man is only as faithful as his options. So it is with great sadness that I confess the one person not in attendance today is my mistress of long standing, Greta Niemi.

Greta was a sexpot who loved me in ways that went beyond Hilda's ability, though I never held it against my wife. Hilda was what she was, and Greta was what she was. I felt fortunate to know them both.

This wake does not seem complete without Greta. How I would have loved to have seen her here. But how could she ever show her face in a room filled with those holding sympathy for Hilda?

Wait. O'Shea was just joined at the front door by Father Terrence Goodlad, the Vatican's man in Hibbing at Our Lady of Perpetual Sorrow. The Catholic parish is right next door to O'Shea's Funeral Home. Goodlad and O'Shea do business. The Ultramontane recommends all local Catholics to O'Shea's Funeral Home, and in return O'Shea buries the nuns for free. Look at them standing at the door. Without me, O'Shea and Goodlad are now the town's leading patriarchs.

Goodlad, Dublin born, now in his late sixties, is a former boxing champion who decided to dedicate his life to fighting for Jesus Christ.

How the Catholics appropriated one of our own rabbis, hailed him as God, and made his death a Jewish crime is for me one of the great lies of history. But I'll talk more about that later.

Goodlad is about to share a joke with his pal O'Shea. Don't ask me how I know; I just do. Those two Irishmen love to swap stories and, even though a good belly laugh is beyond me now, I put myself beside them to listen. It's always easy to tell when Goodlad is about to recite something risqué. He lowers his voice and nervously twirls the end of his long mustache. At the same time, he covers his mouth with the same hand lest any of his parishioners hear his words and find out he has a shadowy side.

"Tim, have you heard the story about the Jewish burglar?" asks Goodlad, with his hoarse voice.

"No," says O'Shea, and he licks his lips in anticipation of the story. "Let's have it."

Oh no, not that Jew joke again. I've already heard him tell it once before. Perhaps if he knew the corpse had a Jewish soul he wouldn't tell it at this wake. Or maybe deep down he suspected I was Jewish and that is precisely *why* he tells it. Here it comes again.

"It seems that there was this Jewish burglar who broke into an empty house one night while everybody was away," began the priest. "As he walked through the rooms with a flashlight, he heard a voice call, 'Jesus is coming. Jesus is coming.' Now the burglar, let's call him Lewinsky, was a bit frightened because he thought the house was empty. But he walked on through the dark house until he came to a birdcage and aimed the light right into a parrot's eyes. He stands before the bird and it repeats its cry, 'Jesus is coming. Jesus is coming.'

"'Who the hell are you?' asks the Jew.

"'My name is Elijah,' replies the parrot.

"'What kind of idiot names his parrot Elijah?'

"The bird cocks his head a bit to the right and says, 'the same idiot who names his German shepherd Jesus.'"

The two men burst into laughter. Several in the crowd see them yukking it up and feel uncomfortable because they fear Goodlad might be laughing about something they shared with him at confession.

Truth is, I never liked Goodlad. But I was obliged to be polite. That's because I was married to Hilda Rukavina, and for the past twenty-five years she, as a devout mackerel snapper, a nickname we had for her Catholic brethren because of their Friday meals, worshipped the ground Goodlad walked on.

"Hey, Goodlad. Here's one for you," I called. "Do you know what the first recorded case of PMS was? It was the day Mary rode Joseph's ass from Nazareth all the way to Bethlehem."

He doesn't hear it on account of me being dead.

Here's something. A brown-shirted man from the United Parcel Service just entered the chapel. With his close-cropped blonde hair and a big toothy smile, he could have passed for a Hitler poster child. When O'Shea signed for the package, the teamster walked back to his brown truck and carried a heavy flat box into the chapel. His neck bulged from its weight and he seemed on the verge of a hernia. However, his red face went nicely with his brown uniform. Tim had him lay the parcel against the wall near the coffin. It was the headstone I had ordered.

How fitting—the monument honoring my life, arriving just in time. For the occasion, Goodlad, standing beside the casket, offered a little eulogy about my civic virtue and my dedication to the people of this community. Oy, talk about being damned with faint praise.

Following the speech, right in the middle of my party, Hilda decides that she wants to unveil the headstone for the admiration of the crowd. So she gets on her knees and begins pulling off the paper as if it were a Christmas present. A crowd of men and women gather around her in curiosity.

The top of the granite stone is the first thing they see. How the crowd oooed and aaahed. "Nice color," they said. Then the name, Joseph Vukovich, cut deeply into the stone in large block letters, becomes apparent to all eyes as Hilda tears the brown wrapping from the top. "Yes, that's him," they all say, nodding their heads in affirmation. The dates of my birth and death come next as Hilda unravels the paper top to bottom. There is murmuring that for a guy way past his hundredth birthday I looked and acted much younger.

As she pulls the paper lower, in smaller letters it reads "Beloved Husband." That really gets the crowd. Sniffles come from the women folk. Finally, Hilda pulls the paper off the bottom and there it is—the hammer and sickle.

It was a big hammer and sickle too, nicely done, engraved in a size even larger than my name. Yes, the great symbol of strength and egalitarian virtue of the twentieth century was featured on my grave marker.

Hilda's gasp was heard across the room. A few men applauded loudly but were quickly censored by their wives. When Hilda looked up and saw Father Goodlad staring disapprovingly into her eyes, surrounded by the parishioners from Our Lady of Perpetual Sorrow, she fainted.

My bereaved widow awoke a few seconds later in the arms of the priest, surrounded by a throng of concerned friends and family. She pointed her finger to the gravestone and started sobbing.

Okay, so I should have discussed the tombstone before I ordered it. After all, she will, one day, have to lie beside it. But I didn't feel like compromising.

Now, I am not the first man on the Iron Range to have the hammer and sickle, the symbol of revolution, on his tombstone. Thousands just like mine grace the graveyards of Saint Louis County, Minnesota. But with the fall of Russian communism and capitalist economies pumping so much money into their propaganda machines, the symbol embarrassed my old girl. Truth is, it shouldn't have. The only reason half the steel workers in northern Minnesota are working these days is because the demand for steel is soaring. And why is that, you might ask? Communist China.

Hilda, still sobbing, unable to express her mortification, set off Maureen O'Shaunessy Rukavina, Hilda's meddling sister-in-law. A dazed look came over Maureen's face, which featured eyes wide open and a blank stare. She stood straighter than I've ever seen before. For a split second, her brown eyes actually turned blue. From around her neck, Maureen removed a pewter crucifix on a silver chain that featured the great Christian savior hanging upon it like a miserable lug. She gave it to Hilda. In a voice that sounded like a zombie's, she said, "Hilda, darling, here, take this cross. Put it in your husband's hands."

My wife rose to her feet. She walked to the casket, kissed my cheek, and before a hundred pairs of eyes, in an expression of reverence before God, put the crucifix standing vertically between my thumbs, which were folded neatly on my chest. She then retreated with her head bowed. This time the women applauded.

"What the fuck!" I shouted. "You silly cow—you ruined my party! Hilda my wife, the bane of my life, peer pressure has always been your weakness. Now you've succumbed and this manly farewell of mine has been spoiled. You put a cross in my hands? Are you nuts?"

All right, so I never told Hilda I was a Jew. It never came up, and she wasn't the kind of wife who asked questions.

Verklempt. I think that word hits the nail on the head. I was verklempt and so distracted that later when red-haired Rosie Meyerhoff, now drunk, grabbed her shirttails and started flashing her breasts to the menfolk just like she did in the old days, I didn't even laugh. I always used to laugh. Nor was there any joy in the tall tales the old men told the young bucks regarding my verve.

So now what am I to do? Throw a temper tantrum? Turn off the Lawrence Welk CD? Hit the circuit breaker and kill the lights? Knock over the flowers? Blow out the candles? Overturn the buffet table and soil the carpet because of my humiliation?

And to think that up until a few minutes ago, I was having a great time.

"Father," said Hilda, "he's never been baptized, and we neglected to give him last rights at the nursing home."

So Goodlad sent one of his altar boys next door to get the holy water and his Bible. Were it not for O'Shea, my executor, complaining that it was not in my will to be baptized and that the holy water might do damage to the makeup he so discreetly applied, I might have gone to the grave as a baptized Catholic.

Walking to the chapel door, I stared at that newspaper photo just to recall what a mean son of a bitch I could be. There had to be some reason for this insult, some trickster, some villain behind all of this. Everything is on purpose, but for what purpose this happened was way beyond me.

As a dead man I now speak the polyglot of spirits. I raised my fists to the heavens and screamed out in fury to whomever was listening, "Fix this, you fuckers!"

It was no impotent rage. I knew exactly to whom I was shouting—the cadres of Communist brethren waiting for me to arrive in heaven. And they knew exactly who was shouting at them because I heard the echo of a small voice with a Yiddish accent say, "Give us just a minute."

I've shot men for less than this. But just this once I was willing to give them the benefit of the doubt. Yet I was seething just the same as I waited for an explanation. I stomped around the funeral home, angry to the point of distraction. Now I'm feeling like a big schlemiel. I don't like it. So I sat there glum among the drunken merriment of my wake.

Have I become a great fool in death? Has my epic journey been reduced to farce? Is my drama now burlesque? Will my long sojourn in the land of lutefisk eaters end in humiliation?

Nobody changes genres on me and gets away with it!

It took a few minutes for words to come back from the great beyond. But the very sound of what was said sent chills down my spine. I was so crestfallen that I almost wished I had curbed my histrionics. I didn't want to hear what I heard.

And what were those words? "Joshua Bronstein."

Joshua Bronstein? No, not him. Say anything, but please just don't say Joshua Bronstein. To suggest that the only man alive with enough chutzpah to pull that cross from my claw is Joshua Bronstein is enough to make a dead man cry.

Who knows from this Joshua Bronstein? That young man is probably dead drunk running around with that Ojibway rock and roll singer of his.

The understanding that only Bronstein could save me from being buried as a Christian impersonator must be someone's idea of a joke. That my legacy on earth should rely on that pathetic ex-Bar Mitzvah boy is ridiculous.

That Bronstein, I'll tell you... I always felt sorry for him. He too was in exile here in Minnesota. Lacking the aegis of the Communist Manifesto, he had nothing with which to battle middle class anxiety. So he drank. And he drank more than I ever did. Of course, I admit that at one time I did have affection for the young man. After all, though he was no relation to my beloved Trotsky—he was a Bronstein.

But now what do I do? Wait for Bronstein to walk through O'Shea's big oak door into this sanctuary with his Jewish kit? He showed it to me once—the blue, velvet bag which contains his black satin yarmulke, his white prayer shawl with the gold fringes, and his old Hebrew Union prayer book that was given to him when he was thirteen.

What I wouldn't give to have him standing over me with his skullcap and shawl—to see him open his book to the appropriate page and read the ancient Hebrew words of the Kaddish, the Jewish prayer for the dead, while rocking back and forth like some Hasid at the Wailing Wall. And then, if he removed that cross, how fabulous that would be.

But only a fool waits for such redemption. After all, I am dead and Bronstein is a derelict. Not only that, he is also O'Shea's disgraced ex-son-in-law and wouldn't be caught dead here.

I will not go gently into that good night. I'll rage like a winter storm straight out of Alberta before I take this insult. I am prepared to hover over this body until my grievances are redressed. I'll stand the fires of hell, but not this insult.

Life doesn't get any easier after you die. You mortals should know that.

CHAPTER TWO

Touch that cross? I ain't touching that cross. No sir, not me. I don't care that it's sticking so deeply between my fingers that it's chafing the sternum of my corpse. These ghostly hands won't touch that cross. No, not even if my fingers were still flesh, blood, and bones and covered with Playtex Living Gloves, I still won't touch that cross.

Oh yes, I know it sounds cowardly, so very un-Bolshevik. I can imagine what my detractors might say. Are you afraid of grasping the Catholic icon of the masses, Kalinsky? Retreating to some bourgeois ivory tower far from the Lutheran symbols of the proletariat, Kalinsky? Afraid to wet your hands with something so Baptist, Kalinsky? Say what you will. I don't care. I ain't touching that cross.

What if that cross is bewitched or infected with something like the Midas touch? What if I touch it and then everything that comes in contact with my fingers suddenly turns to gold? Can you imagine the calamity? It would turn me into the worst kind of plutocrat—a capitalist propagating the gold standard instead of revolution.

What if I touch that cross and it is infected with a celestial virus? What then? I might turn into some Typhoid Mary, infecting the ranks of my heavenly Hebrew comrades until they are forced to quarantine me like some leper.

Of course, there is another possibility. Maybe by touching the cross I'd be engulfed into some gentile agape Jesus Christ was so famous for; that love energy would flow out of me like some Aquarian water bearer; that I might turn the cheek to all insult; that my wounds would be healed and I'd help usher in paradise on earth.

Fat chance.

Let them compare me to some bearded Hasid neurotically twirling his side locks lest something un-kosher violate his living space. I'll take that heat because there is no way in hell that I'm touching that cross. You think I'm being paranoid, don't you? Let it be. In this case, total paranoia is total awareness.

Just look at that cheap piece of jewelry Hilda put in my hands. It's amazing the things they do with pewter. True, it's got weight to it. In miniature scale what we have here is the crucifixion. It's a well-cut pair of two by fours in perfect proportion. There are four red stones, one at the end of each station. Such detail—the planks could pass for knotty pine. Hanging in the middle is Jesus himself. You can even see the nails through his palms and the little stream of blood running down his arm. That's got to hurt.

The stuff Christians do in the name of this graven image has never ceased to amaze me. Don't get me started. I can go off on a rant that will take the better part of an hour.

However, since we're already on the subject let's just mention a few. They decorate their homes with it. It serves as a magic talisman to ward off evil. They wear it around their necks for the same purpose. They bow to it as a sacred icon. They build special wooden rails in front of their church pews so they can kneel before it as an expression of righteousness.

Let a ghost tell you something. The rituals Christians make up about this cross have nothing to do with anything. One day they will stop staring at it, get up off their knees, take responsibility for being blockheads, and become a pain in their own ass instead of ours.

But what do I care about earthlings and their foolish notions about divinity. I am dead now and know a hell of a lot more about it than they do. Still, I've got to get rid of this cross.

Now, I've found that if I really get angry I can move physical objects. Certainly, I'm new here in the realm of shades. In the spirit world, the laws of physics are different. But there are properties here as empirical as any in the mortal realm. I just don't understand them yet.

Just like mortal life, which is a series of trials and tribulations, confusion, false starts, and ambiguity, so life in the spirit world is the same. We stumble forward. Contrary to common belief, there's no instant apocalypse in heaven. Revelation is a slow, painstaking process. We inch our way forward. Besides, if I always saw my way immediately, immaculately, I would be God, instead of just a rebel angel.

Following Hilda's blasphemy, my anger, so spontaneous, poured out like a winter gale. I made the chapel door fly open and sent a gust through the room. Didn't know I could do that. Even the candles flanking my casket were blown out. It knocked the cross from between my fingers and onto my suit. That was good.

Unfortunately, what happened next foiled me. O'Shea relit the candles. When he saw the cross blown over, he reached inside his suit coat pocket and pulled out a small plastic Ziploc bag. Inside was a tube of Krazy Glue. It's a little known fact, but Krazy Glue is the duct tape of the funeral business. A little dab between my thumbs was all it took. The wretched thing is now stuck so solid that no amount of wind will blow it down.

Just look at the face on that cross. Only a mother could love it on payday. Flowing hair and a beard, long straight nose, high forehead. You know, it looks a lot like Joshua Bronstein. Holy shit, it's even got his thick neck.

Bronstein, what the hell are you doing between my thumbs? Idiot, get out of there. Some wandering Jew you turned out to be. Of all places to lay down roots… up on a pewter cross glued to my corpse while I'm lying inside a mahogany casket.

My God, that's exactly who it is—Joshua Bronstein done up in pewter. Who could have cast such a thing? I didn't recognize him at first. Look how his face contorts in pain. It's even got that three-inch scar on his forehead from the car accident.

Doesn't this beat all? Bronstein on the crucifix explains something, but what it explains, I don't know. It seems that this little drama is a two-Jew drama—me being the first Jew, and Bronstein being the second Jew. But why Bronstein should be so intimately involved in my fate beats the hell out of me.

This wake was supposed to be my bon voyage party and the beginning of my great epic journey. Damn, there's an even bigger party waiting for me in heaven. All the old Jewish Bolsheviks from the class of 1917 have been invited. I have RSVPs from Leon Trotsky, Grigory Zinoviev, Lev Kamenev, Ivan Svedlov, Isaac Babel, Julius Martov, Naum Rzosky, and Chaim Bonk. There's half a chance that Vladimir Ilyich Lenin himself will attend. Rosa Luxemborg, my God, what a dame, has promised me a kiss.

Now what is it that I find? My story is not an epic at all. It's a mystery. And the great mystery question is this: why is a graven image of Joshua Bronstein glued upon my corpse?

Now, here's something—I know I mentioned this already, but I'd like to say it again. I'd rather deal with anybody in the world but Bronstein. The man's an embarrassment. He's one of those guys who you secretly hate because when your people are walking that thin black line between assimilation and anti-Semitism, dopes like him reflect badly on the collective identity of the tribe and set us all back.

So I have to tell you that Bronstein is the last person I want to deal with right now. That's right, the very last individual I want to deal with as I leave this earth. He's a combination of two of the worst schlimazels in the Old Testament—Jonah and Job.

A confession is called for here, and now you're going to hear it: sometimes, I am full of crap. Yes, it's true. I've always had a hard time telling the truth, even to myself.

But sometimes the truth can even elude a Bolshevik. For instance, the suggestion that Bronstein might burst into O'Shea's chapel, defying the crowd, and snatch the cross from my casket, will never happen.

It's not that Joshua Bronstein is incapable of such action. He hated the masses. When the spirit took possession of him, no one had more chutzpah. But Bronstein will never set foot within a block of O'Shea's Funeral Home.

It's true, and it came to me the second Bronstein's ex-wife walked through the chapel door. Since the divorce, she, the former Victoria O'Shea Bronstein, now goes by the name of Victoria Bronstein O'Shea. She came into the chapel to say hello to her father, the undertaker, who also happens to be Bronstein's ex-father-in-law. There's also a dead child involved. But wait, my story is running ahead of itself.

Tim kissed his daughter on the cheek. Victoria, the former mother of one, has embarked on a new career—politics. She was once a nurse, a healer, but now she is running for the Minnesota state senate. From the way she looks, it is easy to surmise that she's spent the day campaigning for votes.

Her blue dress has long sleeves and a high neckline but is fitted in such a way as to show off her curves. There is a little makeup, and her bobbed, blonde hair is styled enough to be fashionable but not long enough to be sexy. It's a well-conceived look, suggestive enough to allure certain kinds of men while not threatening their women.

But there are no politics allowed in O'Shea's funeral chapel, and she knows this. Her father admonishes her to take off her "O'Shea for Senate" campaign button. So the martyred divorcee unclasps the pin and puts it in her pocket. Still, she makes the rounds saying hello to everybody at the wake. The old folks have known her since she was a baby and are already telling their friends to vote for her.

There's a picture I'm seeing in my mind's eye right now, and I'd like to share it. It's an image of Joshua standing at the shoulder of a freeway entrance the way he looked six years ago, the first time Tim O'Shea laid eyes on him. I've heard O'Shea tell this story many times. It hearkens back to the time when he was proud to have him as his son-in-law. For a time, he even considered taking him into his business and putting him in charge of Jewish grief.

You see, it was Tim O'Shea himself who brought Joshua to the Iron Range. He actually picked him up hitchhiking one day on a freeway entrance just west of Chicago and brought him home. For some reason, that image of Joshua hitchhiking is as bright and clear as a magazine photo.

As a reporter, Joshua always resented the notion that a picture was worth a thousand words. But that's beside the point. That image is as vital to me as if it was imprinted on the clouds.

If I had to speculate why it demands so much attention, I'd say it's because the sight of him standing on the curb was the epitome of who he was before we tried to turn him into an Iron Ranger. In doing so, we turned him into a derelict instead.

It was a cool spring morning in Wisconsin, and Joshua, the wandering Jew, the California Kid, the romantic outsider, the freelance reporter, was writing a travel article about hitchhiking cross-country from New York City to San Francisco in the new millennium.

Tim O'Shea was lonesome for company that morning. He was on his way back to Hibbing from Chicago. He had driven down to the Windy City in a black Chevy Suburban to retrieve the body of Jimmy McGowan, a childhood buddy of Tim's who had died of a heart attack on the south side. Jimmy had a burial plot in Hibbing. When his family got word of his death, the O'Shea Funeral Home got the call.

It was a routine retrieval. A Chicago mortician had already embalmed Jimmy. All Tim had to do was arrange the wake, the casket, and the priest. He could have had the body flown in to the Hibbing airport. But that wasn't O'Shea's way.

O'Shea had spent his whole life in Hibbing and was now one of its elders. He was proud of that role. He made it his mis-

sion to bring the friends of his Hibbing youth home to their final resting place. He'd get in his car and bring their dead bodies
home. This was his ninth trip and for Tim, probably the saddest.
Jimmy was not only his friend but also his first cousin.

I don't know if Tim believed in ghosts, but he liked to carry
on long conversations with the dead on the road back to Hibbing. Unfortunately, he wasn't perceptive enough to hear what
they said back to him. But that's not important. What was important was the closure that he shared with the departed.

He retrieved my body the night I passed on, and it was
great fun sitting in the back of his Chevrolet listening to him
remind me of the early days. O'Shea was a great storyteller and
every memorable experience that he and I shared together was
recalled with great orchestration. Later that night, in my honor,
he drank Stolichnaya in the embalming room.

There were two other reasons O'Shea loved these retrievals:
fast food and cigars, something his wife Mona never permitted.
That wife of his could be real bossy. So car trips in the company of
dead men who tell no tales had all the excitement of going to the
circus. Topics usually centered on sex, booze, and Elvis. After all,
O'Shea wasn't born an old man and, in his early years, though his
children had a hard time imagining it, he actually had a libido.

But Tim had never gone so far as Chicago before. The long
hours alone behind the wheel were wearing him down. Plus, he
was getting sick and he didn't realize it. He's a diabetic, and
were it not for his wife hounding him about taking his insulin
and making sure he ate well, he'd have been waiting for me here
in the realm of shades when I died.

Tim always enjoyed the bravado of a good shot of insulin
in the tummy before dinner. It was a ritual perpetrated in front
of the menfolk at Mona's dinner parties. For fun, he'd scare his
grandchildren when the family gathered for Sunday dinner. But
earlier that morning, on his way back up north, he lost two small
bottles of insulin in the parking lot of a Burger King when they
fell from his pocket and rolled into a sewer drain.

The sight of Bronstein standing on the highway hitchhiking appealed to Tim. He looked in the rear view mirror at Jimmy's lifeless shape stuffed into the black body bag and thought about how nice it would be, for a change, to have live company.

Bronstein possessed what we Bolsheviks refer to as the 'cretin glance.' It's a facial expression of virility and self-confidence that did not shirk in masculine company. Each man projects it in a different way. On Joshua it consisted of squared shoulders, a furrowed brow, the narrowing of the left eye, and a slight grimace that swore to God that in the face of all indignity he would stand stalwart.

Tim O'Shea was a sucker for that kind of testosterone. As the father of ten daughters and only two sons, he considered the assertion of his manhood as sacrosanct as the Father, the Son, and the Holy Ghost.

He liked nothing more than tough guys who looked their peers in the eye and acknowledged their manhood with a Spartan nod. Joshua Bronstein had that kind of verve the day Tim met him.

Bronstein had no thumb out. Instead, he held a cardboard sign in his right hand extended out straight and almost even with his shoulder. It read "Golden Gate Bridge."

A good sign, Joshua believed, was the key to successful hitchhiking. He would say, 'when motorists knew where you were going, they were more apt to pick you up.'

A sign like "Golden Gate Bridge," fifty miles west of Chicago, seemed like an audacious endeavor. What man would hesitate to contribute at least thirty or forty miles to that effort? Not only that, but Bronstein was in the process of writing a short story about his trip and each driver that picked him up became part of the narrative.

Bronstein had printed the sign in beautiful block letters. In the few seconds that drivers had to consider him, he felt his sign presented him in a good light. He'd been carrying that sign since the George Washington Bridge.

O'Shea was speeding down the entrance ramp when he passed Bronstein who was wearing faded blue jeans, a pair of black army boots, and a red flannel shirt whose sleeves were folded up to the elbow. His beard was two days old. A large, black backpack leaned up against his leg. Tim recognized something from his own youth and hit the brakes. He honked the horn and waved his hand out the window for the stranger to get in.

Tim's decision was made in three seconds. Those three seconds went on to change the destiny of several lives. Destinies change and manifest themselves in intervals of three seconds all the time, I suppose. But now I have to laugh. Because with the discovery of Bronstein hanging on the cross glued between my own two thumbs, it now seems that my life was another that changed the day he entered O'Shea's Suburban.

What happened next is interesting. But it only became part of the story after Joshua fell from grace. Joshua pulled on the door handle and nothing happened. It was stuck. He pulled and pulled on the stainless steel, but the door refused to budge. He didn't want to pull on it too hard for fear of breaking it off. So there was a standoff.

O'Shea was pissed off. He pulled on the handle from inside the car to no avail. He shouted instructions to Bronstein through the closed window. But his words were lost in the roar of passing highway traffic. Then O'Shea got out of the car cursing like a sailor because he had just purchased the vehicle and these things shouldn't happen with new cars. O'Shea bumped it with his hip and the door opened.

Thinking of that scene in retrospect, perhaps it was a sign from heaven. Don't get into the cab, Bronstein! If you do, you're fucked! That meaning is easy to see now but, that day, neither Bronstein nor O'Shea caught it. Bronstein threw his backpack into the back seat with Jimmy and climbed aboard.

"What's with the stiff?"

"That's Jimmy McGowan. I'm taking him home," answered O'Shea.

The two men in the front seat had polite, amiable conversation. Neither one revealed too much. A half hour passed. O'Shea felt himself fading. He needed a sugar fix but had forgotten to buy a candy bar. So he pulled over and asked Bronstein to drive. Twenty minutes later, O'Shea was in a diabetic coma beside Bronstein in the front seat.

Bronstein didn't think much of it at first. He figured since the old man was asleep he could get a little rock and roll on the radio. But, when O'Shea didn't flinch through a heavy metal medley, when his pallor turned pale, when he started to drool from the corner of his mouth and was held up only by the strength of his shoulder harness, Bronstein got scared.

He called to O'Shea. There was no response. He poked him in the shoulder with his finger. He slowed down to forty-five and turned off the radio. He tried shaking O'Shea one more time. Still no response. He tried shaking him again, this time a bit harder. When a pistol revealed itself from a holster at Tim's shoulder, Bronstein looked at the body bag and the gun and, realizing that he had been picked up just outside of Chicago, feared that O'Shea might be a Mafia hit man on the lam.

He pulled the Suburban off onto the highway shoulder. When a police cruiser came by, Bronstein waved it down. The cop examined the body and quickly escorted Tim, Joshua, and Jimmy to a nearby emergency room. It only took a short time for the doctors to diagnose the problem and the old man was stabilized.

When Bronstein later called Tim's family at the farm, Mona was sitting in her husband's own La-Z-Boy recliner at the window of the family room waiting for the Suburban to enter the driveway. She startled when the phone rang and put down her rosary beads to pick it up.

Bronstein told his story. But realizing that a stranger telling a wife that her husband was in a rural Wisconsin hospital might sound fishy, he called Deputy Sheriff Alek Pochowski to the phone to corroborate everything he had told her.

When Tim was able to call her a short time later from his hospital bed, Mona reviled her spouse with great abandon. It's the strange way Catholic women express love for their husbands. When she finished her tirade, she told her husband to bring Bronstein home.

Pulling up to the O'Shea farmhouse with Tim, Joshua arrived to a hero's welcome. The whole family turned out. They made a big fuss over him. He stayed for dinner and the night. O'Shea took him under his wing and showed him off around town—his new friend, Joshua Milton Bronstein.

Bronstein stayed on, hanging out at the local library, drinking bourbon at the Homer Bar, and breakfasting with Tim and his two sons at the International House of Pancakes. He was a minor celebrity—the guy who saved Tim O'Shea on the highway. Everybody wanted to meet him.

He soon forgot all about the cross country, hitch-hiking story. Instead, he got to know the town of Hibbing, Minnesota and decided to do a long feature article on its favorite son—Bob Dylan.

Public opinion was on Bronstein's side. "Who better than a Jew to define for the reading public another Jew. After he left town and changed his name from Zimmerman, we never understood him anyway," said Ralph Dicklich, Hibbing's mayor.

I met Bronstein at a Sunday dinner at the O'Shea farm. The whole clan was there, well over sixty people; sons and daughters, their spouses, dozens of grandchildren of all ages and some extended family. Talk about mayhem.

Babies were crawling up the green-carpeted stairs wearing nothing but diapers. Youngsters chased each other through the house with toy guns. While the women boiled water in the kitchen, the men gathered in the family room around a big screen TV watching golf. In the O'Shea home, pink was pink and blue was blue, and the division of labor held fast. Men changing diapers and women snow plowing a driveway never happened.

Bronstein was still something of a curiosity around town, and I, an old friend of the O'Shea family through our wives, came to find out about him.

When the golf match was over, the men, mostly Tim's sons-in-law, gravitated to the dining room and took their places at the long, wooden dining room table with its twelve chairs. While the men were oblivious to the racket of their children, I had to turn down my hearing aid.

Since I was a Russian immigrant, no one really spoke to me. Truth is, I've never met so many grown men with nothing to say in my whole life. It wasn't even that I disagreed. The issue, I believe, was that they all watched too much television and were programmed to receive images, not discuss them.

Tim held court at the head of the table in his captain's chair with its long, wide arms. Beside him, to his left, was a special chair for the matriarch, Mona O'Shea, whose seat had an embroidered needlepoint cushion with the names of all her children on it. Behind it, on the wall, was a picture of the Madonna and Child, a petit bourgeois kitsch replica from the Renaissance.

Since Mona was in the kitchen, O'Shea's ranking son-in-law, Billy Meyers, sat in her seat. To the patriarch's right was Tim Jr., his eldest son. When two Catholic priests, Monsignor John Jones of Little Falls, Minnesota and his protégé, Father Terrence Goodlad, of Dublin, Ireland, arrived to feast on Mona's slightly overcooked leg of lamb, two younger sons-in-law, both of whom were Lutheran, gave up their seats.

Joshua sat at the far end of the table across from me and he, a former newspaper reporter, couldn't resist the opportunity to dialogue with the shepherds of Catholicism. He had drunk several beers that afternoon and, like most good reporters, thrived on mischief. He began questioning the holy men about Catholic doctrine. It was quite innocent at first; he seemed eager for a clearer understanding.

Jones, the elder, did all the talking. He puffed out his chest, proud that not only was he getting a free meal but the honor of holding forth at a table of men. However, it was Goodlad, the worldlier of the two priests that Joshua really wanted to talk to.

Joshua asked if they really did believe in papal infallibility. Didn't abiding by one man's dogma interfere with an individual's personal search for Christ?

Jones adjusted his eyeglasses and spoke about centuries of Catholic tradition and wisdom, which the basic pillars of western civilization were founded upon. Though everyone listened to Jones' reply respectfully, few were actually interested.

Joshua then asked about the denial of equal rights for women in the church and its resistance to female clergy. Why was the Virgin Mary the only acceptable woman in the Roman Church? Weren't they intentionally repudiating the richness of the human psyche by making only male spiritual energy acceptable?

Goodlad was eager to reply. But Jones made it clear, that as senior clergy, only he would answer the heretic. Schooled in church excuses, he paid lip service to his female parishioners while defending the wisdom of the Holy Father, the pope, which he, as a servant of the Vatican, was obliged by oath to obey.

I sat and watched this exchange in silence. But to myself, I laughed. As a Bolshevik, the idea that a pope could be infallible was something only a fool would believe.

Once Bronstein's beer induced mental sluice opened, it all poured out of him.

"What about the theory that Christianity was really started in ancient Rome by Greek slaves? After all, Christ is a Greek word. Why, if the Christian community began in the Middle East, was that area populated mostly by Jews and Muslims?

"Lastly, Saint Luke was born one hundred years after the crucifixion in a foreign country that did not even speak the language of Jesus. So how can he be so sure that the Jews killed Christ?"

O'Shea's sons and sons-in law squirmed in their seats. Tim Jr., sitting at the right hand of his father, red-faced at such effrontery, lit into Joshua for his disrespect. But Tim Sr., the town's only Catholic undertaker, looked like he was enjoying the show. Jabbing his son with an elbow, he whispered, "This is my dinner table, and here men speak their minds."

With that subtle affirmation, Joshua went off on a tirade indicting the clergy for the way they sought to fit all decent human emotion onto the Procrustean bed of Catholic catechism which, because it was so judgmental, marred so many souls. Then he sought an explanation for what he called 'recovering Catholics.'

He mocked the priests for abandoning the Latin Mass in favor of a language similar to the mundane rhetoric used car salesmen uttered on late night TV.

I wish I could remember more of what the priests gave back to Bronstein, but I was distracted by the tension in the room. It was so thick that the hair on my back stood out straight.

The chubby Father Jones reminded me of a man holding the leash of a French poodle while it crapped on a busy city sidewalk. He made impassioned, sometimes angry, but mostly stern replies. It didn't matter. Joshua was making all the points. The men around the table looked upon the newcomer with dread as if waiting for a thunderbolt from on high to strike him dead at O'Shea's dining room table.

I actually felt sympathy for that priest who came to eat lamb but had humble pie instead. And Bronstein never even mentioned pederasty within the Catholic clergy.

It was Goodlad, the Irishman, who saved the day. He pulled out the trump card, the only one left in the deck. "Excuse me," he said, staring into Joshua's eyes, "what did you say your last name was?"

"Bronstein."

"That's not a Catholic surname, is it?" asked Goodlad.

"No, it's Jewish."

"Ohhhhhhh, a Jew," said Father Jones leaning back in his chair, a smile creasing his lips at this revelation. He nodded his head in gratitude to his Franciscan brother and then gazed around the table making contact with every eye.

Oh yes, it all made sense to Jones. He'd been baited by a Christ-killer. Throwing his hands up in the air, with a sense of resignation, he whispered as if in a soliloquy, "A Jew." He then gave Joshua a quick glance. "Yes, you've got that look."

Turning the other cheek was now easy for the white-collared celibate. Jones gracefully changed the subject to the upcoming fishing opener. Enthusiasm for that conversation lit up the room.

If Bronstein was incensed at being so easily dismissed, he didn't show it. After all, he was a guest in the O'Shea household. Since he could not participate in a Minnesota fishing conversation, he lowered his head and cleaned his fingernails.

Well, I thought to myself, this Bronstein is everything they said he was—a wise guy with a lot on his mind. He didn't fit in here. That was obvious to me, though perhaps not to him. But he decided to stay on.

Bronstein and Father Goodlad actually became friends. Both were outsiders in northern Minnesota, and having seen a greater portion of the world, they met often for coffee and conversation. They even played chess over drinks at the Homer Bar. Lost in concentration, staring at the thirty-two pieces on the checkered board, they'd play for hours, often ignoring everyone else in the bar.

Truth is, Goodlad never liked Father Jones of Little Falls, Minnesota. He thought him a little man with narrow sensibilities. So Bronstein's debate with Jones actually endeared him to the Irish priest. When Jones discovered Bronstein and Goodlad's budding friendship, he was furious. But there was nothing he could do about it.

While many Minnesota men were mistrustful of Bronstein, his charm was not lost on the O'Shea girls. Soon he was sleeping with Victoria O'Shea, who, with her green eyes, leprechaun looks, and pert breasts was the pick of the O'Shea litter.

They married and had a baby whose name was Adam. All was going well for Bronstein, who had surrendered his own identity to the collective identity of the O'Shea family. In order to fit in with his Catholic in-laws, he dabbled in Catholicism under the watchful eye of Father Goodlad, his mentor.

But domestic bliss was not in the cards. Bronstein's life came apart one Sunday afternoon in late November. He was watching the Minnesota Vikings play the San Francisco 49ers in the living room of his brother-in-law, a car salesman named Tom Nelson. They had pizza and a few beers, and then it was time to get Adam home. Adam couldn't have been more than fourteen months old at the time.

Bronstein didn't have a care in the world. The Vikings had won the game, a snowstorm had just ended, and a small moon glowed in the sky. Adam was smiling in the car seat behind him and life felt good. Bronstein felt so secure he never snapped in his seat belt.

But then the north wind began to blow. Snow drifted across the road. It was difficult to see. And then Bronstein turned onto Ugstad road. With its twists and turns and blind spots, Ugstad road has been the demise of many a good man.

Coming around a steep curve, he was surprised by a huge animal in the middle of the road. He swerved to avoid hitting it and slammed on the brakes. The car hit a patch of ice, slipped off the road, and hurtled down into a frozen lake. Joshua's forehead hit the windshield. The car was stuck in the ice at a forty-five-degree angle. Its back tires were suspended in air. Joshua was knocked out, but the baby was safe in the car seat behind him.

A teenager in a pickup truck passed by and saw the wreck. He pulled Joshua, unconscious, from the car, dragging him across the frozen lake to the shore. But now the ice started making funny noises and the teen got scared. In a rush of courage, he went back for the baby. He pulled open the back door and Adam, who had been silent the whole time, started to cry long, loud wails.

But what was this car seat? How do you unlock it? The kid pulled on this lever and he pulled on that lever, but still the baby was not free. When a large crack split the ice between his feet, he got too scared to think straight. The car started through the ice and the teen barely saved himself. Adam and the auto went down to the bottom.

When Joshua came to, he was slightly delirious but happy to be alive. Interrogated at the scene by the police and ambulance crew, he said that he had come across a moose on its knees in the center of the road praying to the crescent moon. He swerved to avoid hitting it and fell into the lake. "It was really weird," he confessed with a loud laugh.

"Are you sure about that… a moose on its knees praying to the crescent moon?" asked the policeman.

"Yes," he confessed, "that's what it was."

Then they told him his son was dead. Bronstein never laughed again.

The teen rescuing Bronstein saw no moose, and no tracks could be found in the blown snow. And in no time the maverick from somewhere else became the irresponsible father hated by the whole town.

The county attorney was called in and charges were filed. A court-ordered blood and urine test was taken the next day. The results were never announced. True, Bronstein did have a concussion at the time he told the moose story. But later, when a lawyer was hired to defend him, under the advice of counsel, he changed his testimony.

You don't kill Hibbing babies with an excuse of a moose on its knees praying in the roadway to the crescent moon. Nobody could stand it, and the accident became the focal point of community outrage. It made the front page of the *Mesabi Daily News* for a week.

"How damn irresponsible of the man to be driving drunk with his son in the car," cried wives and mothers. The men asked, "How stupid does that guy think we are, trying to pass off a bullshit story like that?" There was no excuse for this. Bronstein became the town scapegoat and everyone was glad to have one.

"How Many Beers Does It Take to See A Moose Praying To The Moon On The Roadway?" ran an editorial in the *Mesabi Daily News*, the very paper Bronstein wrote for. Pink elephants they had heard of. But a moose praying on its knees to the crescent moon in the middle of winter? The newspaper suspended him.

Father Jones came after Goodlad with a vengeance. "Didn't I tell you he was no good! The Jewish interloper was not only disrespectful of the Catholic faith, he's now a child murderer too," he said.

Jones brought the matter to the attention of the bishop, who demanded Goodlad sever all ties with Bronstein. The following Sunday, Bronstein's friend and mentor gave voice to the community's outrage in a stern sermon at the pulpit of Our Lady of Perpetual Sorrow, condemning him.

Joshua's good life in Hibbing ended. He was ostracized by the O'Shea clan and soon thereafter divorced.

In the weeks that followed, the town's anger subsided. Laughter and ridicule replaced it. They called him Bullwinkle Bronstein. Jokes circulated about the facial comparisons between the archetypal Jew and the archetype moose with their awkward physique, large noses, and beards.

Though it's only been three years, it seems like a lifetime ago that I last spoke with Joshua. Ironically, our last conversation was in this very funeral home. I cannot remember what I whispered to him amid the throngs of teary-eyed mourners who had turned out for Adam's funeral. I only remember the bandage on his forehead and his vacant look. Grief overwhelmed him. He could not speak or smile or even look me in the eye. He cursed God and turned away.

Wait. O'Shea just walked into the chapel. The wake is over. The undertaker slams down the casket lid and locks down the hinges. I thought he was gone. But no, I should have recognized that odor. He was up in his office, and if my nose is right, he was smoking a Macanudo Robusto.

O'Shea is now wheeling my casket down a hallway. He pushes it off the cart and into a dumbwaiter. The casket fits perfectly into the little elevator. The door closes, a small motor whirrs, and my body descends down, down, down to the basement.

Tomorrow, they will put the casket in the back of a black Cadillac hearse. A small procession will drive through Hibbing on its way to a cemetery in Nashwauk, Minnesota for burial. Two leather straps will loop beneath the wooden casket and four strong men will lower me underground with that cross inside.

What force is drawing me back to this life when I long to ascend to heaven? Who is responsible for this mystery? I have no idea. But they should know one thing. I'll bend over, but I won't take off my pants.

CHAPTER THREE

Joshua. Joshua Bronstein. Joshua. Wake from your sleep. Wake up, you lazy bum. It's morning, and you're still out cold. What's the matter with you? Don't you work? Wake up, Bronstein.

Joshua, you'd think that a man your age could find better accommodations than a one-bedroom trailer out here in the woods. Why do you hide from the world?

Just look at this place. It's a mess. I've seen cleaner pigpens. Well, at least you don't have to go outside to shit. But a home like this would take Hilda days to clean.

When the heater goes on, dust balls roll across the floor like tumbleweed in TV westerns. The dirty dishes, piled so high in the sink, would be even taller except that you own so few. I wouldn't sit on that toilet seat. Look at the clothes. They're thrown over every piece of furniture. Haven't you ever heard of a hamper? What about a closet?

Books are stacked up around the trailer in piles, stacked vertically one upon the other. There are lots of them. Most are from the used book stores so plentiful in Minnesota. I look at the titles. Not much history or politics which was my life blood. No, they're mostly self-help and psychology, new-age theology, and men's movement books from the disciples of the southern Minnesota poet Robert Bly.

The garbage is piled in the corner of the kitchen: plastic bags, take-out pizza boxes, cola bottles, cellophane wrappers, paper towels, and tin cans.

Everything edible was licked clean by the large, brown, male mutt named Shortstop, who is lurking somewhere around here. It was a rescue Bronstein got from the dog pound. It's part rottweiler, part pit bull. For a while it was the only friend he had in the world. Its dog hair adds another dimension to the trailer's filth.

Bronstein, I'm trying to communicate with you, and I wish you could hear me. Unfortunately, shades don't speak clearly to the living. If worse comes to worse, maybe I can get your attention by writing you a note in the layer of dust covering your coffee table. I even know what to say. "You. Fuckhead. Take that damn cross from my casket. Truly yours, Kalinsky."

When I first met you, Bronstein, you were like a mighty swordfish that any angler would have given his eyeteeth to fight. Look at you now. You're a gefilte fish, pickled in a clear glass jar.

Who's that under your blanket with her face nestled up to your chest? Is that your girlfriend?

Holy crap. It's Debra Crow! I remember that Indian girl. In her early days she was a model for the Land O Lakes butter box. I could go on about her personal, financial, and sex life for hours.

How, you might ask, do I know details about Bronstein's lover? It's because that in addition to being a great union organizer and a remarkable Bolshevik, I was also the oldest living bartender in the state of Minnesota. Not to sound immodest, but several feature articles about the strong drink I poured while counseling the working classes graced the covers of some of the finest publications north of Duluth.

Debra Crow sat at my bar on many an afternoon where I would get her drunk, peek at her cleavage, and listen to her stories about bad love.

Look how close she sleeps to him. On a cold morning like this, a naked female is a good thing. She's out cold too. I happen to know that she is a bigger lush than he is. In her defense, she probably has to drink more just to become oblivious to his snoring. How else could anybody get a good night's rest with that cacophony?

I've always admired those breasts. That complexion—it's so dark, so smooth. Her hair is the color of midnight. This girl is an old man's wet dream. And that ass… I like it. So shapely, so round. Feel how firm it is.

"Feel it again, why don't you?"

"What? Who said that?" I called out.

"You could crack walnuts with an ass like that."

"Where you are?" I asked.

"Brother, look… we're over here."

I search around the room and I saw them, the two Hasidic ghosts sitting with their backs pressed against each other on the floor. Both men had their legs crossed. Their shoulders touched. They wore the traditional black caftans of east European Jewry, the kind I remember my grandfather, Morris Broverman, wearing in my early years. One specter was fat, robust, and bearded. He occupied his time by cracking his knuckles. His partner was skinny and pale, like a newborn hamster, his eyes a pale blue. His fingers were intertwined behind his head.

"That Joshua, he's got a nice ass too," said the skinny one.

"Too bad it's on his shoulders," I answered.

Despite my sarcasm, it was exciting to finally see someone else in the realm of shades. It had been years since I heard the Yiddish accent of those Jews dwelling in the Pale of Settlement.

"So there you are, the two of you. I should have smelled your gabardine when I came in."

"Are you making fun of my caftan?" asked the skinny one.

"Maybe."

When the skinny one jabbed his partner with his elbow, the fat man took his turn to speak. "It's good that we are all here now. We need to straighten a few things out."

"Straighten what out? What could you and I possibly have to straighten out?"

Did he answer my question? No. He pulled a face. He raised his eyebrows up to his hairline while at the same time lowering the corners of his mouth in a way that cut me right to the bone. In so many words, what I saw was a shit-eating grin that suggested, "I've got you by the short hairs, Kalinsky, so don't break my balls."

Go slap that supercilious look right off his face, I told myself. Oh that look, you know that look. I've always hated it. The problem was I didn't know why it was plastered on his puffy face. Something was going on. They knew, but I didn't.

What were these two up to? I never understood the Hassidim. Of course, living in northern Minnesota I hadn't seen one in decades. There are many forms of Jewish manhood—the religious zealot, the hustler, the financier, the doctor, the lawyer, the philanthropist, the rabbi, the writer.

Above all, the purest light of the rainbow shines off the forehead of the left-wing Jewish Bolshevik. But the Hassidim were fundamentalists who knew what they knew and nothing more. There could be no international class struggle in their small world.

But then, suddenly, I got this revelation. The truth of it straightened me up like a shot of pepper vodka. I glared at the two of them, taking in the full measure of their betrayal. But I kept my composure because I did not want them to know that it was only at that very instant that the truth dawned on me.

Yes, I got it all right. I've always had a sixth sense about manipulation, especially when being led around by the nose. Moses, in the presence of the golden calf, felt no greater rage. I now knew who was responsible for the cross in my casket. Those bastards sabotaged me at the onset of my trip to heaven. The great mystery of who was jerking me around had been solved. But a more important question now arose: Why?

"Kalinsky, try to understand, this Bronstein is my charge," said the big man, who stretched his hands to the sky and leaned hard against the back of the skinny one, folding him forward like an accordion.

"We've been assigned to be his guides for a while. But as you well know, a Jewish male lost in the wilderness is a difficult responsibility. Look how he lies there on those filthy sheets. A picture taken of him now would embarrass his mother."

"This is true," I said.

"There is a chance he might get the call of Lamed Vav," said the tubby one.

"What's this Lamed Vav?" I asked.

"Mortals call it folklore, but those of us in the realm of shades know better. At any one time there are thirty-six hidden righteous men on whose merit the world depends. They wander in exile, humble and unnoticed, and only assert themselves when they are called. It is from this group of thirty-six that the messiah will be chosen when his generation on earth is deemed worthy."

"What does Bronstein have to do with it?"

"Last Thursday, Harvey Greenberg, a religion professor, and Lamed Vav from Cleveland, died of a heart attack," said the fat man. "There's an opening. The job could go to Bronstein."

"Do you really think that Bronstein can save you all from the ravenous appetite of Muslims and Christians? With a guy like him in charge, it could be Poland, 1944, all over again."

"The reason we are here with Bronstein is because he is not bolstered by politics or money or other complications," said the skinny man. "He lost his faith in those things when Adam died. That is what makes him a candidate for the Lamed Vav. He may be a schlemiel, but he's our schlemiel. There may come a time when his spiritual qualities may burst forth to raise the lumen of his people."

"Unbelievable," I said.

"And now let's cut right to the chase," said the fat man. "You know Bronstein. Since he is the only one who can get that cross out of your casket and save you from the jeers of your Bolshevik peers, we know you will help us."

"I find it outrageous that my ascension to heaven should be undermined by my own kind," I said.

"The notion that all Jews play on the same team is strictly a Christian perception," the fat one answered, and regrettably, he was right.

"What are your names?" I asked.

"I am Herman Himmelman," said the fat man. "My thin friend here is Singer."

"Have you got a first name, Singer?"

"A first name? Of course I have a first name," he answered. "Don't you think I had a mother who pinched my cheek and spoke that name lovingly? Or playmates at school who thought enough of me to call me by that name, which honored my grandfather. A first name? Indeed, I have a first name."

"So Singer, why not sing Bronstein a song of courage... something to strengthen his resolve and show him what it means to be a mensch."

"Every time I do he gets horny. He takes that courage and squirts it in his woman. It's quite a scene. Stick around. You'll see what I mean. His woman is remarkable."

They both stood up and faced me.

"You think I'm kidding?" Singer asked.

"The sex act between a man and a woman has been going on since time began," I said. "It's hard to believe that drunks like Bronstein and Debra do it any better than anybody else."

"It's not the fucking that's so interesting, it's the foreplay."

"Kissing, hugging, oral sex, masturbation?" I said. "I've done it a hundred times."

"Not like this."

"Not like what?"

"It's not about Debra and Bronstein. It's about Debra and us," Singer said.

"What are you saying?"

"Debra starts by smoking marijuana. Then she puts on her Indian drumming CDs. As the beating of the drum intensifies,

Bronstein starts reading out loud," said Singer. "Sometimes it's Henry Miller, sometimes Dylan Thomas, other times it's his own work. This Bronstein's got rage, and when he speaks that stuff out loud it's enough to make your back straighten. If he ever spoke to God in that tone of voice, God would be compelled to listen.

"Meanwhile, the beating of the drum and the sound of his deep voice reading make the woman go crazy. She gets up and starts dancing like a whirling dervish. Ojibway dance steps, hot soul moves. She'd even do the Hora, but Bronstein won't teach her. The more she dances, the hotter she gets and starts ripping off clothes. The whole trailer shakes. Soon she's naked and manic from the drumbeat and Bronstein's angry voice.

"Then she starts to spin," Singer continued. "Around and around she goes with her hands and legs flying about. She spins and she spins until she gets too dizzy to stand and then she drops on the floor like a corpse. That's when she leaves her body and joins us here in the realm of shades. She comes to our world and flirts with us. We talk, she lets us touch her, she touches us, we mess around, and we tell her things, most of which she doesn't remember when she awakens."

"Debra told Bronstein that she gets her best dreams after passing out," said Himmelman. "So he doesn't disturb her. He stares at her naked body crumbled on the floor."

"If she's passed out too long, he brings her out of it with the sex letters from *Penthouse* magazine. It takes a real dirty one to get her attention. When she returns to the mortal world she's like a cat in heat. That's when the passion begins. There's moaning and groaning, and sometimes she gets wild and loses all self-control. He has to put her in a full nelson to restrain her. But me and Himmelman get intimate with her first. A good time is had by all."

I tried to act unimpressed. But to know Debra Crow once before I went off to the promised land would be a beautiful thing.

This Singer not only looked like a hamster. Judging from his hands and feet I'd bet he was hung like a hamster too. From the size of Himmelman's belly, it was easy to assume he hadn't seen his dick in years. Given the opportunity, I knew I could make it with Debra. But I put my reverie aside and spoke.

"Well, a loose woman is nothing to sneeze at," I said.

"You're telling me," said Himmelman.

"How many times have you seen this happen?" I asked.

"Herman, how many days have we been waiting for Kalinsky to die?" asked Singer.

"Singer, let me talk now," said the fat man, his palms over his friend's lips. Then he turned to me and said, "Forgive him for mentioning such things."

"Don't apologize," I said.

"Kalinsky, I knew you when your name was Broverman back in Kiev. Your sister, Sarah, was friends with my sister, Ruth. Can you remember?"

"Yes, I remember you now. Your father, Simon Himmelman, was the accountant for Kiev Fire and Light."

"A pious man indeed," said the son, smoothing the wrinkles in his caftan. "Kalinsky, let us talk plain. You were an angry bastard even then, and I know you're going to be difficult now. Let your trip to paradise steep for a while. This man Bronstein is important to us and you must help him."

"How could I possibly help Bronstein?"

"A man of your reputation and destiny," said Himmelman, "maybe you can do something for him."

Reputation and destiny, now those were the magic words that tempered me. But I was still pissed off about the cross and not about to let them blow smoke up my ass. "How much manipulation did it take to get that cross into my hands?"

"Actually, given the intelligence of your Hilda and her sister-in-law, it was rather easy," admitted Singer. Suddenly, a dazed look came upon Singer's face. His eyes opened wide, as if in a trance. His back straightened, just like Maureen's had. Then, in a voice that sounded exactly like my sister-in-law, he said, "Hilda, darling, put this cross in your husband's hands."

"How did you do that?"

"Oh, Kalinsky, it was easy," said Himmelman, putting his hand on Singer's shoulder in a gesture of admiration. "Death is like high school. You're still a freshman. We've been dead much longer. You may not get it now but you will soon enough."

"Why must it be Bronstein to dig me out of this mess? I'd rather ask Hitler to butter me a bagel."

"It's a compromising position... I grant you that," said Himmelman. "You're a big man though. Take responsibility for this. Your pride has always been your Achilles' heel. We all know that, and that is why we will get our way."

"Such a story I might tell," said Singer, cupping his palm beside his mouth as if he were telling a secret. "Did you know Kalinsky, a life-long Bolshevik, had himself buried with a cross in his hands?"

"Won't that be something to talk about," said Himmelman, laughing.

"That's a lie and you know it," I shouted.

"True enough," said Singer. "But people would rather hear good lies than bad truths. And I assure you that me and Himmelman will tell that story over and over again with great glee."

The short hairs, damn them... they had me by the short hairs.

"How can a shade like me get this drunk to wake up and assume his responsibility as Lamed Vav?" I asked.

"You'll think of something," said Himmelman.

"Then hear me now, you Hasids. You with your long black coats and prayer shawls, you ostriches who express your verve by the rakish tilt of your yarmulkes, all of you who would rather settle for a negligent God than create a new world order—hear this. Three days and that's all. I'll remain for three days. Don't you ask me to stay any longer for this loser. What happens to Bronstein is his luck. You will get three days from me, and in return the cross is never to be mentioned again."

"Pilot him out of his sloth," said Himmelman. "Make him ready for his call. How you accomplish this feat is beyond my ken but no matter now... in three days much can happen."

"Fine. But know this Himmelman—on the third day, complete or not, I'm going to paradise. And don't lobby me to change my mind. I'll not stain myself with bourgeois sentimentality for this schlemiel, not when there's a communist reunion awaiting."

"I ask you, brother," said Singer, "is it not ironic that the first word of what Bronstein is aspiring to is lamed? For what is he, if not lame?"

"True enough, but let an old man stand beside him for a while," added Himmelman. "Jerk him around, Kalinsky. Perhaps you can trick him better. Put something in his path and show him the way. That's what shades do best. And Kalinsky, don't fail. I don't like to be disappointed."

"Someday you'll answer for this," I said.

Himmelman shrugged his shoulders. "Healing Jewish souls is what matters to us. The rest is details."

Then there was silence. The Hasids looked into each other's deadpan faces again. Then the fat man said, "Time to go."

And then, suddenly, they were gone without so much as a good-bye. I was alone and confused in the realm of shades.

Have I told you that in Washington, DC, in the early 1930s, I ran a spy operation out of the Russian embassy, which was responsible for recruiting such noted spies as Alger Hiss and the Rosenbergs? The reason I mention it again is not only to brag but also to bring up the point that I, Kalinsky, the great Soviet gatherer of secrets, knew the form and content of subterfuge.

What I quickly realized was that Himmelman and Singer had been on a reconnaissance mission and that in the parlance of espionage, I'd been played. That's right. I had been played by two men who maybe were Hasids, but maybe were not.

Played. That's the only word that captures their manipulation of me. Not only did they put that cross in my casket... they were brazen about it. Now that's what I call chutzpah. Despite their funny outfits, these guys were professionals.

CHAPTER FOUR

A funny thing happened when Himmelman and Singer made their exit. A sound rang out. *Ping, ping.* Not loud pings mind you; it was soft, but pings nonetheless. And the bell-toned ping their exit evoked was actually pleasing to the ear. And while I felt relieved that they were finally gone, there was also curiosity about this ping and where they went.

Relatively speaking, Himmelman, being of greater mass than his skinny friend Singer, made the louder of the two pings, and following his ping something remarkable happened. Debra Crow startled from sleep. The reason I call this remarkable is that she easily slept through Bronstein's snoring, which sounded like a couch being dragged across a hardwood floor. But this ping by Himmelman, which by volume was no louder than a fingernail against crystal, woke her.

Now Bronstein's hound, Shortstop, a big, brown, lazy mutt asleep at the foot of their bed, saw and heard nothing. But the startled Debra Crow rose from a supine to a sitting position. Her eyes searched the room, her ears listened attentively to the sound of silence, and she sniffed the air. But of course the ping was gone. "I must have been dreaming," she whispered.

When her arms reached for the ceiling in a long sensuous stretch, the blanket she shared with Bronstein fell to her thighs.

The cold morning air made icicles of her nipples. Only a blind man could miss it.

Now to be honest, Debra, who was in her early thirties, no longer had the body of a porn star, but it was close enough. Long, lean women with good boobs was for Bronstein the epitome of Eve. He'd have no truck with fat girls. Being the short-peckered person he was, fucking a fat girl, he claimed, never brought him or his partner satisfaction.

Debra scratched the dark blue tattoo covering her right shoulder with her long fingernails. I never saw a dream catcher tattooed on a girl before. But there it was. It's a spiritual spider web flanked by feathers, symbolically entangling dreams in your memory so you can examine them when you wake. Upon the bed's wooden headboard hung another dream catcher, a real one. Debra made it herself.

When she turned her head in my direction, I swear that girl saw me, eye to eye. We both startled. I admit it; I was frightened. Perhaps I shouldn't have been. What harm could a mortal woman inflict on a ghost dwelling in the realm of shades?

Yet, as the vanguard of the proletariat, I was not unaware of my moral responsibilities. Does a Peeping Tom have the moral right to lead the masses?

On the other hand, I momentarily considered the fact that carousing around the bedrooms of beautiful women at night might be fun.

So there I was, Kalinsky, former Marshal of Conspirators, hanging out in a dark trailer in the early morning hours in the middle of nowhere waiting for Bronstein's girlfriend to go back to sleep. And when I say hanging, I mean hanging.

There was this lamp screwed to the ceiling. It was a purple Tiffany lamp hanging by a brass chain. Debra Crow made it in an art class at Mesabi Junior College, and there it was above their bed. It was one of the few things of color in their squalid quarters.

Taking advantage of my weightlessness, I had wrapped my legs around the brass chain and sat on the top of the fixture as if I were once again a young boy at Aunt Ida's kulak farm on the banks of the River Don. There I'd swing from a rope tied to an oak tree and splash into its dark, rushing water.

Debra Crow never looked at the ceiling. The angle required of her neck was too sharp, and the girl was no contortionist. Perhaps she thought I had been scared away. Then she lay back down, rolled her body on the side, and nestled up to the body heat of Bronstein, who had momentarily stopped snoring. Still, I could look down and see that her brown eyes were still open.

The knowledge gleaned from this little encounter heartened me. Debra Crow was aware of life beyond the veil, and perhaps she might assist me in my effort to turn Bronstein into a grave robber.

There in the ghostly silence I apprehended the relentless communication teeming through the spirit world. I had never noticed it before, but in the pre-dawn silence I became aware of this innate activity buzzing around the ether.

Now how, you might ask, could I ever fathom such information while holding on to the brass chain of Debra Crow's purple Tiffany lamp? I'm going to tell you a big secret—the wind carries information around the realm of shades.

The wind, harnessed by mortals to sail their ships, turn windmills, crush grain, and fly kites, also serves as a cosmic internet that collectively informs the spirit world.

It makes sense. The etymology from which the ancient Hebrew tribes of Israel named their God, Yahweh, stemmed from the sirocco wind, which blew in sandy revelations to their pre-feudalistic society while they sat beside their camels in the moonlight. And suddenly the truth of that revelation came to me. Those ancient tribal members were right to put such stock in the whirling revelations of dry desert breezes. I repeated the word in a whisper—"Yah-weh, Yah-weh, Yah-weh." It even sounded like the wind.

I listened carefully for any information floating around the ether about our communist reunion. I heard nothing. Then a spirit came by. That was surprising. She was a young innocent trying so hard to be a good Samaritan. "Come," she said with a quiet smile. "You must be lost. I am Holly. Let me show you to the gates of heaven."

Certainly, she was not one of us, more like the midwest country club type. She had long blonde hair, a creamy complexion, and big white teeth. The end of her nose was so sharp it could cut cheesecake. There was a time in my life when I would have led a woman like that right to bed. But not today... I'm dead.

"Come," she implored me. "I will show you the way."

"No thanks," said I, "trying to quit." It was a queer answer, I know. But this interference was a distraction from my predicament. I had to think fast. And who came to my rescue? You won't believe it. It was Singer. All I could think of was that Jewish schnook, who was so emotionally distracted by his own internal drama that the world around him made little or no impression.

So I gave Holly my best Singer imitation. I looked askance into space, stooped my shoulders, hung my head down, and bent my wrists. And now I suddenly witnessed the virtue of Singer's behavior—Christians found it repulsive.

"What is your name?" she asked, her maternal solicitude undaunted.

"My name... my name is Nudnik."

"Nudnik, when did you die?"

"When my heart stopped."

"Come with me," she whispered. "You're dead now. I'll take you home."

I made a slight gesture with limp wrists, saying in the same sing-song as Singer, "Dead, me? No. Maybe tomorrow. Who knows? I might wait. I'm off now for some gefilte fish and a glass of hot tea."

Turning away, I began muttering the highlights of my bar mitzvah speech from Temple Beth Shalom in Kiev.

She touched me gently on the shoulder and gave me a lascivious wink suggesting that intimacy would be mine if only I accompanied her. I didn't take the bait.

"I'll see you later," she said.

No sooner had Holly gone, with an absolutely delightful ping, than Singer stood before me. He had seen the exchange between us and was insulted.

"Are you're making fun of me?" he asked.

"Landsman, I meant no offense," I answered. "But I have my own issues. And while I love women, the last thing I need is some beautiful blonde hanging around trying to make me wolf down her ways."

"I understand," he said. "The questions they ask... it's enough to make you crazy."

"So, Singer, you're back so soon? Let me guess. Bronstein screws this woman in the morning too, and you've come to watch?"

"You're very cynical, Kalinsky. That's why I hate you."

"Hate? Hate did you say? Singer, your hate couldn't ripple water in a bathtub. If you ever really learn to hate, there might be some hope for you."

"I don't trust you or what you have in store for Bronstein," he said. "You'll rob him of all his virtue, make him a Bolshevik instead of a Lamed Vav."

"Make Bronstein a Bolshevik? Never. The Christians have put an evil spell on him. He's heard their cheerless anti-Semitism so often that he no longer doubts it. He's so steeped in their judgment, catechism, alcohol, and the devil knows what else, that they've crippled him."

The sun rose. The two of us turned at once when Debra Crow pulled back the covers and jumped out of bed. The argument now meant nothing. A naked woman can do that.

Her long black hair, parted in the middle of her head, hung down. It covered her chest except for the nipples poking through. An appendectomy scar was at the bottom of her tummy. A big wad of bathroom paper left over from last night was wedged inside her vagina so that Joshua's sperm didn't drip down her leg. She ran to the bathroom, which was the warmest room in the trailer.

"Well Singer, looks like we missed the sex show," I chided.

"Maybe, but today is Saturday. They'll try again tonight. Sex on the Sabbath, as you well know, is a double mitzvah."

At the bathroom mirror she studied her own face which consisted of thick lips, high cheek bones, and brown eyes. There were two small marks, one on her cheek, the other on her forehead—maybe the result of chicken pox. She brushed her teeth. She got dressed. A pair of blue jeans came up over her cute butt, no underwear. Boots were pulled on with no socks, and an old, blue turtleneck sweater came over her head.

We were so entranced by the sight of her that we got careless. When the sun penetrated the windowpane, it cast our dim shadows upon the wall. The two of us scrambled out of the light and headed for dark corners. But the sharp-eyed Debra saw us.

I found this somewhat remarkable since during my wake neither my friends, family, nor the union rank and file ever considered that I might be lurking in the shadows of O'Shea's Funeral Parlor.

And so my opinion of Joshua Bronstein rose a little bit. He was not making love to some dull, bourgeois floozy. In addition to her fabulous breasts, she recognized spirits when she saw them, perhaps even realizing that we were leering at her. It made me feel somewhat ashamed. But if she didn't care, why should I?

Debra Crow put on a light jacket and went out the door to her garden plot. Most of the snow surrounding the trailer had melted, and little green shoots of wild onions—the northland's harbinger of spring—emerged from the earth. Taking a spade, she began turning over the moist soil. That job kept her busy.

A few sparrows gathered in the trees above her. They chirped several songs that Debra listened to attentively.

She was so lost in her labor that when a wayward mosquito, which you don't usually see this early in the season, landed on her neck and dipped its needle nose into her skin, it brought no reaction. For some reason she didn't mind playing host to a bloodsucker.

Perhaps she understood the little known fact that mosquitoes are the soul's very first incarnation on earth. Those insects cannot evolve physically without a little human blood in their mix. That's why in many quarters of the universe, Minnesota, the Land of Lakes, host to millions and millions of mosquitoes, is considered the fertile crescent of North American civilization. For many of them, it's their first tour of duty.

Many great future personages of history will one day admit that their formative years were spent as insects flying through the downtown corridors of Hibbing, Minnesota. But wait.

Joshua Bronstein woke. Naked from bed he came, mumbling and stumbling from too much booze. Peeling off blue, sperm-stuck bathroom tissue from the shaft of his penis, he marched to the bathroom. A Kleenex commercial like this you will never see on television.

His five o'clock shadow was fourteen hours old. His black hair had tufts sticking out in every direction. His head was pounding. Looking in the bathroom mirror, he gave himself a goofy smile. Today he was the one with the hangover. Yesterday, it was Debra.

He ambled to the refrigerator and poured himself a glass of grapefruit juice, the pink kind. True, he was mumbling and stumbling, but not so mumbling and stumbling as to forget that when one drinks grapefruit juice in the morning, it's best to do so before brushing your teeth.

He returned to the bathroom, grabbed his toothbrush, and began brushing. He did the top row, then the bottom row, then his molars on his right side, then molars on his left side. He ran into trouble while brushing his tongue.

The toothbrush went too far inside his mouth and he gagged. Quickly, he swung his body two steps to the left until his face was over the toilet. He assumed the hurling position. Rum, Pepsi, and stomach acid was a flash flood up his throat. He tightened every muscle in his body in response and let out a loud, "Oooooh."

Anyone who knows will tell you that rum and Pepsi never tastes as good the next morning. Fortunately, his strong stomach muscles helped keep the potion down.

"Behold the man. This is your Lamed Vav, Joshua Bronstein." I chuckled. "You fellows are on a fool's errand. Of course, I shouldn't gloat since I'm only here to convince him to rob my casket."

The two of them shrugged their shoulders and said nothing. After more careful brushing, Bronstein dressed. He, being a west coast native, never felt comfortable in this cold climate. So he donned long underwear, pants, a T–shirt, a flannel shirt, a jacket, and a wool hat so he might go outside and greet his sweetheart.

Debra was on her hands and knees now. Her fingers were caked with mud. A bag of seeds was beside her. She rose when Joshua appeared.

"Peanut, my head's killing me," said Bronstein.

"What's the matter, didn't you have a good time last night?"

"I had a great time last night. It's just that this morning I'm paying the price," he said.

"Are you going to work today?"

"Not sure. I'll make a big breakfast. If I can keep it down, I'll go in late."

"I like my eggs sunny side up," she said.

"Okay. But first I'm going to need aspirin and more grapefruit juice."

"If you don't go to work maybe we could go to a matinee in town?"

"Don't even ask, baby. I can barely put two sentences together. I might have to go back to bed."

Bronstein was older than Debra. Did she remind him of how he felt as a younger man, filled with passion and virility, a time long ago before his troubles began? That was my opinion. As for her, my impression was that she liked the fact that he was older, worldly, and smarter than most of the men she knew. Plus, he talked. The stoicism that marked most Minnesota men was missing in him. He loved to tell her stories about life beyond Minnesota borders. What he knew about culture was exchanged for what she knew about spirituality and reckless abandon. That's not a bad trade.

"I'll be done soon," she said sweetly. "After breakfast I'll go to the grocery store and buy something for dinner and pick up some booze at the bottle shop. Tonight I'm going to do stuff for you that I've never done to another man before."

"Debra, you don't have to lie to me. What you'll do, you've done a dozen times to a dozen different men. And that's why it's good—you've perfected it."

"Maybe. But tonight I'm going to raise naughtiness to a new height."

He smiled a mischievous grin and took a moment to consider the possibilities.

"Hey, do me a favor. When you go to the bottle shop, don't buy rum and Pepsi. I can't stand that shit."

"Why not?"

"It's too damn sweet. All the sugar mixed with alcohol is what caused my hangover."

"Oh it did not. It's the bubbles in the Pepsi that got to you, not the sugar."

"Baloney," he said, "that candy-ass sweet stuff is enough to cause diabetes. Pick me up a bottle of Scotch."

"Damn, Joshua, I'd rather slurp turpentine."

"Baby, I ain't drinking rum and Coke tonight and that's that."

"What about what I want? Don't I count?"

"Get both."

"I don't have enough money to buy you Scotch and rum and still have enough money for dinner tonight. Have you got any money?"

"No."

"Well, maybe if we eat noodles tonight and skip the meat and vegetables we'll have enough money for Scotch and rum."

"We're not that hard up, are we?"

"I think we are."

"We have to eat," he said.

"What are we going to do then? It's Saturday night, and I always get drunk on Saturday night."

"You get drunk every night."

"So?"

"So, let's compromise," he said. "How about some red wine?"

"The sulfites give me a headache. How about beer?"

"Not beer," he said. "It's not economical. You've got to drink a shitload to get drunk, and then you end up running to the bathroom every five minutes to piss it out."

"Yeah, but at least it's cheap."

"How about vodka? I could drink it on the rocks and you could mix it with whatever you like. If you buy the cheap brand we'd have enough money for dinner too."

"Okay," she said.

"Make sure you get the biggest bottle you can because tomorrow is Sunday and the liquor stores are closed. If we run out we'll have to drive all the way to Wisconsin."

She nodded in agreement.

"Breakfast will be ready in twenty minutes. Finish up your gardening."

Himmelman, standing between me and Singer, was mooning over Debra. "Man, what I wouldn't give to have a woman like that."

"You wouldn't know what to do with her," I said scornfully. "You and your narrow Hebraic world, living and working among the Jews, marrying and siring Jewish children. It's a big, complicated, multi-cultural world out there that you Hasidim know nothing about."

"Listen to you talk," Singer said.

"You think that I'm full of shit, don't you?"

"Yes, I do," said the skinny fundamentalist.

"Let me show you something about shit, gentlemen."

Did I tell you that Bronstein had a dog named Shortstop? I don't remember. This hound loved the freedom to run loose in the north woods, without leashes or chains. The mutt was to be envied, since he actually got to be a dog with all his instincts instead of some stinky, couch-bound sleeper. Being part rottweiler, he took some pretty big craps and, for some reason, he always did it near the front steps of the trailer.

Bronstein, so hung over, so oblivious to everything, was not paying any attention. So when he walked to the front door I gave him a little push. He stepped right into a pile of dog shit, which was still steaming. With his size ten sneakers, Bronstein marched through the front door of his trailer.

To the bathroom he marched grabbing Kleenex to blow his nose. Then he walked to the kitchen. At the cupboard he reached for some aspirin. At the refrigerator he pulled out the grapefruit juice to wash it down. Ah, he had forgotten the bacon and eggs and a stick of the Land O Lakes Butter, lightly salted, whose label had an image of an Indian maiden that was his girlfriend. He carried them to the stove where a skillet awaited. Suddenly, the path of filth revealed itself.

"Boy, he really stepped in some shit this time, didn't he?" Himmelman said.

Bronstein looked around to see if the dog was nearby. Good thing for Shortstop he was gone. He temporarily escaped a beating. Fortunately, the linoleum floor would not be that hard to clean up once he found a scrub brush, soap, and a bucket.

While the three of us sat outside in the cool morning breeze lusting for Debra and the pleasures of the flesh which were no longer ours, Bronstein was on his hands and knees scrubbing shit from the floor. I could hear him muttering under his breath as he made it clean.

He rushed through the job because he did not want Debra to see the mess. Not that she would have cared much. After all, it was his trailer. But he was still conditioned from his years with

Victoria O'Shea and her famous Irish temper. Should the wife have come upon a scene like this, insults and invective would have made Bronstein feel like a dunce.

That's when it happened. Two hostile ghosts appeared. They were dressed in black pants, white tuxedo shirts, black bow-ties, and black shoes. Seeing that Bronstein was on his knees and ripe for abuse, they flanked him and, in stereo, shouted insults at him as he scrubbed dog shit off the floor.

"Are they Mormons?" I asked.

"No," Singer and Himmelman said at the same time, while staring at their shoes.

Bronstein was *monkey in the middle* between the two of them. The one on his right straightened his back, gave the Nazi salute and shouted, "Sieg Challah!"

"Look at this Jew scrubbing shit off the floor," said the second one. "Damn, you are one stupid fucker."

"It won't be long until his entire race is making their living the same way," said the partner.

"You can say that again, Hans."

"Give him a good kick so he feels our presence, won't you, Fritz?"

"A kick in the ass is too good for him. Better to ram something up his ass?"

"I'd pull down his foreskin but it's already gone." They laughed.

"Hey, Jew-boy, are you and your girlfriend going to get drunk again tonight?" asked Fritz. "She better not leave her body, because if she does me and Hans are going to violate her so that she'll never do you again."

I was puzzled by this spectacle. "Who are those guys?"

"Hans and Fritz," said Singer nonchalantly.

"Who are Hans and Fritz?"

"Twins. A couple of dead Germans who take great delight in badgering Bronstein."

"They rail against your boy and you do nothing?" I shouted.

"It's the Sabbath, and we don't work on Saturdays," said Himmelman. "These men know this. They stop by once a week."

"You lazy trade unionists—"

Himmelman cut me off. "Kalinsky, keeping the Sabbath holy is one of the watchwords of our faith. We don't work on Saturday."

"Isn't Bronstein allowed to enjoy the Sabbath?"

The Germans were invisible to Bronstein. But somehow he was hearing everything they said. And such mimics they were. Fritz's imitation of Victoria O'Shea was remarkable. His feminine voice chastised Bronstein for being the reckless driver who killed her only child.

Hans' voice spoke the eloquent Irish brogue of Father Terrence Goodlad, whose passionate pulpit speech made Bronstein the bane of Hibbing society.

As Bronstein cleaned, their rhetoric orbited his mind like a satellite. It stoked his self-hatred into an inferno. I could tell by the manic way he scrubbed the floor and splashed the brush back into the bucket.

Debra Crow heard him muttering from her garden. She peered in the window and interpreted the scene. Was she angry as Victoria O'Shea might have been?

No.

Did she castigate him for his incompetence or hold a grudge? No.

She tilted her head, giggling at him softly, and went back to her garden. In truth, she was happy, because now she would have an extra fifteen minutes to work in her garden.

Bronstein finally finished his chore. He threw the dirty water out a window on the other side of the trailer where Debra Crow couldn't see. He felt so bad about hiding it from her that he felt ashamed.

He walked into the bathroom to wash himself clean. After all, not even Bronstein, with his truncated level of personal hygiene, would wash shit off the floor and then go directly to bacon and eggs.

He grabbed soap, razor, and shaving cream and jumped in the shower stall. There was a mirror just below the spigot where Bronstein intended to shave his blue jowl. He smoothed a handful of shaving cream across the right side of his face. He was just about to do the left side when he stopped and tried to figure out just who was staring back at him.

Yes, it was a good question. Who was that fucker who stared back at him in the mirror? Instead of finding a friend, Bronstein found the image of someone he hated.

He started muttering to himself while the two German dybbuks stood back and watched the result of their taunts. Vile accusations of judgment swirled between Bronstein's ears that he could not silence. He defended himself desperately in an imaginary conversation, hardening his features, so as to give his words extra strength. Then he slipped into a combative stance, ready for a fistfight.

Now he was shouting in a fine alcoholic's rage. "Bring it, bring it, bring it on, you fucking fuck. Come on bitch, you want to cha-cha? Come on. I'll cha-cha. Let's go. Me and you. Once and for all. I'm sick of all your bullshit. Show your fucking face so I can punch it out."

His hands began to fly in mock battle, his back arched, and his muscles bulged. His fist banged hard against the wall. It was an impressive display of manhood, but futile.

His woman, working peacefully in the garden, heard his tirade. It was not the first time. Debra ran to him.

She opened the bathroom door with such speed that it startled him. His flying fist went astray and smashed the bathroom mirror that hung below the spigot, breaking it into twenty shards. One hit Bronstein right above the eye. He sliced his knuckle too. Blood gushed from both wounds.

Debra pulled back the shower curtain and, seeing his wounds, said, "Oh, Joshua, what have you done?"

She grabbed a bath towel and pressed it against his forehead. A wash cloth went around his hand.

The sight of his own blood cooled Bronstein's rage. He was quiet now, naked before his woman and mortified by what his wrath had wrought. The look on his face was one of disbelief. "I don't know what came over me," he said.

"Don't move," said Debra. "There's glass all over the place." She ran and got him a pair of slippers and he put them on. Then she led him naked to the toilet seat. While he sat there, she sprayed water against the bloody wall and swept up the broken mirror.

His self-contempt was such that emotionally he just shut down. He tried to speak, but humiliation robbed him of words.

"She doesn't care that he's a wreck," I said. "She's just happy that he doesn't beat her when he drinks."

"How do you know this?" asked Himmelman.

"Trust me, I know."

Debra gave the bleeder a hug and left him alone. I walked into the kitchen with a gait that I had seen in a John Wayne movie as I looked for the Germans.

At last, the opportunity to redress my grievance at having missed my turn against the Wehrmacht on the Eastern Front with the Red Army had arrived. I confronted the anti-Semitic shades, mad for revenge.

The smug grimaces they wore were the result of them thinking I was a just another putz like Singer and Himmelman. I slapped it off both of them. First one, then the other. My anger was white hot and they, having been dead for so long, were no match for me. They immediately recognized my hegemony and backed down.

"Jews fear Nazis no longer." These were my words. "Go back to hell, you filthy vermin. If you ever return, you'll face my Bolshevik wrath."

I could see that they might have been formidable in another day. They were big and strong and agile. But I was stronger and knew I could kick both their asses.

"Nazis? Us?"

"Yes. You must have been in the war. Were you in the sixth army that met its doom at Stalingrad? Were you in German tanks in North Africa with Rommel? Did you march with Von Runstedt at the Battle of the Bulge? Were you SS murderers in Poland? Did you man the death camps at Auschwitz?"

"We were none of those things," said one of the twins.

"You must have had some place in the Nazi hierarchy."

"To tell the truth, me and Fritz were waiters at the Airport Club in Berlin."

"The Airport Club?" I asked.

"For twenty years. We saw all the big shots."

"Then you served the leaders of the Nazi Party?"

"They knew us on a first name basis."

"Really?" I asked. "What were they like?"

"For the most part, lousy tippers," answered Hans. "But always amusing."

"Hey Fritz, remember the night Hermann Göring brought those two call girls to booth seven?"

Fritz laughed out loud.

"What? Tell me," I demanded.

"Göring had these two floozies in for dinner. He orders caviar and a 1923 bottle of Veuve Clicquot," said Hans. "It must have been back in 1937 before the war started. Then, Charles Lindbergh, the famous American aviator who was visiting Berlin, walked in.

"Göring and the girls were on their second bottle of champagne. They found out that the American hero was sitting ten feet away. They left Göring, who was the head of the Luftwaffe, and sat down next to Lindbergh. They touched his leg and giggled. They whispered things in his ear. Göring was getting really pissed because he was picking up the tab for those dames, and there they were swooning over another man."

Fritz picked up the story. "So Göring calls Hans over, grabs him by the lapel, pulls his ear down to his lips, and pointing to Lindbergh, whispers, 'Kick that bastard out.'"

"It was an awkward situation," Hans said. "So I told Göring, 'I cannot *mein herr*. That's Charles Lindbergh.'"

"I don't care who he is," said Göring.

"But he's meeting the American ambassador."

"What did you do?" I asked.

"I walked over to Lindbergh's table and told him there was an important call for him," said Fritz. "I took him to the quiet of the manager's office and handed him the receiver. When the American picked up the phone, Hans was on the other end. He pinched his nose to change his voice and said, 'Please hold for the Führer.' He waited with the phone at his ear while Göring collected the girls and walked out."

"That really happened?" I asked.

"That's just one of the stories I could tell. I even penned a book," said Hans. "But unfortunately the manuscript was lost in the Berlin bombing."

"Too bad," I said. "You could have called it, 'Third Reich Schlep.'"

"Hey Fritz, tell him the Jewish penis story," said Hans.

"Oh, that night? Sure. Joseph Goebbels, Field Marshal Wilhelm Keitel, Rudolf Hess, and Dr. Joseph Mengele were all sitting at a big round table in the middle of the restaurant. They kept us there almost until dawn talking Nazi theology."

"What did they say?" I asked.

"They debated propaganda. Should the Jews be portrayed in the press as monsters with big penises or sissies with small penises? It was a question posed by Minister of Propaganda Goebbels. They brought in Mengele for his medical opinion. They drank one-hundred-year-old Louis the Thirteenth brandy and argued all night."

"It was Goebbles' contention that propaganda must portray the Jews as having giant penises to evoke the envy of the working classes," said Hans.

Fritz cut in. "Nothing should be permitted to compete in size and hardness with the Aryan penis, claimed Hess. He made reference to the Nazi salute which was just an imitation of a big boner anyway. It was his opinion that the Jewish penis only appeared bigger because it was circumcised."

"Then they asked Mengele for a medical opinion. Mengele's idea was that on average the Jewish penis was no different from the German penis."

"But Goebbels claimed that would never do," Fritz continued. "He felt a ripe distinction between the two versions of manhood—Aryan and Jew—must be made in the minds of the German people. So in the early years of the Reich, Jews had large penises. Later, when they were all rounded up and sent to death camps, the rhetoric changed to reflect the fact that their penises had shriveled."

"Fascinating," I said.

"Thank you," they answered together.

"But tell me, why do you pick on Bronstein?"

"We're bored. It's the only fun we have left," said Hans.

"Don't you know you're dead?"

Now silence became them.

"How can you be in such denial and not know you are dead?"

"I suspected it, Hans, right after the kitchen exploded during that air raid," said Fritz. "I just never wanted to say anything."

"We're servers with no one to serve," said Hans. "For a waiter, that's a terrible thing."

"Do you still feel great allegiance to Nazi leaders?"

Fritz rolled his eyes. "No man is hero to his waiter," he said.

"Wait right here gentlemen. I might be able to help you."

I walked to Himmelman and Singer as the Germans watched from a distance.

"How much misery do Hans and Fritz cause Bronstein?"

"Quite a bit," said Himmelman.

"I think I know a way to get rid of them," I said. "I'm going to ask Holly to take them to the pearly gates. How does one summon her?"

"Scratch your balls," Singer said.

"What?"

"Scratch your balls," he repeated.

I looked him in the eye. He was dead serious. It made sense in a way. She seemed a little horny when I met her. So I scratched my balls and waited. Nothing happened.

Singer stared at me and said, "Try again."

So I reached down and scratched my balls again—this time with greater fervor. Nothing happened.

"Maybe you're doing it wrong," said Singer. "Try with both hands."

So I tried with both hands and this time with more vigor.

The two of them howled with laughter. "Kalinsky, stop it already. I was just kidding," said Singer.

Between giggles, Himmelman said, "Just whisper her name into the wind and she'll come when she can."

So I did. Then I returned to Hans and Fritz.

"I know this blonde. Better looking than Eva Braun. She can take you to a place where restaurants and clubs abound. There's a big reunion of Bolsheviks meeting this week. The party's going to be enormous. They're looking for waiters."

"You'd do that for us?"

"Sure," I answered.

"Is there anything we can do for you?" asked Fritz.

"I'll think of something," I answered.

"That's big," said Hans.

"Wait here. A woman named Holly is on her way."

"We'll wait," said Hans.

I returned to Singer and Himmelman. We saw Holly arrive. She had a conversation with Fritz and Hans. She led them off with such a ping that I was surprised that Bronstein, seated on the toilet seat with a white towel pressed to his bleeding forehead and a wash cloth twisted around his knuckle, didn't hear it.

Debra realized that Bronstein's duress was coming from the realm of shades. She was as angry as a hornet. Reaching into a kitchen drawer, she pulled out what looked like dried purple stalks wrapped tightly by a thin thread. Her eyes scoured the walls and the ceiling. She closed her eyes and went into a trance. It took a few minutes before we realized who she was looking for. It was us.

Somehow, she got a bead on us. It must have been Singer she saw. The fool was so busy leering at her that he must have revealed his shadow.

She walked to the bedroom in long strides and returned with an electric fan attached to an extension cord. We looked at her curiously as she plugged in the fan and set the control on high.

At the kitchen stove, she lit the herb until it was on fire. Then she blew it out. Burning coals emitted thick blue smoke. Putting the herb in front of the spinning fan, she was ready for war. With smoke shooting out of the whirling metal, she came hunting.

"Yuck," cried Singer. "What's that horrible smell?"

"It's sage," said Himmelman.

"That shit will kill you," I said.

"What did we do to deserve this?" protested Himmelman. "It wasn't us. Kalinsky, tell her it wasn't us. It was Hans and Fritz. This is just plain anti-Semitism."

"Run for it!" yelled Singer.

Himmelman and Singer flew from the trailer like bats out of hell. I slipped under the closed bathroom door to be beside Bronstein who was still on the potty, while Debra spread the smoke all over the trailer.

"And don't you ghouls ever come back!" screamed the angry woman.

Returning to the bathroom, she found Bronstein where she had left him. "Let me look at that," she said, pulling back the bloodstained towel. "Your forehead is going to need stitches. Get dressed. I'll take you to the hospital."

When Bronstein and Debra jumped into her rusting Delta 88, Singer, Himmelman, and I were already in the back seat. She drove down the unpaved road and turned onto the Spudsville road. When they came to Highway 169, she made a left and put the pedal to the floor.

Bronstein, beside her, towel pressed up against his head, watched as the speedometer went from fifty to sixty to seventy-five to eighty miles per hour. But when she got close to the Hibbing exit he yelled at her.

"Hey, slow down already," he said. "It's not a life threatening wound. It's just a cut. I'm not going to die. Chill out."

She slowed the car down to the speed limit as she entered the city limits. There was a line of cars at the stop sign waiting to turn onto First Street. They were fifth in line. Ironically, they found themselves right in front of Our Lady of Perpetual Sorrow. And who should be out front sprinkling salt on the sidewalk?

Father Goodlad.

The priest noticed the man in the front seat with a blood-stained towel pressed against him. Staring at the passenger, he took a few steps to get a closer look. When Bronstein saw Goodlad, he mumbled a soft, "Oh shit, not him." He ducked down in the seat. Fortunately, the way opened to First Street before Goodlad recognized him.

"Why does he hide his face like that?" Himmelman asked.

"See that priest? That's why."

So I told them the story of the once budding friendship of Joshua Bronstein and Father Terrence Goodlad. In an earlier time, the Dublin priest and his Semitic stalwart spent hours and hours in long private conversations in the priest's study and on long walks around the rocky shores of Hibbing lakes that were formerly strip mines.

Certainly, Bronstein vibrated at a pitch different from the locals. But Goodlad, being a Dubliner, did too. At the outset of their friendship, a common topic of discussion was the culture shock of coming to this part of America so very different from the place each was born. For me, this friendship was a Communist friendship because it sought to transcend the twin scourges of the twentieth century—nationalism and religion.

I remember one night when they were leaving the Homer, Father Jones entered with a priest visiting from Duluth. So intense was the conversation between Goodlad and Bronstein, that Goodlad barely acknowledged his cohorts, much to the chagrin of Jones. Bronstein was just more interesting.

Given the media coverage in the days following Bronstein's car crash, it became socially untenable for Goodlad to continue their friendship. Peer pressure forced him to pull up his emotional drawbridge in order to protect his own castle, lest the flash flood of public outrage wash it away. Their meeting of minds ruptured, with each retreating back to the tiny orthodox corner they knew so well—the martyred worlds of the Irish and the Jews.

Bronstein might have pulled it off, this synthesis, this intellectual marriage of the two faiths, were it not for the death of little Adam. Joshua might have melded with the masses and found a solid footing among them. But a baby Jesus had been taken from the manger and someone had to be blamed.

Victoria's nine sisters closed ranks around her during the divorce. They helped harden her heart against him until it became like Iron Range earth in January. Bronstein surrendered almost all their mutual assets. In part, it was to expatiate his guilt. But so implacable was his ex-wife's team, that it would have taken a fifteen-round, knockdown, dragout fight to get anything more. Washing his hands of the whole affair was enough. He asked for money to make a fresh start.

Unfortunately, he hadn't reckoned with his woe. Leaving town was out of the question. He felt an overwhelming need to stay near Adam. So he got a job at the very graveyard where his son was buried, and that became his life.

Now that the obligation to maintain a solid middle class persona was no longer his to abide by, freed from bourgeois constraints, he went on a tear against those very values. And it contributed to his deepening alienation.

I told Himmelman and Singer the story of how Bronstein embarked on a series of sexual escapades at the Homer Bar. Joshua had always been discreet about the profligate campaign but not so the young Hibbing women he slept with. Several came to unburden their consciences to Father Goodlad before morning mass following a Saturday night of reckless abandon with Joshua Bronstein.

At first, morbid curiosity engulfed Goodlad. He asked for the entire story. Eager to talk about it from behind the screen, these girls told all. Maria Moran, Mary Jo Bielatski, Mary Ann Jones, Mary Pat O'Donnell, Mary Therese Grimaldi... the list went on. Bronstein targeted Marys.

The priest might have pressed charges against Bronstein for the lewd acts he perpetrated against the female members of his flock were it not for the excitement that sometimes accompanied their verbal account of it.

Sworn to the secrecy of the confessional, Goodlad said nothing. Yet he realized that Bronstein was taking revenge on him by making himself a menace to Catholic womanhood. It got to the point where Goodlad no longer had to ask the stud's name... he recognized Bronstein's modus operandi.

First, Bronstein, the silver tongued devil, would woo these unsuspecting maidens with his swarthy good looks and witty remarks. He had a competitive advantage over other locals since he actually knew how to carry on a conversation. Drinks would be consumed, cigarettes smoked, secrets confessed.

Then he'd invite them outside to his Jew canoe, the infamous, powder blue, 1979 Cadillac Coup De Ville. It was always in a dark corner of the parking lot. How Bronstein managed to keep that car rust free through so many Minnesota winters was a mystery. For Goodlad, it was ample proof he had a deal with the devil. On warm evenings Bronstein would take them to a remote campsite near Side Lake. In cold months, it was back to his trailer.

I witnessed a confrontation between Goodlad and Bronstein one night at the bar. Seeing Bronstein sitting by himself, Goodlad walked right up to him and verbally accosted him for his wanton sexual mores.

Bronstein had been there three hours. I know, because I was serving him drinks. He listened to Goodlad's umbrage for several minutes and when the priest was finally done, Bronstein, with slurred words and a fake Italian accent replied, "You no playa da game, you no maka da rules."

Himmelman and Singer listened to my story attentively. It gave them insights into aspects of Bronstein's life they didn't know. I think they were daunted by the realization that his predicament was so multi-dimensional.

"Well, at least we got Hans and Fritz out of Bronstein's life," said Himmelman. "Nice work Kalinsky. But how we are ever going to make him ready for the Lamed Vav is beyond me."

"You think you have problems? How am I going to get him to rob my casket?"

"Looks like we're all screwed," said Singer.

CHAPTER FIVE

It was nurse Audrey McBride, her hair in a brown-gray bun neatly wrapped behind her head, who attended Bronstein in the emergency room of Holy Ghost Hospital.

In her first contact with Bronstein, nurse McBride pulled down the corners of her mouth until her bottom lip stuck out. She then furrowed her brow to sympathetically mirror his pain. It was an emergency room ritual she'd been doing for years. I haven't the faintest idea why.

Touching him maternally on the shoulder with her delicate hands, the nurse asked his name, what happened to him, and how he felt. When Bronstein noticed the gold crucifix on the lapel of her white uniform, he knew he was in trouble.

As intake nurse, it was Audrey's job to assess the patients and decide who the doctor would see first. When she reached for the blood-stained towel Bronstein held against his head, he recoiled and stuttered out, "Maybe we should just wait for the doctor."

"Just relax," she said softly. "Let go of the towel and let me look at your forehead."

"I'd really prefer if..."

"Nooooo," she said gently as her fingers brushed across his lips. This gesture was intended to put his fears to rest, and it worked. She even managed a smile for Debra. "It's okay... let go of the towel."

Reluctantly, Bronstein removed his hand.

Dried blood glued the towel to his skin. It hung down over the left side of his face. When the nurse reached for it, fear came to Bronstein. But being the dutiful patient, he let her have her way.

When she pulled the cloth away from his skin the gash re-opened. A stream of blood ran down over Bronstein's eyebrow, down the side of his nose, over his lips, and down his chin.

Bronstein, never known for his high pain threshold, let out a defiant yowl that blew back the nurse's eyelashes. Now a dozen pair of eyes from all over the emergency room were trained upon them.

"That's a nasty cut," said the nurse as she dabbed the wound with his towel. When dripping blood stained the purple and green plaid of Bronstein's favorite flannel shirt, it was too much.

"What are you, a moron? Of course it's a nasty cut. That's why I'm here."

"Excuse me, sir, but I am a trained medical professional who has been at this job for twenty years. I know what I'm doing and do not appreciate being talked to like this."

"Trained medical professional my ass!" muttered Bronstein, brushing her hand away and retraining the stained white towel against the wound.

"Some nurse she is. She'd make a better shoemaker," muttered Debra.

Nurse McBride pulled back her shoulders and put a stern look on her face so that the other emergency room patients would not lose confidence in her as a representative of Holy Ghost Hospital.

Yet, I could see that Debra and Joshua's remarks stung her because she assumed that archetypal pose that all numbskulls in positions of authority take when confronted with their own incompetence—a bureaucrat.

"Before we can attend to you, I'll need you to fill out these forms, dear."

The word *dear* was a nice touch, and she said it with just the right effect. She gave him a sincere smile and to the dozen locals looking on, that simple utterance of compassion reclaimed for her some of the moral high ground.

She returned a moment later with a clean white towel for Bronstein and held it out as a peace offering. But his stiff-necked umbrage was in full force now and he clung to his own. "No thank you," he said. "I'll just keep this on until the doctor can see me."

"Suit yourself then," said the nurse patiently, returning to her position behind the counter.

"Isn't it just like a Catholic to tear at somebody's wound until it bleeds," said Debra.

"How can you tell she's Catholic?" asked Bronstein.

"I can recognize one a mile away."

"What do you look for?"

"Anger and indifference."

"You can see that in her?"

"Sure, her attitude was a Catholic school standard at Our Lady of Perpetual Sorrow. There are a dozen angry adults in that place whose only job is to make everyone around them miserable."

"I didn't know you went to Catholic school."

"I did."

"Did they have a spanking machine?"

"No, the nuns used wooden rulers on our knuckles," said Debra, looking down at her hands. "That's how I first found out about Christ's mercy."

"Sounds awful."

"It was. Those idiots have absolutely no sense of humor. That's the whole problem with Christians. They're so busy imitating a crucified God that they mistakenly think that only pain is real. God, sometimes I hate white people."

"Well, we're not all bad," answered Bronstein.

"What do you mean 'we'?"

THE SHADY ELDERS OF ZION

"I mean that not all of us white people are bad."

"Hey Joshua, I hate to be the one to tell you this, but you're not white."

"What do you mean I'm not white? Of course I'm white."

"No, you're not. Do you think I'd be sleeping with you if you were white?"

"Look at this arm, Debra. This arm is white."

"You're not white. You're a Jew."

"I am too white."

"No, you're not."

"Yes, I am."

"Don't be fooled by what you see in the mirror, Joshua. The color of your arm has nothing to do with it. People don't hate minorities because of the pigment of their skin. They hate them because of the contents of their soul. And let me be honest, the content of your soul is anything but white. Only Christians are white."

"Oh really?" he asked, sarcastically. "What about the Black people?"

"Don't know any, and it doesn't matter," she said. "We are talking about you and your problem. You think you're white and that you should be just like them. But you'll never be just like them. They are small-minded and have no knowledge of how the great trickster gods goof on us all. That's what makes white people ignorant."

"I don't know about tricksters."

"Joshua, ditch those history books about Jewish misery and start paying attention to the great funny men of our time, all of whom are Indians."

"Bullshit, all the great funny men are Jewish."

"You don't really expect me to believe that, do you?"

"Have you been living under a rock? Jerry Seinfeld, Don Rickles, Lenny Bruce, Alan King, Jerry Lewis, Rodney Dangerfield, Jon Stewart? What are they, chopped liver?"

"Those punks couldn't get a belly laugh out of a hyena. I'm talking about tricksters like George Yellow Chicken, Coyote

Gray Sky, Billy Ten Trees, and Jimmy Skin Rash. That crew will unscrew your penis while you're sleeping and put it in your pajama pocket just for laughs."

"I never heard of any of those guys."

"Well, it's not my fault you're ignorant."

Bewildered by their exchange, Joshua decided to abandon the conversation altogether and concentrate on the hospital form that, fortunately for him, contained no ambiguity.

Bronstein walked up to the nurses' station five minutes later with the paper completed in his finest handwriting and handed it to the nurse. Examining it, two facts caught McBride's eye.

The first was his name. Now, she had been told his name twenty minutes earlier, but the fact that he was Joshua Bronstein, *the* Joshua Bronstein, had not dawned on her until that minute. Nurse McBride was an acquaintance of the O'Shea clan and knew all the stories about this drunken father, the phantom moose, and the dead baby.

The memory of Father Goodlad's tirade against this very man at the Sunday church service she attended three years ago returned to her mind. She decided, in the name of morality, to jerk Bronstein around as much as possible so he would know that guys like him do not have the approval of law abiding, God-fearing Minnesotans.

Another thing that raised her ire was the blank spot regarding health insurance.

"Do you have health insurance?"

"No, ma'am, I'm afraid I don't," he said apologetically.

"And how do you plan to pay for this?" asked the nurse.

"I'm not sure."

"Lucky for you we now take credit cards."

"I don't own a credit card."

"Check perhaps. You do have a checking account, don't you, Mr. Bronstein?"

He hesitated. A momentary sense of relief came to his face when he remembered that inside his thin wallet was a blank check he kept on hand for just such emergencies. When it dawned on him that he only had five dollars and forty-four cents in his account, he put on his poker face.

"Yes, I do. I'll write you a check." But his response was not very convincing and the ice queen pegged him for a deadbeat.

"Christ," she muttered under her breath, gazing away from Bronstein and at the dream catcher tattoo on Debra's arm. "You're the third one this morning. People like you are going to put this hospital right out of business."

The nurse turned and walked through the two white swinging doors. She went to a nurses' station out of the patients' sight where her friend, Dorothy Peterson, was reading charts. McBride slumped down in a chair next to her and opened a can of Seven-Up.

"You'll never guess what I have out there," said McBride.

"An interesting case?"

"I'll say, a Jew without money."

"Really, a Jew without money? I didn't know there was such a thing," Dorothy said.

"I can spot a deadbeat a mile away," said McBride.

"What does a Jew without money look like?"

"Like any other low life, I suppose, only circumcised."

"Well, we're obligated to treat deadbeats too, you know."

"This isn't an ordinary deadbeat. It's Joshua Bronstein."

"Joshua Bronstein... the baby killer?"

"Yep."

"He's got his nerve coming in here after killing that child. What's he here for?"

"Judging from the company he keeps, the Indian whore he's with probably slashed him."

"Is that what he told you?" asked Dorothy.

"No," said Audrey with a smirk.

"Oh, Audrey, you're so bad." The two friends looked into each other's eyes and began giggling.

"He says he cut himself in the shower, but I can't believe that."

Dorothy rose from her seat, snuck up to the door and peeked through it. She gave Bronstein and Debra the once over. "You'd think these idiots would come up with an original story once in a while."

"I know. It's pathetic, isn't it?"

"I was at Bernice Paulus' house just last week," Dorothy said. "She had a luncheon for Victoria O'Shea. She's running for the state senate. I heard her talk privately about the arm twisting Father Goodlad had to do on her behalf in order to get their marriage annulled. Her ex would have none of it. It got really ugly. But the priest finally won."

"She's lucky to have a guy like Father Goodlad in her corner," said Audrey. "At least now she can remarry in the church if she wants to."

"I heard he's a gravedigger at the Nashwauk cemetery."

"It doesn't surprise me at all," said Audrey. "Given his reputation, that's probably the only job he could get."

When McBride reemerged from behind the swinging doors, Bronstein walked up to her and asked her how much longer it would be. She deliberately ignored his question and pretended he wasn't there.

Now, Bronstein was no stranger to discrimination. Many times his Semitic facial features singled him out as a Jew. He bore the disdain of individuals who didn't even know any Jews, only the ingrained prejudicial rhetoric against them. But this was the first time he had ever been the victim of class struggle. And because his Jewish family viewed poverty as a condition worse than syphilis, it stung him.

The nurse, so solicitous to every wounded soul coming in to this healing place, now purposely avoided any eye contact with Bronstein. Everyone was taken before him. This included a strapping young man with a migraine, two dehydrated babies with the stomach flu, a boy who gashed his leg with a chain saw, and a mother with cramps.

The fact that he was now certified trash in the eyes of nurse McBride made a deep impression on the former suburban schoolboy, the former Washington reporter, and a former member in good standing of the O'Shea clan.

It convinced him that what Debra said was true. He wasn't one of them. The realization of how far he had fallen from grace, to such an extent that a little Christian charity was being denied him in the basement of Holy Ghost Hospital, had a sobering effect.

"God, I hate white people," muttered Bronstein.

Time went by and then went by some more. Perhaps this gatekeeper, so disdainful of Bronstein's past, so concerned with hospital economics, hoped the wounded deadbeat might get tired of waiting and go to the Lutheran hospital twelve miles down the road. But Joshua had no such inclination. So he waited in that sterile basement emergency room, where white curtains covered tiny windows. Long fluorescent bulbs lit the room. There was very little to look at except the cinder block walls painted white and the long rows of pipes that ran along the ceiling servicing the hospital with its heat, water, and sewage removal.

A set of chairs with orange, vinyl seats were lined up in rows against the walls and clustered in the middle of the room. Music might have helped, but they were too cheap to buy a boom box.

It was there on the pipes that Singer and I and Himmelman sat looking down upon the wounded below us. It was so tedious that even *we* were bored. "These doctors, they must be getting paid by the hour," said Singer, with a heavy sigh. Nobody disagreed.

Time passed.

Then Joshua started making music with his palms. To free his hands for music making, he tied the towel tightly around his head in a thick knot. This made him look like a pale-faced Sikh, but not a white man.

The air in that room was so dry that Bronstein was able to make a percussion type sound, like a drummer with brushes at the end of his sticks, by rubbing his hands together. Making his palms straight and stiff he rubbed them, back and forth and back and forth in a rapid motion. It created enough of a rhythm to carry a tune. The song he rubbed out that afternoon was from "Fiddler on the Roof." Debra Crow didn't recognize it. We, however, did.

This Jewish hand rubbing was a musical tradition that went back to Babylonian captivity where musical instruments were denied to the Hebrew slaves. Their music making was an act of defiance to their fertile crescent captors. Few souls actually remember this, but between hand rubbing and whistling softly between their teeth, these ancient Jews created the superstructure for what later became the Klezmer music tradition of eastern Europe.

Of course, the musical hand rubbing was lost on the tone-deaf Babylonians. Those pagans couldn't understand how a tune could be made from the friction of fingers and palms. But they didn't listen too well anyway. If they had cocked their ears just a smidgen, they might have been amazed by the songs. For to my mind, this Jewish hand rubbing represents our Semitic genius at its best. And Bronstein, his eyes narrowed and his shoulders squared, was really rocking out. Losing himself in this ancient musical tradition made him forget his woe.

Like most Jewish traditions, this musical hand rubbing was misunderstood. Christians thought the ancient musical art was a gesture of avarice. Shakespeare's Shylock in the "The Merchant of Venice" made it famous. But the bigots got it wrong. The delight of hand rubbing stemmed from Hebrew musical abandon and not from lusting for money.

Now it is true that this musical tradition was atavistic in that it skipped several Jewish generations at a time and then, as if by miracle, suddenly reappeared. According to Singer, not only was it big during Babylonian captivity but also at the time of the 1648 Chmielnicki massacres against the Jews in eastern Europe. Singer was an eyewitness. And I began to worry that perhaps the resurgence of this hand rubbing was an unconscious harbinger of Jewish doom.

Regardless of what the approximate meaning might be, the three of us—Himmelman, Singer, and I—actually enjoyed Joshua's hand rubbing performance. We knew what he was doing, and to tell you the truth, it wasn't bad.

Singer even sang along. "If I were a rich man, bah, bah, bah, bah, bah, bah, bah, bah, bah, bah, bah, bah, bah, bah, bahhhh."

Bronstein rubbed his palms together. We bobbed our heads and clapped our hands to the beat. As we did, more time passed.

But soon he grew tired of making merry. All that joy was making his palms chafe, his heart race, and his body perspire. Carefully, he unbuttoned his favorite flannel, removing it so as not to disturb the towel. It was thrown to the floor. There he studied the blood-stained collar, which provoked his anger at the nurse.

He slumped forward in the chair. Sweat glistened on his forehead. He suddenly realized that following the incident at the trailer, in his panic to get to the hospital, standing buck naked in the bathroom, he had grabbed the first piece of clothing within reach. As it turned out, it was one of Debra's T-shirts.

The shirt was tight around the shoulders and came up so short that it didn't even hide his hairy belly button. He knew it had something written on the front. He just hoped that he hadn't grabbed the shirt that read, "Just Say No to Sex with Pro-lifers," a quote that might only provoke McBride further.

But tough luck was his. Looking down at his own bosom, it was that very one. Realizing that fact, he folded his hands across his chest so no one would see.

Every muscle in his face went limp. A look of utter dejection appeared. Like he always did in these situations, the urge to flee seized him. It seized him like a panic. But where was he going to run? He beat back the fear. Bitchy McBride couldn't hold him off forever, he thought. He might just as well stay where he was. In an effort to relieve his humiliation, he started to cry.

There was no loud sobbing that might attract attention and further damage what was left of his male pride. No, it was just three or four tears that welled at the corner of each eye and dripped down his face.

The tears on the shaven side made it all the way down his cheek and dripped on the T-shirt just above his heart. On the unshaven side they were caught in a roadblock of stubble and formed a little swamp on his cheekbone.

Every so often, almost religiously, he would look longingly at those two white swinging doors for the medical treatment he hoped lay somewhere beyond. Except for the nurse, with the fine lines in her white skin, he had no idea if anybody else actually worked back there. But like God, who mortals hope dwells somewhere beyond the veil, Bronstein hoped that someone back there might bind his wound.

However, the chance that it was someone as negligent as Yahweh himself did not escape him. And as he speculated about who actually worked beyond those swinging doors, more time passed.

The tedium was even killing *me*. But how could I complain since it was me who, in a fit of impatience, pushed Bronstein's foot in the dog waste. It contributed to his initial humiliation and the following events that caused him to slice his head in the shower.

I'm humble enough to take some responsibility for this mess. If he were on this side of the veil, this is what I would say to him. "Bronstein, I just felt like yanking your chain a little bit. I had no idea that the likes of Hans and Fritz would arrive and fuck with your head. For this I apologize."

Now his girlfriend became uneasy. They had not talked or looked at each other for some time now.

"Joshua, why don't you talk? What's the matter? Are you getting sick of me?"

"No, don't say stupid stuff like that."

"Oh, so now I'm stupid."

"I didn't mean that."

"Tell me what you do mean. You know I can always tell with you. You get these shifty eyes and you can't look me in the face. I can always tell. You are sick of me and want me to go away, don't you?"

"No, that's not it."

"No? I think maybe you are sick of me and you're blaming me for what happened."

"No, I tell you I'm not sick of you."

Bronstein sat there totally demoralized. And now he was getting pissed off because she was interfering with his pity party. All he wanted was to be left alone.

"Then tell me what it is, Joshua. And tell me now or I'll leave you here."

"I'm sick of myself, okay? Can you understand that? I'm sick of myself. I'm sick of feeling like there's not a good place for me in this world. I'm exhausted by the humiliation. If I could cure myself of all this, maybe I could make something of my life. But God help me, I'm stuck and can't get out of it. Every time I think I've escaped it all, something ridiculous happens to remind me of just how fucked up I really am."

"I don't understand. How can you hate yourself when I see so much good in you? Maybe I'm the moron. But maybe it's you. I'm pretty, and I know how much pleasure I give you. Why isn't that enough?"

"I really don't know."

"My grandmother used to say that it is difficult to love a man who doesn't love himself. Is that you?"

"Yes, it's me and my bad karma."

"I don't know about your bad karma. It sounds to me like tricksters. Why can't you just lighten up? It's not like you're white or something."

"Stop saying that!"

"Besides, didn't you tell me that when Sigmund Freud developed his psychological theories most Christians dismissed it as Jew science? I think if you had a better understanding of the spirit world you could work with your spirit helpers and overcome your so-called bad karma."

"I don't believe in spirits," said Bronstein, and he said it as adamantly as a Stalinist.

"Well, you might as well, because they believe in you."

"What do you mean?"

"They're all over the place. They follow you around like a puppy. I figured it out this morning. I thought perhaps those spirits were my people. But they're not my people at all... they're yours."

"How do you know?"

"I've never seen an Indian with a yarmulke or those Jewish dreadlocks over their ears."

"You saw that?"

"Yes. There were two of them, and then there was a third one who looked like the devil himself."

"The devil himself?"

"Pretty much. I didn't get a good look at his face, but I'll tell you... he was scary."

"You can really see that kind of stuff?"

"Sometimes. And let me tell you something else... they don't have any intentions of going away. I suggest you find out what they want before they drive us both crazy."

"How do I do that?"

"How should I know? They're Jew spirits. Speak Hebrew at them."

"I don't speak Hebrew."

"Well, I don't know what to tell you."

Debra was satisfied with their exchange. Then she walked right up to the nurses' station as bold as brass and banged on the bell. It's shrill sound got everybody's attention.

"My boyfriend's cut," she said sternly to Nurse McBride when she appeared. "And we've been waiting a long time."

The nurse didn't like being lobbied by Debra. It was obvious from her face. "We know you're here," said McBride. "The doctor will see Mr. Bronstein when he is finished with the more serious cases and not before." The nurse turned abruptly and went through the swinging doors.

Debra returned to Bronstein and slumped down on the chair next to his. "Why do you hurt yourself?"

"It's the voices. They make me crazy. They keep screaming at me. They blame me for every problem of the world. They blame me for their own bad moods. They blame me because I am a Jew. It's like there's a pogrom going on in my head."

"They called you a Jew?"

"Yes."

"What do they say?"

"They say everything. They constantly tell me to shut up. Shut up, Bron-stein. Shut up, Bron-stein. And they say the last syllable of my name with scorn, just like that nurse did."

"When do they say it?"

"In my daydreams and in my night dreams. Last night I dreamt that I was watching television with a big group. They were all O'Shea family members. We stared at the screen together. It was like a Mass. I had a big smile on my face and I called out. 'Here's something… this television stuff is horseshit.'

"And they all looked at me. In unison they said, 'Shut up Bron-stein. Who are you to criticize television?'"

"Really, they got mad at you just for saying television is crap?"

"Yeah, they all raised their eyebrows, and after that a dozen of them, one right after the other, hollered, 'Shut up Bron-stein.'

"Debra," he continued, "when I tracked that dog crap all over the trailer, I was so humiliated that the voices returned to taunt me. They became so loud that I couldn't hear myself think. All I could hear was them mocking me for being stupid. I was afraid that you would hear it too and that you would agree with them and dump me. I tried to protest my innocence. I went thrashing at them. That's when I accidentally broke the mirror in the shower."

He felt much better after his confession. His girlfriend felt compassion and put an arm around him.

"I feel terrible, Debra. I want to go home," he said softly.

"Not yet. Wait for the doctor."

Some more time passed.

They squirmed once in a while, but mostly they sat in silence listening to the hum of the fluorescent bulbs. Finally, Debra spoke.

"I need a drink. There's a liquor store about two blocks from here. How much money do you have?"

Bronstein searched his pockets and pulled out what looked like about two dollars in change. Debra had a few munched up bills in her purse.

"What are you going to buy?"

"I don't care, as long as it's a lot," Debra said.

She put on her coat and quickly buttoned it up. She put a wool hat on her head, grabbed her purse, and rushed out of the emergency room without saying good-bye.

Joshua sat back in a chair with his bloody head resting against the cinder block wall and tried to forget his pain.

Someone had left yesterday's *Mesabi Daily News* on a chair. A paper like that you can read cover to cover in fifteen minutes. So Bronstein picked it up. Having stolen the nurse's pen, he worked the crossword puzzle, perused the sports page, and finally came to the obituaries.

It was then that he saw my death notice. He read it ravenously. And then he stopped and read it again. He buried his face in his hands. When Debra Crow returned he showed it to her.

"Wow, the old guy finally kicked, huh?"

"Apparently."

"I used to sit at his bar in the late afternoon when it was slow. He'd only charge me for one drink after serving me four. If I unbuttoned my sweater, he'd throw in a shot too."

"This has been a bad day," Bronstein said. "I feel like the last Hebrew on the Iron Range."

"Well," she said rather tentatively, "you still got me."

He did not respond.

Debra reached for the tequila bottle in the brown paper bag. She twisted off the cap, which had already been unsealed, put her hand against his chin, opened his mouth, and poured the Mexican whiskey down his throat.

For fear of the nurse, they retreated to the far corner of the emergency room and sat on the floor side by side doing shots. Now they no longer cared how long the doctor took. They passed the bottle back and forth and back and forth until Bronstein's pain became a faint, dull twinge.

"It's just past noon and they're drinking together?" asked Singer, awakening from a dream.

"Those two don't call it drinking... they call it foreplay," I said.

"Oh," said Singer. "That's different. Wake me up for the main event."

He closed his eyes and went back to sleep.

"Kalinsky," said Himmelman, "you were going to tell us a story about the night Debra Crow met Bronstein, remember?"

"I was an eyewitness."

"Good. I want to hear about it now before they run off somewhere." Himmelman gave his buddy Singer a nudge. He woke up.

"It's okay with me if he wants to talk," said Singer, startled from sleep.

"Good," said Himmelman.

I could tell that Singer was hoping for a lurid story more appealing than sleep. Not wanting to disappoint him, I tried to construct a tale that was true to the actual events while making it interesting enough to stimulate Singer's imagination.

"What I remember best was that Debra had a voice like a meadowlark," I said. "She sang in a rock and roll band called 'The Ravens.' It consisted of two guitars, a drummer, and her at the microphone. Now how would an old man like me know this? Tending bar at the Homer.

"While she played, I shuffled slowly back and forth serving drinks. My hearing was already shot, so they gave me the stools closest to the speakers. And it should be said that I had a following among the Iron Range regulars.

"Alcoholics came forth to seek my counsel from all over Saint Louis County while sitting at the big oak bar in downtown Hibbing. And man alive, was I ever famous for my Black Russians, which I concocted with vanilla vodka and a secret ingredient.

"When Peter Knutson, the bar manager, wasn't looking, I poured them all free drinks. I listened to their problems and gave them advice as good as any of the wonder rabbis the Hasid's brag about.

"Several times I had the good fortune to talk to Debra Crow alone. On quiet afternoons, she'd sometimes stop by for three or four. To me, she opened up her heart. Were I fifty years younger what I might have done to her. Instead, I set her up with Bronstein.

"I was one of the few people in town who would still talk to him. So I invited him to visit me on a night when Debra was singing. He arrived with a woman he was seeing, a lush from North Dakota named Kim Massingale. Having a warm woman who drinks is an essential component for getting through a long Minnesota winter.

"The band played, the place was crowded, and Bronstein and Kim sat at the bar. Bronstein put up a dollar on the bar's only pool table. Soon it was his turn to shoot. He was hot and won three games in a row. It's true that Bronstein could cut balls into pool table pockets like nobody's business. But the real energy behind his performance stemmed from the contempt he harbored for his opponents.

"Debra had finished her first set with the band. And now Bronstein and his eight ball competitors became the bar's entertainment. A long row of dollars went onto the table belonging to a half dozen men eager to play.

"Kim got impatient. Bronstein won too many games. She felt neglected and, with her alcohol intake increasing, she got testy. She pounded down four or five beers and then started rooting for his opponents, hoping that someone might retire him from the table so he would start paying attention to her. She made catcalls like, 'bad shot, Hebrew,' when he missed.

"This conflict between a man and his woman caught Debra's attention because those were the songs she loved to sing about. She started rooting for Bronstein just to piss off Kim. Her attention was nothing dramatic. She gave him a dreamy look, complimented him once on a good shot, and winked at him. For his part, Bronstein ignored her. But Kim did not and her jealousy grew. Leaning back on the two hind legs of her bar stool with her arms against the bar for support, she raised the volume of her insults. The crowd started to notice and people gathered around her to share in the mirth.

"Kim called to him. 'Hey Joshua, did you hear about the new Jewish car? It not only turns on a dime, it stops to pick it up.' That delighted the men who were rooting for John Gunderson, Bronstein's opponent. The pool players ignored the insults. But Kim was relentless and the men watching the game loved it.

"'Hey, Joshua, know why Jews like to watch porno movies backwards? They like the part where the prostitute gives the money back.' That one brought peals of laughter, and Kim was a star.

"But Debra didn't like the abuse Kim was dishing out. As I mentioned, she hovered about Bronstein in her skimpy shirt and tight jeans. Then she walked past him, touched his ass, and continuing through the crowded bar, surreptitiously kicked the back leg of Kim's bar stool. It gave way.

"The big mouth's head hit the bar with a thud, and she fell onto the floor with a splat. Debra strolled lazily along to the lady's room. Everybody was so busy watching the pool game that no one saw Debra's fancy footwork. But I, Kalinsky, the master tactician, saw it all through the blue-gray haze of cigarette smoke.

"When they pulled Kim to her feet, her head was spinning. Bronstein thought it was her just deserts and made no effort to help. Two women helped Kim to the bathroom where she threw up in the toilet. Debra, who got there first, even took a turn holding her head over the bowl.

"Then Debra Crow walked up to Bronstein and introduced herself. She said, 'You're good.'

"Nobody had told Bronstein he was good in a very long time. Considering all the humiliation he had suffered from Kim, he was grateful. But now it was time for Debra to go back on stage.

"'Bartender, how about a couple of shooters for me and the pool king here,' said Debra.

"What'll you have?" I asked.

"'A couple of Dead Nazis, please,' she said, staring into Bronstein's eyes. He did not flinch.

"I mixed Rumple Minze with Jagermeister, threw it into two shot glasses, and set them down. They grabbed the drinks, tossed them down their throats, and banged the empty glasses on the bar at the same time.

"'Got to go to work,' she said.

"Debra went back on stage. But she had Bronstein's attention."

"It was that simple?" asked Himmelman.

"It was that simple," I said. "But I have to admit, Debra did most of it herself. I just provided the necessary propaganda to get her interested."

"Did he take her home that night?" asked Singer.

"They exchanged phone numbers. That's all," I said. "She knew it was Bronstein for her after a short conversation."

"Really?" asked Singer.

"Absolutely," I answered.

"I pity the poor girl," said Himmelman.

"Poor? This girl has a dowry."

"Where does a rock and roll Ojibwe singer get a dowry?"

"Desmond Grouch."

"Desmond Grouch? Who has a name like Desmond Grouch?" asked Singer.

"Her ex-husband, the Mdewakanton Sioux elder Desmond Grouch from down in Shakopee, Minnesota. The man is close to being a millionaire from the Indian gambling casino he started outside of Minneapolis," I said. "He first saw Debra on stage singing with her rock band at one of the clubs near Prior Lake. They were married for a few years, but he beat her. He also skimmed casino profits. One day she cleaned out his bedroom safe of nearly three hundred thousand dollars and ran back to her people up north. It was dirty money, so he couldn't call the cops. Debra's four brothers threatened to castrate Grouch, should he ever come after her. A week later an attorney was sent to negotiate a settlement. After a difficult back and forth, she agreed to keep a third of it and give the rest of it back. She was also granted alimony and a divorce. So there, now you know a secret about Debra Crow. She has money of which Bronstein knows nothing about. In addition, she wants this Jew to impregnate her."

"Why would a rich girl go for Bronstein?"

"Because he is a Jew, and they have a head for money."

"Oy vay, does she have the wrong guy," said Singer.

All of us had a good chuckle.

"This is one time that a Jewish stereotype worked to his advantage," I said.

"Kalinsky," Himmelman said. "I don't get it. If it's such a secret, how do you know about it, but not Bronstein?"

"Every word I've spoken is true... I swear."

"But how do you know?" he repeated.

"I've heard stories."

"Did she confess it to you at the bar?"

"No."

"Then who told you?" Himmelman asked.

"Greta Niemi, a friend of Debra's family."

"Who?" asked Himmelman.

"Greta Niemi."

"Who is Greta Niemi?" Singer asked.

"The greatest witch in the north woods. Gentlemen, you can ogle over Debra Crow if you want to, but this Niemi, what a woman."

"Tell me about her," demanded Singer.

"Okay, here's the lowdown on Greta."

And in anticipation, the two Hasids gathered around me. Stories of women who are a wonder are something every man longs for. So I told some tall tales about my little psychic baby, Greta Niemi, my paramour in the old days. And if I embellished things a little bit, it was only because I was bored.

Everybody was intimidated by Greta Niemi, I told them. She had more money than her suitors. A pretty face she possessed her whole life. Her breasts were like ripe plums. And smart? You have no idea how she befuddled the tough guys who courted her. But those weren't even her best features. Here's what was.

She percolated estrogen. It's true. It bubbled out of her from some hidden aperture and collected around her in a cloud. It put men into a spell. Breathe the same air as she and you were smitten. At least that's the way menfolk reacted. She hypnotized them.

With women, Greta provoked a whole different reaction. I remember walking down a downtown sidewalk with Hilda at my side one day when Greta passed us by walking in the opposite direction. It was a shock to see her so suddenly before me. We were lovers then. I kept my composure, but not Hilda.

The minute we were within five feet of Greta, Hilda started to sneeze. Loud, body-wrenching *achooos*, which didn't stop until Greta turned the corner.

At one point I considered the power she had over men a major act of manipulation. Now, in retrospect, I'm not sure how much control she actually had over it. Whatever it was, it was. There's no doubting that. But I think she was as much the victim of this phenomenon as the men she made swoon. The reason I say that is because whenever men swooned, her nipples hardened. It drew attention to her breasts and embarrassed her.

Plus, there was that psychic stuff. She noticed every detail. It was her belief that even tiny, seemingly insignificant details were morally instructive. For her, everything passing before her eyes was a legitimate telltale. That minutia was as significant as one's actions and as one's speech.

One winter evening, when I was leaving her house, the key went into the ignition of my car and snapped in half.

To her that was the harbinger of our coming break-up. That's how spirit guides communicate with mortals, she said. And now that I am a spook myself, I realize that those little coincidences are the only way that those of us living in the realm of shades can push mortals onto a better path.

Cultivating those spiritual gifts took her years to hone. And because of her many spiritual trials, which taught her tough lessons in tough ways, she was critical of the New Testament idea of Jesus. To Greta, all that hero worship was a bunch of hooey because it denied the hard work, wrong turns, the doubt, and spiritual crisis that Jesus endured to reach the level of consciousness that inspired the following generations. "Immaculate? No. That's bullshit," I once heard her say. "He worked his ass off."

Truth is, the first time I really noticed her, years ago in a liquor store, she was the town kook. Recently released from Moose Lake State Mental Hospital, she was a divorced woman in her late twenties trying to contend with a difficult bout of mental illness.

In part it was Iron Mike Niemi's fault, though it was a well-kept family secret. For the great Hibbing capitalist was merely a stepfather who had married Greta's mother shortly after the real father abandoned the family. Mike rescued the mother, Greta, and a younger sister, Andrea, from poverty.

When teenage Greta sprouted breasts, Iron Mike began
creeping into her bedroom at night. Her mother never knew, or
if she did know, she chose to say nothing. It was Greta's fear that
should she refuse the stepfather sex, he might throw the three of
them out in the cold or worse, that he might go after her younger
sister, Andrea. So she let him have his way. Iron Mike got his
way with everybody.

Years later, she broke down. The secret was too hard to bear.
Unfortunately, at one point, so very confused, she began throwing herself at every man who gave her a look. She went from
town kook to town whore. That's when a court order committed
her to a psych ward. She was released after six months. And it
was the beginning of her psychic stuff. She found it so unpleas-
ant to be in her body that she cultivated a strong bond with the
spirit world as a means of escape.

It's the reason she took such glee in the betrayal of her stepfather. For the truth is, I'd never have successfully engineered
the Great Steelworker Strike of 1968 were it not for Greta spying
on Iron Mike in his own home. She reported about his finances,
his deals, his political allies, and battle plan. I used every piece
of information against him. He never knew what hit him.

★ ★ ★

Back on the hospital floor, Debra and Bronstein made a toast to
me with a long gulp of tequila and asked that the life I have in
heaven be more satisfying than the one I had on earth. They toasted the dead boy, Joshua's son, Adam. They toasted blowjobs and
orgasm and the clitoris and the penis and best of all, tequila. And
then laughter returned to their hearts and they were happy.

When Debra Crow drank, she underwent a remarkable transformation. Her posture and her very body language
changed, taking on this slutty hoochie-coochie pose that made
her so compelling. She partied hard, and for the first two or
three hours she was a work of art—just like other femme fatales
like Mata Hari, like Delilah, like Eve.

After a while she got a little sloppy and on the tail end of a two-day bender she was dangerous. And I knew this because she came to me at the Homer regularly. I gave her free drinks when she came in with the shakes but no cash.

So there they sat, the two of them in the back of the emergency room and out of the peripheral vision of the rest of the patients who were all facing forward.

"Let's play dragons," said Debra. Joshua had never played the game before so she went first. She put her head on his lap and stared into his eyes. She took a large mouthful of tequila and swished it around her mouth. Then she took a match from her pocket and, pursing her lips, lit the match and exhaled. Orange flame hovered around her lips. The flame was extinguished when she put her lips back together.

"That was cool," said Bronstein, in a bit of a daze.

"Now you try," she said.

Following her instructions, Joshua put his head upon her lap, careful not to upset the towel. He opened his mouth and Debra poured a healthy dose of tequila down his throat. "Now, don't swallow it," she said. "Swish it around your mouth. I'm going to make you breathe fire, Joshua."

She took out a match and lit the tequila in his mouth. An orange flame issued from his lips. Unfortunately, Bronstein caught the hiccups, and to prevent himself from choking on the tequila, he swallowed.

"Aaa—!" A thwarted scream issued from his mouth. He jumped to his knees, holding his throat with both hands.

"I told you not to swallow," she said.

Every patient in the emergency room turned to look. But since Debra had hidden the tequila bottle, they thought the reason for Bronstein's outburst was the reason he needed to see a doctor. Debra gave them a friendly wave of her hand and a timid smile. So after one quick glance, they turned and faced forward because, as everybody knows, Minnesotans are exceedingly polite.

"Damn," he wheezed, his hands holding his throat, "that burns." He made a trilling sound from his throat, hoping that it might ease the pain of his singed uvula.

"Watch this. I'll show you again." She rolled around, put her head in his lap again, and looked at the ceiling. She took a big swig from the bottle and arched her back. She handed him the matches and motioned with her hands for him to light her up. He lit it on the first try. When she exhaled, the fire flew out of her mouth and almost as high as Joshua's chin, just like a fire-breathing dragon.

When McBride reentered from behind the two white doors and saw what was going on she screamed across the room. "There is no drinking in the ER!" Upon seeing the flame, she added, "There's no smoking either."

Debra swallowed the liquor and raised her head a few inches off Joshua's lap to offer the nurse a drunken smile.

"Mr. Bronstein, the doctor will see you now... alone."

Debra turned her head away from the nurse's face and nestled her face into his crotch, hoping to get him hard.

"Save it, Peanut," said Bronstein. "We'll be home soon."

Joshua entered the medical area bloody and drunk. The doctor was one Steven Ginsberg, a Chicago native doing his residency at Holy Ghost. He recognized Bronstein as a member of the tribe immediately. The fact that it was early afternoon and he was wearing a woman's T-shirt that smelled of girlie deodorant, and had a gash on his head that might have been caused by his Indian girlfriend in a drunken rage, made Ginsberg pinch his chin with the fingers of his left hand and raise his eyebrows.

"Truth is, Himmelman, I feel sorry for this Bronstein," I said. "He was born into a bad era. That's the real wound he bears. His anger would have found a creative outlet as a Bolshevik. As it stands now, he longs to be a man of passion able to stand with other men who have ideas, purpose, and nerves of steel. But poor Bronstein, he was raised into a middle-class American family in the latter part of the twentieth century. What options lay ahead for a man like that? Another Jew doing retail? How about a big house in a sterile suburban neighborhood in a post-modern age? There's no life for real men today."

"That's not his problem," said Himmelman.

"His problem is that he's a bum," I said.

"What do you mean, a bum?" countered Himmelman. "If he was a lazy bum they wouldn't have assigned us to rehabilitate him."

"Bronstein is a working man doing menial labor in order to find time to think, read, and contemplate," argued Singer. "I knew Baruch Spinoza. He was the same way. He grinded lenses all day just to keep his mind free for scholarship at night. That physical labor should yield time for spiritual contemplation. Is that not at the heart of the Communist Manifesto, Kalinsky? Why do you belittle this man who lives up to your working class standards?"

"I don't know why. It's my own prejudice, I suppose."

"You're such an idiot," mocked Singer. "If you hadn't made him step in that crap this morning, he'd have gone to work and would probably be the man digging your grave right now. And let me tell you, such a grave he digs. The corners are sharp right angles. He picks the floor clean of stones so when they lower you into the ground it's like lying on velvet."

"Singer's right, you know," said Himmelman. "He'd have had ample opportunity to steal that cross for you too. But no, you had to be a tough guy."

"I make no apologies for what happens to mortal men."

"Kalinsky, tell me more stories about this boy," said Himmelman. "We're his guides. But we've only been on the job a short time. We need to know."

"Come outside, we'll talk," I replied. We went out into the cold, cloudy street and I told them stories about Bronstein's rescue of Tim O'Shea, his marriage to Victoria, the death of his son, and other details of the miserable life he had carved out for himself in northern Minnesota.

An hour later, bandaged and ready to go home, Bronstein emerged from behind the emergency room door with nine stitches in his forehead. Debra was nowhere to be found.

He called out her name. She did not appear. He went searching for her. He stood outside the lady's toilet calling her name. No one answered. He walked down a long corridor to the cafeteria—not there. He felt somewhat better when he discovered her car was still in the parking lot. Where could she have gone?

It was not uncommon for her to do this. Sometimes, on some sort of unnamed whim, which he never really understood, she would take leave of him and disappear. It usually happened when she'd been drinking. Perhaps she had a boyfriend somewhere else. But she was really loaded now and could be just about anywhere, doing just about anything, he thought.

Twenty minutes later he discovered Debra sitting on the front steps of the hospital. And it was only by chance that he saw her. A small part of her shoulder, visible from behind the pillar she was leaning against, caught his eye when he walked out the front door. Her eyes were droopy and she seemed barely conscious. He walked up to her gingerly and sat down beside her. It started to snow.

"Pathetic punk. What do you want?"

"They put stitches in my forehead," said Bronstein. "I'm healed and ready to go."

"They healed your head? They didn't heal your head. You're still a fucking mess."

"What do you mean?"

"I mean you said some things in there that just sucked. I don't even like you anymore. Get the fuck away from me."

"What did I say?"

"Oh, I am a Jew lost in the wilderness," she mimicked. "I can't find my place in the world, I am so misunderstood, the O'Shea family thinks I'm a dirt bag. You know what? Everything you said is true, and do you want to know why?"

"Okay, tell me," said Bronstein.

"It's because you're white and you know what? I don't fuck white guys."

She reached for another swig from the bottle, but the bottle was empty.

Dorothy Peterson walked by on her way home. She cast a glance at Debra up against the pillar. "Oh," she said, sarcastically. "Here's something new and different, a drunken Indian."

"Shut up, bitch," screamed Bronstein.

Then, turning to Debra, he said, "I am sorry I put you through this. Look, it's snowing. We better head home."

"I heard from the liquor store clerk that we are going to get twelve inches," said Debra.

"Great," he said sarcastically. "Just what we need, Indian winter."

"Don't blame this on my people. Some Jewish hardware store owner with too many snow shovels to sell probably paid off the weather gods so he could clear his inventory."

"What did you say?"

"You heard me."

She was right. Bronstein did hear her. It's just that he had no snappy comeback. He asked her to repeat what she said hoping that some smart aleck remark might come to him in the meantime. But nothing came, so he sat in silence.

"Come on, let's go." He reached under her arm and picked her up.

"Let go of me." She pulled away from him and slipped after one step. Were it not for Bronstein's quick hands she might have fallen head first on the stone steps.

When they got to her car, he warmed up the engine and scraped the snow from the windshield. She immediately fell asleep. On the drive home Debra briefly awoke. Lifting her head from his lap she looked to see where she was. "Where are you taking me?"

"Back to my place."

"I don't want to go there," she said.

"Where do you want to go?"

"The Indian burial ground," she said.

"In a snow storm?"

"Especially in a snow storm. That's where I want to be."

"That's ridiculous."

"You don't have the balls to come with me."

"No, I guess I don't," he said.

"I'm getting on my snowmobile and I am riding to the Indian burial ground. Too bad you're too much of a wimp to come along."

"Who are you calling a wimp?"

"Wim-py Bron-stein, Wim-py Bron-stein," she chanted with slurred words.

"Shut up. It's a stupid idea to go there in the middle of a blizzard."

"I'm not going for me, Joshua. I'm going for you."

"Oh really? And why is that?"

"Because you're a little bitch. Maybe out there you can find your balls."

"That's mean. Today has already been an ordeal and we're both loaded. Don't add to my problems."

"If you were a real man we'd take my snowmobile there and build a campfire and a snow house. Do you remember the last time we went there?"

"Yeah, I remember," he said. "It was a blue, autumn day. The wind was blowing just hard enough to keep the bugs away. We put up a tent, made a great dinner, and made love for the first time. It was our third date."

"With this big snowstorm you can't go to work and dig graves anyway."

"That's true," he said. "Okay, I'll think about. Go back to sleep."

Debra loved the Indian burial grounds and Bronstein knew it. She had played there as a child. It was where her great, great, great grandparents were buried in unmarked graves. The site was located in a meadow surrounded by birch trees. It had a marvelous view of Bug Lake whose shoreline was down a steep hill.

Singer, Himmelman, and I were riding in the back seat. I repeated the words *Indian burial ground*. My face lit up like a lantern. Himmelman and Singer noticed.

"What's got you so happy, Kalinsky?" asked Singer.

"This is a stroke of luck. The Indian burial ground is less than a mile from Greta Niemi's home."

"Will we get to see her?" asked Singer.

"You will if I have anything to do with it," I answered.

The roads were slippery and the wind was blowing snow right into their windshield. The wipers didn't work well. It was hard to see. Bronstein braved his way into the storm drunk and driving too fast. Fortunately, no moose appeared.

CHAPTER SIX

By the time they made it home, four inches of snow had covered the ground. In anticipation of additional accumulation, Bronstein parked the rear wheel drive Delta 88 in a makeshift little shelter made of pine branches beside the Spudsville road, lest the car get stuck on the dirt road on their way to the trailer. They walked the rest of the way.

In the kitchen they downed two glasses of water each to help ward off the inevitable alcohol dehydration. They popped aspirin too. Then it was naptime.

The two of them undressed and spooned in each other's arms. The front of his thighs pressed against the back of her thighs, his chest against her shoulder blades, his arm firmly wrapped around her, his hand cupping her breast. Even their toes made contact. His head lay close to her hair. The smell of her herbal shampoo made him long for spring.

As a bartender it was my opinion that Debra had done the right thing drinking tequila that afternoon instead of Bronstein's favorite Scotch or her own rum. Tequila is more of a body high, and I calculated that the recovery time needed to freshen up, compared to the other two liquid concoctions, required less time and sleep.

For our part, Himmelman, Singer, and I went outside to watch the snow blowing in from the west. In Minnesota we call such storms Alberta Clippers because they blow straight out of the North Pole, slide along the eastern ridge of the Rocky Mountains through Alberta, and veer left to pummel the northern plains and prairie. It was my first snowstorm as a ghost and I was enjoying it. Want to know what it reminded me of?

It reminded of a late spring morning in 1921, standing beneath a shower of confetti falling down from tall buildings as I led a column of shock troops along a parade route to Red Square during the Moscow May Day parade. Cheering crowds swarmed the parade route, beautiful women threw flowers, young boys saluted. Our boots swooshed through three inches of confetti piled on the pavement.

How could I not remember that parade? My family was watching. Back then I was the young Captain Ivan Kalinsky, tough guy, leading his cadre past the reviewing stand. All the Bolshevik heroes were on that podium—Vladimir Ilyich Lenin, Leon Trotsky, Gregory Zinoviev, Lev Kamenev, and of course that Georgian weasel, Josef Stalin.

Years have passed since that event branded itself upon my memory. The reason it remains so bright is that it made me feel like an active participant in the epic march of history.

But now, caught in the company of schnooks like Singer and Himmelman, that reverie, which at one time was the center of my world, seemed like the dank fiction of a world that was no more.

That May Day parade is etched as a legitimate point of reference in my memory, like true north on a compass, amid the thousand directions my life has taken during my many decades as a man. It was a defining moment of my manhood for which I have always been grateful. And it's a brag book of sorts. I admit it. The opportunity to tell the story remains one of my great treasures.

I loved to hold court and gush it out with full orchestration to the drowsy drunks sitting on the stools before me at the Homer Bar... but only after last call had been given to the likes of Rick Rinaldi, bartender at the Kahler Hotel, Russell Nelson, a local painting contractor, and George Mooney, who cooked in the Homer kitchen.

Now why, you might ask, did I only pull out such drama to that doddering crew after last call? It's because after so many ounces of alcohol they never remembered anything the next morning. I got the pleasure of telling a good story while not risking my secrets.

Of course, it was like speaking Chinese to a schnauzer. Minnesotans don't give a damn about what happens in the rest of the world. They possess a regional nearsightedness whose vision stops at the border.

Now dead, and soon to be back in the bosom of my comrades, I dream of regaling my men with stories of the cold northern Minnesota winter, of exile, loneliness, and despair. And though it may not bring tears to their eyes, I'll have to be careful about provoking my own.

The pride stemming from knowing so many great Russian men of the last century is also an example of what we Semites call Jewish geography. This is not an insignificant point.

As a people, we Jews have always been wanderers. Until the state of Israel was reestablished, we knew no land to call our own. And so, as a nation of peripatetics, it wasn't where you came from that counted... it was who you knew that mattered most. That's why name-dropping is a Jewish art form. Having no connection to the land, our only reliable link in life was to each other.

For example, I have never witnessed a sunset from the Tolstoy Bridge in Pinsk. But I did know a Jewish dance hall singer named Rena Pensky from Pinsk who loved cocaine and was grateful to any man who could provide it. And she was famous too. Ask any Pinsker from the days before the first Five Year Plan. They'll have heard of her. But enough of that.

Bronstein woke from his nap. His hangover was tolerable due to the large amount of water he had consumed before his head hit the pillow. However, he was still sore from the stitching of his forehead, and his singed uvula still smarted.

Debra woke too. Looking out the window, she estimated that it was now snowing about two inches an hour. Bronstein did not doubt her. For though she was born near International Falls, it was said that her maternal grandmother was an Eskimo.

She called the weather line at a local radio station for the latest forecast. The twelve inches the liquor store clerk quoted earlier in the day was upgraded to twenty.

"Are you still up for a visit to the Indian burial ground?" she asked Bronstein.

"If you can stand it, so can I," he answered.

Wilderness was always Debra's answer to Bronstein's problems. When he pined for the Pacific Ocean with a homesickness that oppressed him, she drove him east to the North Shore of Lake Superior, two hours away. They'd camp out on the rugged cliffs overlooking that vast body of water, which her father's people called Gitche Gumee. It allowed Bronstein to pretend he was back at Bodega Bay.

When he felt disconnected from the rest of the world, when his small life in the north woods became too much to bear, she drove him north to Lake Itasca, about an hour and a half away. There, where lake water poured out into a small brook and became the headwater of the Mississippi River, she had a stranger take a snapshot of the two of them walking barefoot across the rocky stream.

That spot, Debra said, was the true head of the American spinal chord, the mighty Mississippi, which geographically rushed down the center of the nation to the Gulf of Mexico.

Today, following his mishap in the shower, feeling that something was askew, it was Debra's idea that a trip to the old Indian burial ground at Bug Lake was what he needed. She considered his accident big medicine... too dramatic, too significant to ignore.

"Joshua, you're being stalked by spirits," Debra said. "Maybe out there without distractions we can figure out why."

Now you might think that with all the experience Jews have waiting for the messiah, that waiting for spring in northern Minnesota might not be difficult. Unfortunately, it was. It's a collective hardship, for Jews and non-Jews alike, since spring arrives on the calendar long before it arrives on the thermometer.

He tried to think of the last time he had some color on his face. September? That was over seven months ago. The lack of light and heat resulted in a spiritual fatigue that enervated him, accosted his abilities, and drained his resolution. It's a fact that ninety percent of all Minnesotans are vitamin D deficient by January.

How he ached for a trip to Florida where he might waltz around in Bermuda shorts down Collins Avenue in Miami Beach, see his favorite baseball team in spring training, or swim in the ocean. But he was too poor for a plane ticket, and Debra refused to leave Minnesota in winter.

While more manly Minnesota men were drinking themselves into oblivion and beating their wives and children, he was drinking himself into oblivion and beating up himself.

But now, instead of the bright promise of spring fever, here was another winter storm. Who was it that said, 'April is the cruelest month'? Was it T.S. Eliot?

Anybody living in northern Minnesota would readily agree. At this time of year, the idea that you might wake up one morning to a warm blue day was what we lived for. But a spring snow storm? It was an emotional setback.

He was also suffering from Minnesota hat hair, a local phenomenon pervasive in winter months. So many cold, arid days with a wool cap on his head turned his hair into straw. His cowlicks had cowlicks. From the neck up, he resembled a pale scarecrow.

He reached for some toilet paper. Blowing his nose yielded no green snot like it might on a humid August day. No, the dry cold air parched his mucous membranes and what appeared was dried blood. No big deal, it's just something that happens up here.

Naps in the afternoon were frequent for the two of them. That's because Debra and Joshua lived for 9:09 p.m. They cherished that minute and built their whole romantic schedule around it. It's when they'd break out the booze, smoke some pot if they could find some, blast the stereo, and forget about their problems. According to Joshua, 9:09 was the time on the old wall clock at the Homer when he began his first conversation with Debra.

Such rituals shouldn't surprise you, given the Jewish penchant for ritual. On nights they were together, they began anew at this time. On most days it was zero hour, the starting point for their intimacy.

They'd light candles, they'd burn incense, they'd drink, they'd talk, they'd look at dirty magazines, they'd get horny, they'd dance, they'd confess, they'd get mushy, they'd make love. Can you think of anything better to do on a night when the thermometer was at single digits?

"Singer," said I, "you look like you just bit into a lemon. What's the matter?"

"What is this wild goose chase? Why is she taking him into the woods during a snowstorm? Who is crazier, she for taking him, or him for his willingness to go along?"

"They're going into the woods. What's the big deal?" I answered.

"What is the future of a relationship like this?" asked Himmelman. "Such sloth is unbecoming a Jew."

"Unbecoming a Jew?" I repeated with a tone of disbelief. "Himmelman, let me tell you something. In the last half of the twentieth century nobody wanted to be a Jew. They just want to live their lives unencumbered by their Semitic baggage."

"That's baloney, Kalinsky," Himmelman said. "If Bronstein didn't want to be Jewish he could have requested to come into this life as a Presbyterian. But no, he chose Jew and a Jew he must be. That he sets such low standards for himself is what bothers me."

"I can tell you some things about him that not even he will admit to himself," I answered. "When it comes to Jew stuff, he doesn't know much. He grew up in the shadow of the Holocaust. Who'd want to be a Jew after the Holocaust? As if the event itself wasn't bad enough, his parents' generation was so shell-shocked by it they didn't even know how to discuss it. Was it tragedy? Certainly. Was it God's will? Apparently. Was it because the Jews deserved such treatment at the hands of Christians? Who knows? In the absence of real understanding, bewildered Jews let Christians frame the dialogue. Thus, all his life Bronstein was teased in the schoolyard that all Jews cared about was money, that they were hated by God, and they brought the Holocaust down upon themselves."

"Is that true? Christians think that Jews are only about money?" asked Singer. "What about commerce and literature, medicine and philanthropy."

"Usually, the more anti-Semitic a man is," I answered, "the less educated he is too."

Suddenly an air of excitement came to the trailer. We dropped our argument to check it out. It was Shortstop, the dog, who got our attention. When Debra broke out their sleeping bags, which still had the faint aroma of campfire, the hound went mad. He jumped about, barking loudly with his large tail clapping against the door and his teeth nipping at the hem of Debra's jeans.

Bronstein threw things from the kitchen in a large cardboard box—peanut butter and jelly, a soup pot, a can opener, a loaf of bread, toilet paper, rice, butter, and apples.

Debra had a collection of animal hides she kept for such occasions—one bear, one moose, and three deer. They were thrown into two large boxes along with two Swiss army knives, candles, matches, two flashlights, a tarp, some rope, KY Jelly, and some green herbal love ointment.

When they had gathered up their provender, they met in the bedroom and standing before each other, stripped off their clothes. On came the long underwear, the T-shirts, flannel shirts, old sweaters, heavy socks, hats, mittens, down jackets, boots, and scarves. When they were done, they examined them-selves, side by side, in the mirror that covered the inside of the bedroom closet door. They looked like a couple of overstuffed yahoos. But yahoo apparel is what it takes to battle the cold in northern Minnesota.

Carrying their commissary to a shed out back, Joshua pulled out Debra's sleek black snowmobile. Joshua, who rode motorcy-cles when he was a young man, loved this machine. It started on the second turn and while it was warming up, he hooked a small wooden sled to the back of it. They piled boxes on it and tied them down with bungee cords. Shortstop sat between the boxes covered by a quilt.

Joshua drove. Debra sat close behind him. Ten minutes later there was a pit stop at the SuperAmerica store to gas up their machine. When Joshua went inside to pay, he also bought a lighter and two small boxes of Red Hots.

The snowstorm was the evening's big event and everybody came out for milk, bread, and coffee. There was a prideful siege mentality among the locals gathered at the store's coffee pot. Most of them had seen storms like this dozens of times before. They stood in a pack and chatted amicably about the cold white face of Mother Nature still so formidable in early April.

At the cash register, two people were ahead of Joshua in line. The old man behind the counter had a television to keep him company. Tuned to CNN, it showed the image of a serious newscaster staring into the camera and telling of the dire cir-cumstances resulting from the biggest spring blizzard to hit the upper midwest in twenty-five years.

From the scene of the storm, the broadcaster, microphone in hand, and wearing a hooded down jacket, stood beside Interstate 35 outside of Duluth. A snowplow sped by in the background. He recounted a tale of how the storm had already claimed three lives. Ten thousand homes were without power, and the inter-state was about to be shut down. At least ten more inches were predicted on top of the ten inches already on the ground.

Everyone stopped talking and stared at the screen. They stood a little straighter when they realized they'd become the topic of a CNN headline. Though Minnesota ethics demanded that they be more stoic than CNN broadcasters, deep in their hearts, they too longed for spring.

"That's a pretty frightening image you're painting there, sport," said Joshua out loud, speaking to the television screen. "But I suppose that's your intention, isn't it? Fear and chaos... it's all fear and chaos on television. Those are the values you assholes propagate. In Minnesota we ain't scared of no stinking snowstorm."

"Oy vay," said Himmelman. "He's become one of those crazy fucks who talk back to television."

The cashier glanced beneath the counter to see how handy his revolver was, just in case this guy with the loud voice was dangerous. Wary of the bandage on Bronstein's forehead, he feared that perhaps it covered up some unnamed insanity.

Joshua nodded his head when their eyes met. The cashier relaxed when he realized that Bronstein was just mad at the world in general, instead of someone inside the store in particular. He began writing a check for the amount. Then he proclaimed, "You have no idea how much wisdom I've gained since the old days. I used to peddle that same tripe to the unsuspecting masses during my early years as a reporter."

The cashier froze upon the realization that it was now his turn to speak. He was at a loss as to what the correct response might be. After a long pause he blurted, "Yeah sure, you betcha boy, that's one hell of a snow storm out there."

When CNN broke for a deodorant commercial, Joshua gazed out the store's big, broad window. The wind had stopped. Snow was coming straight down. Then he lowered his eyes and saw Debra Crow sitting on the snowmobile staring back at him. She waved her blue mitten when their eyes met, and he laughed at his good fortune at being caught in the middle of such a killer storm.

Bronstein got back on the snowmobile and raced down the snow-clad roads of Saint Louis county. His woman wrapped her arms around his waist, his white bandage fluttered in the wind, and his body pumped so much adrenaline that he loved being in it.

Now all of us shades agreed that, as a member of the bourgeoisie, Bronstein was a failure. The ups and downs of Wall Street stocks and bonds bored him to tears. Talk of mutual funds and individual retirement accounts made his butt itch. The form and content of American middle class values, for him, was the claptrap of cowherds. Of course, sometimes when life frightened him, he longed to be normal and surrender to a respectable career. But it never lasted long.

With Debra out in the woods in the middle of a storm that the national media had already heralded as a killer, was where he was good. I know I've said this before, but let me reiterate. When it comes to the Jews, there are only two choices in life— toil in the land of Pharaoh or wander in the wilderness. And this Bronstein, when he was out in the wilderness, was as strong as a Bolshevik. Out here on an evening like this, a man could still pretend he was a man, battling the elements in heroic fashion.

Now, let me tell you about that sled. It was no Cadillac. Riding on the two steel runners made for a bumpy ride. A couple of shocks and a little suspension would have helped. But Bronstein didn't care about the comfort of the three ghosts along for the ride.

Sharing it with Himmelman and Singer was bad enough. But we had to make room for the hound too. And the answer to that proverbial question, "Does a fat dog fart?" I now know the answer. Let the truth be told—one's olfactory abilities do not change with death.

Regardless, Bronstein was happy. Debra was happy. So did it matter that we shades were miserable?

No!

I figured that my funeral had been canceled due to the snowstorm. So I had nothing better to do than to tag along with the two mortals, the dog, and Himmelman and Singer. Why, I thought, should I sit around and watch my wife's family, whom I never liked anyway, pretend they were upset at my death?

Now let me tell you about the Indian burial ground. It's at Bug Lake, whose size is about five hundred acres, located miles from nowhere. At the north end of the lake is a great swamp. Clouds of mosquitoes rise from it in summer. Because of its remote location, not many anglers fish there. So Bug Lake has an enormous stock of walleye pike which, as every Minnesotan knows, is the filet mignon of fish.

There is a well-sculpted pit, dug by Bronstein, that magnificent gravedigger, the first time Debra took him there. He had lined it with plastic to protect the shovels, a lantern, fire starter, wood, and extra blankets from moisture. On top was a piece of plywood, camouflaged by leaves and branches to hide their cache.

When they arrived, the snow, falling through the arms of the bare trees, showed no sign of letting up. It was already to their knees. The temperature felt like twenty-eight.

Bronstein picked up a shovel and went to work. His calloused palms, accustomed to long wooden handles, piled the snow into a great heap—flake upon flake, shovelful upon shovelful, cubic foot upon cubic foot. Tossing so many heavy shovelfuls of snow made the muscles in his neck bulge. And in this work he found the best part of himself. He kept a steady pace throughout the hour and did not tire as the snow fell.

While Bronstein worked, Debra tended to a roaring fire five yards away. Because the wood had been kept dry in Bronstein's sculpted grave, it burned with almost no smoke. She tied ropes through the loops of her tarp and linked it to the three birch trees beside the fire. It shielded them from the falling snow.

Then she rolled two snowballs, first one, then another. Around the compound they rolled until they were big. She situated them near the fire. Out of those balls, she sculpted two comfy armchairs and covered them with animal hides.

Having finished her tasks, she started to sing and dance around the fire—cool rock and roll action I had seen her do on stage many times. She carried it off with a raw enthusiasm that, for the three of us shades, was like eye candy.

At last Bronstein had a snow pile standing six feet high and seven feet wide. He smoothed the outer layer of the structure with the back of his shovel and was pleased by his good work. Then he rested.

Together they sat, side by side, in their snow chairs near the fire, upon the animal hides, under blankets, shielded by the plastic tarp. They ate the peanut butter and jelly sandwiches. Beyond the flames was Bug Lake, fading in the twilight.

Joshua went back to work. With a small garden spade, he began scratching out a chamber. He delighted in his digging. In the course of the next hour, with industry and artistry, Bronstein dug a beautiful chamber inside the large mass of snow. It was like a womb. For them, it was more romantic than the honeymoon suite at the Kahler Hotel downtown.

He sang while digging out the snow. The song he sang was so compelling that all three of us stared at him. It was, "Joshua fit the battle of Jericho, Jericho, Jericho." The tune gained notoriety in the 1960s when it was rehashed as a TV commercial. "Can't get enough of that Sugar Crisp, Sugar Crisp, Sugar Crisp."

While he sang, he created enough space inside the snow house for the queen sized inflatable mattress they brought along and carved shelves to hold beer cans and candles. He dug a little air hole at the top so moisture could escape. He might have given them a little more headroom, but maybe next time.

When he was done sculpting the interior, Bronstein lit six votive candles. The heat from the flames made the walls inside their snow house sweat. When they were removed twenty minutes later, the walls refroze and became durable like sheetrock.

It now fell to Debra to make the snow house a home. She hauled in a plastic ground cover. It became the floor. The remaining animal hides went on top of it. The queen sized air mattress came next. Their bed was complete with the next layer—sleeping bags, blankets, and pillows.

She moved around the chamber, careful not to knock down the walls. Because they had the same brand of sleeping bags, she opened them up and zipped them into each other so they could share body heat.

She burned a bit of sage inside the snow house while chanting an Indian song to protect their privacy against the likes of me, Himmelman, and Singer.

She strung a dream catcher above the pillows so that any dream coming their way might remain in their minds for further consideration.

Then they were done. The thick walls offered protection from the wind and the snow. The air mattress, the sleeping bags, and the animal hides prevented the cold ground from stealing their body heat. They crawled into the bags, took off their clothes, reached for each other, and fell into another deep sleep. Shortstop at their feet kept their toes warm.

"Seeing the two of them together reminds me of the affair Leon Trotsky had with his Mexican mistress," I said. "I think she was a painter. How tenderly he spoke of her in his last letters before his assassination. She was a dark beauty like Debra Crow. In the arms of that woman, old Trotsky found peace."

"Your boss, Trotsky, was a loser," said Singer. "When Stalin beat him out of power in Russia, it was a tragedy not only for the Jews, but for everybody."

"I'm going to tell you both a little secret now, so shut up for just a minute," I said. "Trotsky had no interest in ruling over two hundred and fifty million Russian dolts in the 1930s. It was a bad job. He wanted to be pope.

"There, I've told the truth and I am glad," I continued. "He'd have given Russia to the barbarian Stalin in a heartbeat. Who'd want the Kremlin when the Vatican was up for grabs? Communism had so much more to offer the masses—culture, theater, and literature. Revolution in Vatican City was one of our real goals—to seize the reins of spiritual power and liberate the gentile masses."

"Trotsky wanted to be pope? I don't believe it."

"It's true. It was his idea that religion was so rooted in the past that it had no mechanism to incorporate revolution, or revelation."

"You must be kidding," said Himmelman.

"Every word of it's true," I said. "When cardinals and bishops got wind of our intentions, it was decided that the entire race of Jews must be crushed. To Stalin and Hitler, they appealed. The results are well known."

"Himmelman, how many more days do we have to hang out with Kalinsky?" sighed Singer. Then looking at me he spoke. "Don't you have a reunion to go to? Communism, catholicism, capitalism, revolution. I'm so sick of this crap. Let's talk about something interesting, like women. You can have your battle between Christians and Jews, between capitalism and Communism, rich and poor. Nuts to all of it. The only battle worth fighting is the battle of the sexes. Everything else is bullshit."

"Brave talk from a virgin," commented Himmelman.

"Kalinsky, what about that woman, Greta Niemi?" asked Singer. "I'd rather talk about her."

"She owns a house one mile up the road," I said. "It's still a little early. She sometimes holds séances in the late evening."

"I don't want to wait."

"Then walk down the road yourself and peek inside her window, Singer. I'll join you later."

"Herman Himmelman, come with me," said Singer. "Let's see if Kalinsky's ideas about women are as wretched as his ideas about politics."

The two of them went over the hill while I remained.

Debra awoke. She looked at the lighted dial of Bronstein's wristwatch and saw it was 9:09. She quietly moved around their snow house while Bronstein remained asleep. Upon her hands and knees, she turned her naked body around so her face was at his toes. She spread her arms and legs far apart. Goose bumps appeared on her skin. Straddling him, she backed her private parts up past his waist, past his belly button, past his neck. I thought she was going to sit on his face.

She grabbed the corner of Joshua's bandage and ripped it off his forehead. He jolted. She continued. Bronstein's eyes were wide open when, to his great surprise, he saw her vagina slowly inching its way toward his mouth. He thought to stick out his tongue, but didn't. The soft skin covering her thighs shuddered in the cold. He noticed it not from the thigh itself but from the quivering shadow cast by the pale candlelight.

She backed her vagina past his mouth, his nose, and then past his eyebrows, stopping at his forehead. Her vagina was now inches from this morning's wound.

She carefully placed her hands against the ceiling of the snow house for balance so as not to put too much pressure against its fragile ceiling. So much heat issued out of her hands that the ceiling began to melt. Clear water ran down her outstretched arms, across her breasts, and down her stomach, finding its way beside Joshua's ear.

She lowered her vagina gently down upon the nine black stitches painted with iodine.

"Debra, what are you doing?" he asked, reaching for her hips.

"Shhhhh," she answered. "Don't touch me."

Quietly, and with great physical grace, she rubbed her clitoris against his stitches. She moaned softly while moving back and forth, back and forth, back and forth.

I could tell by the look on Bronstein's face that he didn't have a clue what she was doing. But lifting my gaze to Debra's face, I saw something different. It was the look of confidence, so much so that you just knew it was all being done for an expressed purpose. I only wish someone would have explained it to me.

CHAPTER SEVEN

The next morning, the alarm on Joshua Bronstein's wristwatch went off in bell tones. He was startled out of sleep. He lay motionless, waiting for the tolling to stop. Was he awake? Yes. Was he emotionally present? No. He felt dazed and disoriented. A frightening dream concluded. Part of his mind remained in that drama, while his body lay inside the igloo deep in the forest.

He lay there like a frozen stiff, but not from the cold... from fear. Naked in his sleeping bag, arms flush against his flanks, he slowly flexed his shoulders and butt. Then he arched his back and looked over his shoulder just in case some unnamed evil might be lurking. Fortunately for Bronstein, it was only me.

As his first act of confidence, he moved his fingers, but cautiously, for he was still playing 'possum. He pulled his hand out of the sleeping bag, and his palm went flat upon the snow floor of his shelter. He looked around and slowly remembered he was in their north woods snow house.

Debra Crow snuggled up beside him. Now, I could see it on his face. He was again feeling at ease and it wasn't hard to intuit what he was thinking—Debra's here. I'm safe.

Dim morning light seeped in through the two openings of the snow house—the small blowhole on top and the other at the entrance. He exhaled and his breath resembled a lung full of cigarette smoke. He rolled Debra over and spooned his body into hers, wrapping his arm around her. But his comfort was short lived.

It felt as if every ounce of liquid he imbibed in the past twenty-four hours was now in his bladder and trying to push its way out.

But it was cold outside. The last thing Bronstein wanted was to leave the warmth of his sleeping bag and walk out into the snow-filled forest to piss. So he held it in. Perhaps he figured that the longer he waited, the warmer the temperature would be when he emerged.

He reached up above his head, pinched a little snow off the ceiling and brought it to his mouth. It quenched his dry throat but not so much as to bring more pressure to his bladder.

From what he could see, the snowstorm had ended and the morning sun appeared. That was a bad sign. Without the clouds acting as a blanket, the earth's heat escapes into the atmosphere. Bronstein guessed the temperature had plummeted. He reached for a string hanging down from the hole above him. When he pulled at it, a small quicksilver thermometer fell into his hands. Reaching for his flashlight, he cast the light upon it. It caught Debra's attention.

"How cold is it outside?"

"Too cold."

"How cold is that?"

"Nine above zero," he said.

"Let's sleep in. It will warm up in a few hours."

"No, I have to go out."

"Why?"

"I have to pee."

"Use the chamber pot."

"I left it by the snowmobile."

"That was a big mistake."

"I know."

"Can't you hold it in?"

"No," he said.

"When you're done bring the pot in for me," Debra said.

He lit a votive candle, which sat on the snow shelf he meticulously dug out. After careful deliberation, he decided that his boots, his long underwear bottoms, and a flannel shirt would be enough protection for the short time he would be outside. He began dressing carefully. Then he crawled out the door.

Twenty feet from the igloo, he relieved himself against a birch tree. He called out to his sweetie while swaying his hips. "Hey, honey, how do you spell your name? It's D-E-B-O-R-A-H, isn't it?"

"No," said the muffled voice from inside the igloo, "It's spelled D-E-B-R-A."

He stopped squirting. "No kidding?"

"Why would I kid?"

"I just assumed it was D-E-B-O-R-A-H."

"Well, you never asked before, have you?"

"No, I guess I haven't," he said. "Well, fewer letters will make it easier."

"Are you pissing my name in the snow?"

"Hold on, honey, I'm almost done," he said, as he squeezed out the last ounce. "I've almost got the A. There, it's done."

"Joshua, that's gross."

"Honey, what a beautiful tribute. I put a heart around it too. I hope somebody comes by so I can show them."

The top third of her body appeared at the entry. Crouched on all fours with her dark hair hanging down, she scowled and threw a small spade at him. "Cover that up."

He caught the spade with one hand. His smile was so bright that she realized he was teasing. "Rat," she grunted and slipped back inside.

He walked to the snowmobile, which was buried beneath a large drift, fetched the chamber pot for Debra, and crawled back into the shelter. She startled when he pressed his cold fingers against her.

"Stop that," she said. "Go back to sleep."

"I just had the weirdest dream. It scared the hell out of me."

"What was it?"

"I was lying here in this snow house and a bright blue arm appeared," he said. "It had fingers and a hand and ended at the elbow. It moved around like it was attached to a body. But I never saw anything beyond the elbow. It grabbed me by my right hand and tried to pull me out of the igloo. I actually got halfway out of the igloo and went right through the walls as if I were a ghost. But when I saw the snowmobile and the fire pit I realized what was happening and let go. Then I got really scared that whatever it was, was going to come back to kidnap me. So I got into this karate pose and started kicking my feet to ward it off. After a minute, it disappeared.

"The next thing I remember I was in this giant parking lot looking for my car. Rows and rows of cars were there in every make and model. I couldn't find mine anywhere. I wandered around looking for a white Cadillac, but then I remembered that I own a blue Cadillac, not a white one. Just then my alarm went off and I woke up. And here's something else… I don't remember setting the alarm."

Debra was silent. She looked at the dream catcher strung above their pillows and smiled. "Good dream."

"Weird dream," he said. "I wonder what it was all about."

"I think you just had your first out of body experience. Somebody was going to take you up to the astral plane."

"Who?"

"I don't know who. Was it a man's arm or a woman's?"

"I think it was a woman's. I noticed the shadow of a gold ring with a big red stone in it. I thought maybe it was you, Debra."

"Sorry, it wasn't me."

"Man, it was all so real."

"That's big. If you're serious about healing yourself, being able to get out of your body is an important step. It suggests you're rising above your problems."

"Yes, but now I'm mad at myself because I didn't go. I think I missed out on a great opportunity."

"No, you should never go unless you feel comfortable. But next time ask the hand who it belongs to and where it wants to take you," she said. "I never go anywhere unless I'm sure I know who it's with. There's a lot of weird energy in the spirit world, and sometimes a bad spirit will try to get your soul out of your body so it can jump in and take over."

"You've been telling me about this stuff for months now. It's beginning to make sense. You're a pretty smart girl for—"

"An Indian?"

"Yes, for an Indian," he said.

"I'll take that as a compliment."

"You should, one outcast to another."

"You've got a long way to go yet, Joshua."

"How can you tell?"

"You're still too angry to understand this stuff," she said. "That's the problem with white people... they're angry about everything. To get healthy you have to lose your anger."

"That New Age stuff is..."

"New Age nothing," she interrupted. "My people have passed this wisdom down for generations. Just because a bunch of Johnny-come-latelies start writing books about it, they call it New Age. It's not new to us, it's as old as..."

"The Jews?"

"Older."

"There's nothing older than the Jews," he said.

"Keep telling yourself that and you'll never heal. One of these days I'm going to heal all your wounds, and then we'll go flying on the astral plane every night together."

"And what can I do for you in return?"

"You can buy me a big mink stole like those rich Jewish yentas you told me about in Miami Beach. I swear I'll only wear it when we're out in the woods fucking."

"It's a deal, but only when I'm healed."

"You'll know when I've healed you."

"How will I know?"

"You'll be crazy about me."

At this the man hesitated. He'd have liked to take the language of love a step further and frame it into some poetic sonnet to express his devotion. But he could not. The realization that he was resisting an opportunity to let love into his life made him sad. And the insight reminded me of something Debra had told him—that a man can't embrace the love of a woman until he first loves himself. With this, Joshua Bronstein was still struggling.

You could tell by the look on Debra's face that she was crestfallen. She loved him more than he loved her. Finally, he found the presence of mind to change the subject. But what a schlemiel. It was only to repeat a question he had already asked. "Who do you think it was?"

"I'm not sure," she said. "I'm going back to sleep. Maybe I'll have some ideas about it when I wake up."

"Hey, where's Shortstop? I haven't seen him in a while. He shouldn't be outside for too long in this cold. I better go find him and bring him inside."

"Good," Debra said. "We can use the extra body heat."

It took him a few minutes to get dressed what with all the layers of clothing required. He also replaced the bandage over his wounded forehead. Then, crawling out the front door, he braved the cold a second time. He walked down a steep bank to the frozen lake.

He called to Shortstop. No dog. He began to whistle. He walked down the fire trail and called his name again. No dog.

"Shortstop! Shortstop! You son of a bitch, where are you?" yelled Bronstein. About thirty feet from the snow house he discovered a few paw prints. But there were only about a dozen.

We shades, Himmelman, Singer, and I, began searching too. Were it a cat, we'd have had an easier time because cats, trees, and humans all share the same kind of soul. They're easier to find when lost.

But a dog? Who knows from a dog? True, they make better Bolsheviks. But cats have always been my preference.

Back in the igloo, Debra dressed. By the time Joshua returned to tell her about the missing dog, she was lacing up her boots. She stepped out into the daylight and cast a glance around the winter wonderland of snow. Suddenly, a strong wind blew. She took a deep whiff.

"Do you smell that?"

Joshua hesitated. "It smells like marshmallows. I wonder where it's coming from?"

"Fire up the snowmobile, I think I know where your dog went."

He cleared off the snowmobile. Debra put a purple scarf around her head, just like a Russian babushka. Then she jumped on, throwing her arms around his waist. He cranked the throttle. She directed Joshua around the lake to a high bluff a half mile in the distance. Once over the top, they saw a house standing in a large meadow of snow. The snowmobile raced toward it at such a high speed that the cold bit through Bronstein's gloves, burning his fingers.

The white stucco house seemed like a mirage in a white sea. Were it not for the decorative red of the door and the red window shutters, Bronstein might not have even noticed it. A broad front porch faced east. Three wooden Adirondack chairs, also painted red, were side by side on the porch. It gave the place a welcoming look. The two snow mounds out front were cars buried beneath the drifts.

Joshua thought to ask Debra if she knew the owner, but the noise of the engine prevented conversation. He pulled up to the house, parked behind the cars, and shut off the engine.

They walked up three steps to a covered porch and a thick oak door. Debra rang the doorbell. No one answered. They waited patiently. After a minute she sheepishly rang it again. After all, it was still early. When she rang it a third time, Shortstop started barking. They stopped worrying.

"Greta's a night owl. She's probably still asleep," said Debra.

"You know who lives here?" asked Bronstein.

"Sure, Greta Niemi. She's a witch."

"A witch? Get out of here."

"No, it's true," Debra said.

"You mean with a broomstick, a tall black hat, and a wart on her nose?"

"No way, Greta's a babe. She's lived out here since I was a girl."

"Is she married?"

"No. She lives out here alone."

"Then who does the other car belong to?"

"I don't know. Maybe she has a boyfriend."

"Will he be a witch too?"

"Maybe. You never know with Greta."

"I never met a witch before. Should be interesting."

Now Debra ignored the bell and began rapping on the door with her fist. No one answered. Debra turned and saw the sun rising. "What time is it?"

"Almost seven o'clock," answered Bronstein.

"We might have to come back later."

A window opened from upstairs and a woman's voice called, "Who's down there?"

Debra walked down the stairs and into the front yard. "Hi Greta. It's me, Debra."

"Debra Crow, what brings you out here so early?" asked the voice from the upstairs window.

"We lost our dog."

"Oh, he came over last night and started barking at the door. It's a good thing I was home. He might have frozen to death."

"Did I wake you?"

"I'm up, just too lazy to get out of bed. There's a key under the mat. Come in and make yourself at home. I'm going to jump in the shower. Then I'll be right down."

Debra climbed back up the stairs.

"If she's so smart, how come she didn't figure out that you came for the dog?"

"It happens all the time," she answered, ignoring his question. "She's a magnet for stray animals."

Joshua found a key under the doormat and brought it to the lock. They walked inside the warm house. A faint smell of birch bark came from the fireplace.

I could tell that Bronstein thought her house was beautiful. Of course, compared to his trailer any domicile was beautiful. Inspecting her first floor, he ran his hand along the soft velour cushions of her couch and chairs. He admired the woodwork that framed the windows and the area between the ceiling and the walls. The living room colors were green and purple. Oriental carpets blanketed the floor. The lamps were antiques.

Her wall art had religious themes. There was a pencil sketch of a bearded rabbi reading a book Bronstein examined carefully. There was also a Buddhist temple rubbing, a large mandala, and a framed bronze crucifix on the wall beside the hall closet.

The painting that interested him most featured the corpse of a dead woman in bed. Two angels, one at the head and one at the feet, were gently rocking her soul from her body. The heads of four other angels waited lovingly in the distance for her to enter the gates of heaven.

"Shortstop," called Debra. From a basement door they heard a yelp. When they opened it, the canine emerged, happy to see them.

Bronstein wanted to punish the dog for running away, but he held back. "Don't you do that to me again!" he shouted. "Look at him, Debra. He's warm and happy, and I'm cold and hungry. Don't I feel like an idiot."

Joshua started sweating. "Let's get going. I'm roasting in here."

"Now that we're here, we can't just leave. We have to say hello to Greta. Take off your coat."

She hung their down jackets on hangers and closed the closet door.

Then he caught sight of something that stirred him. It was a bookcase built into the living room wall. His eyes lit up like flashlights as he beheld what was for him hidden treasure—a library. His feet sunk into the thick carpet as he made his way to it.

Then he realized the snow on his boots was melting into the deep pile. "Oh shit," said Bronstein. Debra winced at the volume of his words. They were a little too loud for Greta's house. He retreated to the front door and removed his boots.

And suddenly, from a corner of the ceiling, Himmelman appeared and called out, "Singer, where are you? It's almost time."

What were those two Hasids up to?

"I used to spend a lot of time here when I was a girl," Debra said. "Want to see a picture of Greta and my mother when they were young?" She grabbed it from an end table and handed it to him.

"That's your mother?"

"That's Iris. She lives in Arizona now with my stepfather. She visits in the summer and usually stays here with Greta."

"Is that Greta standing next to her?"

"Yes. That picture was taken thirty-two years ago, just after I was born."

After he returned the picture to its place, Joshua examined her library. Each shelf had its own subject. One featured occult texts about reincarnation and channeling. There was another for Carl Jung. Another focused on shamans and Wicca. Religious tomes about Christian saints and interpretations of the Bible were on another. Near the bottom was one devoted to trashy romance novels by women authors. What surprised Bronstein most was a small collection of books on the top shelf about the Russian Revolution and European Jewry.

"Is Greta Jewish?"

"No, I told you… she's a witch."

"She wasn't born a witch, was she?"

"No, I think she was Lutheran. But she doesn't believe in that anymore."

Joshua reached up to grasp a red book: *The History of the Russian Civil War*, by Mikhail Klimenko. He thumbed to the back of the book searching its index.

"What are you looking for?" asked Debra, standing beside him.

"To see if the name Kalinsky is mentioned."

"Who is that?"

"Vukovich. He said Kalinsky was his Bolshevik alias."

"Is it?" she asked.

"Hold on, I'm looking."

I suddenly began to bubble. Holy crap, at long last me, the Great Kalinsky, was about to be rediscovered by a new generation. Now I know what Plato felt like in the Renaissance. I called out in glee, "Turn to page twenty-eight, Bronstein. Turn to page twenty-eight!"

"There's his name," she said looking over his shoulder at the index. "Try page twenty-eight."

Joshua turned to the page. There was a picture of three soldiers standing in front of a railway car brandishing rifles. Among those listed in the caption was Comrade Ivan Kalinsky, leader of the Ukrainian Red Legion, with Sergei Kirov and Chaim Bonk.

"That's him," said Bronstein. "Ivan Kalinsky, hero of the battle of Minsk."

"Wait. I don't get it. What's so important about him?"

"It's Vukovich, the bartender."

"The old guy from the Homer?"

"Yes, I went drinking with him years ago at his cabin. He told me this wild tale about how he was the cousin of Leon Trotsky, and in his early years he was a Bolshevik hero. He said the only reason he came to northern Minnesota was to escape Stalinist agents and the FBI."

"You never told me that."

"I didn't believe him."

However, another surprise was about to reveal itself. When Bronstein turned to see if the book was a first edition, he noticed a nameplate opposite the title page. There was the name—Joseph Vukovich. He took down several of the other books and he found my nameplate in each. And then Bronstein, the former investigative reporter, was lost in thought, pondering what it all meant.

Debra did some exploring too. There were several Chinese opera masks hanging on the wall. She took one down and walked to the hallway mirror. She tried it on. "How do I look?" she asked.

"It's not as pretty as your face," he answered.

She returned the mask to its hook. A white collar, which lay on the coffee table, caught her eye.

She wrapped it around her neck and fastened it at the back. She tucked it inside her gray sweater, and returning to the mirror, stared at herself.

She liked the way the collar looked. She played with her hair, searching for the right effect to go along with the white, starched dickey.

First, she grabbed her long hair in her hand and pulled it up in a ponytail high upon her head. No, that wasn't right. She looked like Pebbles Flintstone. So she let her hair drop so it draped on both sides of her chest in pigtails. Its jet-black color was a pretty contrast to the white collar. But that wasn't right either. What she finally settled for was collecting all her strands, throwing it around her neck and having it lay upon her left breast.

Having found the right hairstyle, she searched for a sexy facial expression to accompany it. She tried a big broad smile but decided that it was too girlish. She narrowed her eyes and turned down the corners of her mouth in anger. But she realized Joshua would never find that alluring. She liked a pouty face best. It suggested she would be cross unless he gave her all his love.

Confident that the collar now had its proper accompaniments, she walked back to the living room hoping to seduce Joshua's imagination with her new look. She struck a pose. Her arm reached high against the doorframe, her hip jutted out at an angle, and she pulled her shoulders back so her breasts looked bigger. He noticed her and stared for several seconds.

"How do I look now?"

"Good enough to fuck."

"Shhhh, not so loud Joshua. Greta might hear you. I'll ask her where she bought this dickey. I want one."

"I'll be right down, Debra," called Greta from upstairs.

"She doesn't know I'm here, does she?" asked Joshua.

"She might. Remember that blue hand you felt this morning? It might have been Greta's."

"Do you think so?"

"Ask her."

"Are you nuts?"

"No."

"I'm supposed to look her in the eye and say, 'Excuse me ma'am, was it you attempting to take me out of my body this morning? Was it for a little seduction or a walk around the lake? Perhaps a chat about the Kabbala?'"

"The two of you together, that would be interesting." Debra laughed.

"Tell me about her."

"Greta's heiress to the Hanna mining fortune. She never had to work a day in her life. So she devoted her life to spiritualism and actually teaches religion and spirituality at Mesabi Junior College. I've taken two of her courses. They're great."

"You mean all this Native American wisdom you talk about was taught to you by a Minnesota Finn?"

"Yep."

Let me just interrupt. When Greta walked down the stairs, my heart felt a spasm and it wasn't even in my chest. After all, I'm dead. She was thirty years younger than me and still beautiful.

I loved her large, gray eyes and big silver hair. She was more woman than Bronstein would ever know. Her body was my sanctuary, and I was ready to give him such a smack should he show Greta any disrespect.

Greta hugged Debra and then noticed the collar beneath her sweater. "Nice look."

Then she noticed Bronstein. "I didn't know you brought a friend, honey. And you are...?" she asked, staring deep into Bronstein's eyes, ignoring the bandage on his forehead, waiting for him to complete the sentence.

"Joshua Bronstein," said Debra.

"Welcome," said Greta, examining him through narrowing eyes. Bronstein knew from her expression that she'd read about him in the papers. And I sighed, for so many times was that same look cast upon me in disapproval from this woman, my mistress of many decades.

She winked at Debra. It might have been a gesture of approval. You never knew with Greta. Perhaps she was just trying to put Debra at ease. They followed her to a bright, white kitchen that was large enough to fit a table with four chairs.

"Sit down. We'll have some pancakes. Debra, make the coffee, will you?" said Greta. "I have some bacon." And then she paused as if she knew from Bronstein's name that he was a Jew, and as such might have a dietary restriction against swine.

"I eat bacon," said Joshua.

"Real good then." And she placed the entire package on several napkins and put it inside the microwave.

"May I use your bathroom?" asked Joshua.

"It's right through that door," said the hostess.

He went inside the bathroom and was heartened to find that not only did he now have a warm place to shit, but that there was also a ceiling fan. This was good for two reasons—the noise coming out his ass would not prove indelicate to the hostess, and it would whisk away the stink without having to open the window and expose himself to the cold.

There were also magazines to read—*Wiccan Gazette, National Review*, and *Minnesota Monthly*. He crapped, he wiped, he flushed, he washed his hands without incident.

"Singer," said Himmelman. "Come on... it's time."

My shady friends were up to something. As if inspired by great expectations, Himmelman and Singer came together. And with such alacrity too, the likes of which I never saw between them.

"Finally! I thought I might die of boredom," said Singer, sighing with relief to his chubby colleague.

"Wait, a minute," I said. "What's going on here?"

"You think we've been hanging out here just to listen to your nonsense, Kalinsky?" Singer asked. "I don't mean to brag, but we staged this encounter on purpose, so step back and let us do what we do."

"And what might that be?" I asked.

"I told you already," said Singer. "We're preparing this Bronstein fellow for the Lamed Vav. We had a long talk about it last night with Greta while you were at the igloo. That witch of yours is quite a woman."

"Easy to do business with," added Himmelman.

"What kind of business?" I barked.

"None of your business," answered Singer.

"As her former lover, I am making it my business."

"You'll not be making any more monkey business with her," Himmelman said. "So keep still and pay attention."

"Are you ready, Himmelman?" Singer asked.

"Yes, Singer." And suddenly they were mumbling Hebrew in unison while looking squarely into each other's eyes. I didn't recognize the prayer.

Then it happened, simultaneously. Two doors swung open to the kitchen. Bronstein, straight from the toilet, walked into the kitchen through one door while another man entered from the living room through the other. Both startled, shocked to be face to face.

"Oh, it's you," said the older man who was taller and heavier than Bronstein. He wore a black jacket and black pants.

"Oh yes, it's me," said Joshua, immediately seething with anger.

The tension in the room grew, and everyone was uncomfortable except Greta. She wore a big smile.

"Debra, allow me to introduce my old friend, Felix Culpa," said Bronstein sarcastically.

"Hello, Felix, it's nice to meet you," said Debra, reaching out her hand.

"Your friend is making a bad joke. My name is Father Terrence Goodlad," he said in his Irish brogue.

"Oh, sure, I've seen you around," Debra said solicitously. "You're the guy with that bumper sticker that says, 'Jesus Is Coming. Look Busy.'"

"You're confusing me with someone else," said Goodlad. "Excuse me, but I'll take my collar back." He spun Debra around and unlatched the clasp from the back of her neck. He put it on and now his uniform was complete.

"You'll have to excuse him, Debra. Without the white ring of the Holy Mother church, he's actually quite vulnerable," said Bronstein.

Goodlad stared at the bandage on Bronstein's forehead. He smirked. "Run into a door, Bronstein?"

"Please sit down all. Breakfast is ready," said Greta, beaming at her guests.

"So what brings you out here, Father?" asked Bronstein with the look of a fox.

I could tell the priest was calling on all his self-control to remain at the table. He might have made a hasty exit except his car was under a mound of snow. So there he was, stuck in a compromised position with Joshua Bronstein.

"Actually, I came out here to tell Miss Niemi about the death of her old friend, Joseph Vukovich," said the priest with the air of a man strictly professional.

"His name was Kalinsky," Bronstein said.

"How did you know?" asked Greta.

"He was my friend too."

"We shared that secret," Greta said.

"I was surprised to find several of his books in your library," said Bronstein. "How did you meet him?"

"I heard his name several times back in the 1960s. I wouldn't have dared associate with him. He was a union organizer. At my father's dinner table, the name Vukovich was profanity. A few months before the big strike, I ran into him at a liquor store. We found ourselves side-by-side in the vodka section. I greeted him as 'Mr. Kalinsky.'

"I don't know what prompted me to call him that. It was an honest mistake. I said it quite innocently. Well, he turned pale as a ghost. Then he got indignant."

"'My name is Vukovich, you silly cow.' Well, I didn't like being called a silly cow, so I just walked away."

"What happened then?" asked Debra.

"He began stalking me. Every time I turned around he was right there, staring at me. He was convinced that I was a Russian spy out to get him. It was right after I divorced my husband and I was living out here alone. One night, he came with a gun to murder me."

Everyone gasped.

"You're kidding," said Debra. "What happened?"

"I told him I wanted to die naked. I took off all my clothes. I had a pretty good body in those days and I was able to seduce him instead," she said with a wry smile.

Bronstein looked over at Goodlad. The priest would not return his look. Joshua broke into a mischievous smile. He had caught the local Catholic priest with a north woods witch. The satisfaction was more delicious than breakfast.

Were Goodlad and Greta lovers? For Bronstein the possibilities for conversation at the Homer had just grown enormously.

It took Goodlad several minutes before he found something to say. He grabbed a plate and pushed it in Joshua's direction. "More bacon, Bronstein?"

Joshua emptied the remaining four pieces onto his plate.

"You might have saved some for the others," scolded Goodlad.

Bronstein began eating the strips as delicately as one might eat Russian caviar on a cracker. Several morsels were also dropped to the floor. Shortstop was happy to have them.

Greta and Debra were absorbed in gossip and old stories of family gatherings in this very house. They were laughing and finishing each other's sentences. They ignored the fact that their men were glaring at each other.

Greta ignored the tension between the two men. When she tried to include Goodlad in their conversation, he rebuffed her with a sarcastic remark. She got the message.

Greta touched Debra's hand. "I was downtown yesterday. I found the greatest pair of high heels. Do you want to see them? Come upstairs with me. Terrence dear, entertain Mr. Bronstein, won't you?"

The ladies rose and walked from the room. Both men stopped breathing. Neither wanted to be alone with the other.

I followed the women upstairs for a moment. I wanted to see Greta's bedroom again. I had slept there for years. But did she break out her high heels and model them for her young friend?

No.

They sat on the floor, listening by the heating vent for whatever conversation might transpire between their men in the kitchen. They lit up two Virginia Slims.

"Under no circumstances are you to interfere with whatever goes on downstairs," Greta said. "It might get ugly. But it has to be. Do you understand?"

Debra wasn't sure what Greta was talking about. But the warm maternal look on Greta's face was enough to reassure her.

Debra gazed at the cigarette pack. There were only two left. Realizing her concern, Greta said, "Don't worry... I've got a whole carton in the closet."

Back in the kitchen, Goodlad began with Bronstein. "You're a perfect example of how first impressions can be so wrong. I thought you were different when I first met you. But you're just like all the rest of the Jews—too busy to scratch yourself. And I can tell from your demeanor that you still carry that interminable hubris."

"It's not hubris. It's disdain."

"Listen to what I say," countered the priest. "You can hold a grudge if you want, but it wasn't me who drank beer and drove off that night with a little boy in the back seat... it was you. It wasn't me who claimed a moose praying to the moon caused your car to crash into that frozen lake... it was you. It wasn't me who let that boy die... it was you. Take some responsibility for your action, for God's sake. When I found out you had been drinking it was my duty to make an issue of it to the community. You're just lucky that you got such a light prison sentence."

Bronstein finished the last bite of breakfast. He was surprised how quickly they got down to cases. "After the crash, I confessed to you. I unburdened myself of every memory, every insight, and every idea I could think about it. Then you used it publicly against me."

"You're not a Catholic and never showed any desire to convert. My allegiance is to my congregation and that little boy I baptized at birth, not to an outsider. I spoke the whole truth, and it was certainly more than the newspapers reported. I did it so everybody would understand."

"And so I got what I deserved," said Bronstein with a grimace. "I lost my son, my wife, and my life. And if I ever want to be reminded of how the story ended, I only have to remember that Sunday morning service. I showed up late and stood in the back. I must have been crazy to think I could find solace there. And when you denounced me before the whole congregation, the O'Shea family ostracized me for fear of your holy wrath. Terrence Goodlad, God's man in Hibbing, denouncing a Jew to that flock of fools to maintain the sanctity of his holy house of worship."

"A baptized son of the church had been slain by your negligence and an accounting of that death had to be made."

"He wasn't a baptized son of the church. He was my son. Do you hear me? He wasn't your son. He was my son. Do you even remember his name? Do you? Tell me what his name was, Father."

"It was Adam."

Goodlad got it right and Bronstein backed down.

"I befriended you and took you into the bosom of my flock," Goodlad said. "I stuck up for you when people complained about letting you in our midst. And after the car crash I caught holy hell. Father Jones went to war against me. I was reprimanded by the bishop and was almost discharged, all because of our friendship. It was a hot mess."

Joshua cast a glance across the kitchen to the phone hanging on the wall. It was a white round dial phone with a curly cord long enough to hang somebody. Goodlad noticed him eyeing it too.

"I did what had to be done," Goodlad continued. "Drunk driving was a plague in my parish. I made an example of you. No one's died since that crash. I'd say that the end justified the means."

"Does Tim O'Shea know that the local representative of the Catholic Church is shacking up with a witch?"

"That's none of his business."

"Perhaps I'll make it his business."

"Will it be blackmail, Bronstein? It would seem right up your alley."

"Blackmail has a nice ring to it."

"And what will be the price for your silence? You Jews always have a price. How much will it be?"

"Come on, Father, let's hear some more. I love your anti-Semitic rhetoric. It comes straight from the heart."

"It's not anti-Semitism—it's the truth. Jews act egregiously and shriek when you call them on their bad behavior. History doesn't lie. It goes on all over the world, and has for centuries."

"The verdict of history is not the verdict of God," said Bronstein. "I expected you to at least pay lip service to that."

Goodlad paused and gave his words their due.

"Let me ask you something, Father," said Bronstein. "Which do you think is more important—the sanctity of confession or the religious hegemony of Catholics?"

Then Bronstein started to laugh. It was a long hard laugh that carried on so long that he lost his breath. Goodlad thought him mad. He laughed and laughed and laughed and did not stop. He didn't want to stop.

Was it that something buried so long in his heart had finally been released, the result of which made him feel such joy? No. It was Singer underneath the table tickling his foot.

"You know, I haven't felt this good in a long time," said Bronstein, when his laughter subsided.

"Enjoying the fact that you might have the upper hand?"

"Absolutely."

"Every dog has his day. But if you think I'm going to let a drunkard bring me down you're wrong."

"Don't get scared, Father. Despite the revelation that Greta Niemi is your mistress, I'm sure your congregation will rally behind you."

Of course, Goodlad reasoned, Bronstein was right. If it came down to a public showdown, his congregation would certainly rally behind him. But most certainly, allegations of cavorting with a known witch, and a Lutheran to boot, would undermine the ties that bound his community.

Bronstein stood to refill his coffee. But from where he was sitting, Goodlad only saw him eyeing the phone which was two feet from the pot. Recognizing the differences in the two men's visual perspective and eager to exploit it in Bronstein's favor, Singer started slapping the white phone cord. It swayed back and forth and back and forth before Goodlad's eyes like the pocket watch of a hypnotist.

The priest hadn't felt this vulnerable in a long time. The thought of Bronstein wrecking his reputation made him furious. Was he to sit back and let that outcast scandalize him? Embarrass him in front of his flock? The former Dublin Golden Gloves champ decided it was not to be.

"No, you don't," said Goodlad, springing to his feet and cutting Bronstein off. Violence seeped out of him. I could see it like steam. His eyes were wide open, his muscles were tense, and his blood pressure was off the charts. Goodlad shoved Bronstein into the wall and away from the phone.

Bronstein was shocked by the swiftness of his attack, but Shortstop wasn't. The hound was alerted ten seconds earlier by Himmelman, when he blew into his nostrils.

Protecting his master, the eighty-pound dog lunged at the priest and sunk his incisors deep into Goodlad's palm. He chomped down deep into his flesh and shook his head violently. Goodlad's hand shook with it. The dog's momentum pushed the priest backward into the refrigerator. He lost his footing and his ass hit the floor.

"Hey, stop it," shouted Bronstein. He kicked Shortstop. The dog yelped and ran to the bathroom to hide. He now towered over Goodlad with a taunting look as if he were going to kick *him* too. Goodlad, wincing in pain, stared at his bleeding palm.

Back in the realm of shades, Singer looked like the cat who just swallowed the canary. Himmelman shook his hand in congratulations. Then they strutted around the kitchen table in a cakewalk with their skullcaps tipped rakishly across their brows. Singer had the end of his prayer shawl in hand and was swinging it around in circles like a burlesque queen.

"Bubbella," said Himmelman. "Today, we did good work."

And looking at me, Himmelman added, "Kalinsky, this is what real revolution is about."

CHAPTER EIGHT

Given their history, revenge is an event rarely celebrated by Jews. Except maybe at Purim. So watching the scene in Greta Niemi's kitchen with Father Terrence Goodlad down on the linoleum, back against the white refrigerator door, blubbering quietly about the pain from his bleeding hand while Joshua Bronstein stood over him, was, for the three of us shades, a salient image.

I'll tell you something else. Bronstein's satisfaction was such that if North Korea pushed the button, launching a nuclear attack that incinerated the entire state of Minnesota, our boy wouldn't have minded a bit.

That's because having Goodlad prostrate before him bleeding from the palm, like some crucified Jewish messiah, after getting caught red-handed in violation of his celibacy vow, (or maybe not—did it matter?) made Bronstein feel great. Since we all have to die, why not go out on a high note?

Now you might ask, what was it that gave Bronstein this feeling of strength? Was it getting even with a priest who had persecuted him?

No, that was not it.

Was it that the situation presented a rare victory for Jews over Catholics, reflecting, in a microcosmic way, a religious feud with roots over two thousand years old?

No, that was not it either.

Let me say what it was so no one gets it wrong. The truth, as Bronstein saw it, was that Goodlad finally had to admit a wound. There was no denying it now. He had a dog-chewed palm. No verbal gushing in the confessional booth would relieve the misery. Ten Hail Mary's and ten Our Fathers would not bind the gash. No Catholic catechism claiming black is white and white is black would wash away the blood. Praying the rosary was not going to alleviate the scar.

Six inches above his smile, Bronstein's fingers touched his forehead where, just yesterday, stitches closed his own wound. He was no longer ashamed. His opinion of it had changed. Suddenly, there was pride in it. Now both men were wounded.

Singer and Himmelman had played both Bronstein and Goodlad like marks in a con game. They diligently studied the drama they created. It made me wonder how long they conspired to get these men in the same room.

But I took no delight in their triumph. For I can remember a time when the two men took pride in their friendship.

Of course, being the opportunist I am, I saw in this drama an opening for myself. Perhaps this day might provide the chance for me to reach Bronstein with the messages I'd been trying to send him from the realm of shades. "You. Numbskull. Pull that damned cross from my casket."

I had this idea that Greta, my former psychic baby, could help me convince Bronstein that the will of dead Jews everywhere commanded him to act as a grave robber so I might rejoin my Bolshevik brothers in heaven free from such embarrassment.

Then, of course, there was Singer standing beside me. He rolled his ghosty eyes left, he rolled his ghosty eyes right, and he seethed at what transpired between the two mortals. This puzzled me because I had never seen the weak-wristed fool do anything but whine.

"Singer, relax," said Himmelman. "I know you don't like Goodlad, but we've made progress today."

"Oy, these priests," said Singer, "you should hear what they say when no one's around. They're so close to God, they deserve entitlement, they claim. The masses are gullible and must remain yoked, they claim. There's no such thing as anti-Semitism. We hate all Jews individually, they claim. They make me so angry I could shit."

"Relax, bubbella, you no longer have a bowel."

"I know."

"So," Himmelman started.

"So, excuse me if we don't celebrate together," Singer shouted. "I'm going upstairs with the women. I prefer their company. They're smoking cigarettes huddled around the heating vent. Who knows, maybe one of them will undress."

"Why are the women listening upstairs?" I asked, interrupting the two friends.

"Kalinsky, how long did you have an affair with this Niemi woman?"

"A long time."

"Not long enough," said Singer. "You don't know anything about her. This is her doing too."

"How?"

He swatted my question away in disgust and vanished through a kitchen wall. Singer was not the only one pissed off; so were the mortals.

Bronstein was the first to act. Reaching up, he grabbed the tape holding his forehead bandage and ripped it off. The bandage dangled from his hand. He reached down and handed it to Goodlad, who taped it tightly over his wound.

Goodlad looked at the wall clock. It was 8:20 in the morning. He thought about it for a moment, weighing the hour of the day against his need. No, he decided, considering all that was happening, it wasn't too early for a drink.

"Go to the cupboard. There's a bottle of Irish whisky on the top shelf. Bring it to me," said the priest, as he reached into his pocket with his good hand. He pulled out a white handkerchief to wipe off some of the blood.

Bronstein laughed. "So if you just came by to tell Greta that her old friend Vukovich had died, how is it that you know where she hides the whiskey? Does your big Irish nose detect its home brew through cabinet doors, or are you a regular here?"

"Just get the bottle."

Joshua opened the cabinet and examined its contents. There were two bottles of Red Breast Irish Whiskey on the shelf. He grabbed the open bottle, which was two-thirds empty, and two water glasses, and closed the cabinet.

"You know Father, now that I have you by the short hairs and could nail you to the archdiocese wall, I suddenly have a newfound respect for you. It suggests that you are human after all and not some repressive prude void of all human feelings."

"Yes, I'm sure you are enjoying all of this. And what sort of blackmail do you have in store for me?"

"I haven't decided yet. But rest assured it's going to be ugly."

"No doubt," said Goodlad.

"Help me up," said the priest, and he held out his good hand for a boost. But Joshua stuck a glass in his palm instead.

Goodlad hesitated. He didn't want Bronstein to have any control. But he had commanded Bronstein to break out the whiskey and since he obeyed, Goodlad remained on the floor and held out the glass, waiting for it to be filled.

Joshua unscrewed the bottlecap and poured himself two fingers while Goodlad's hand remained in the air like the Statue of Liberty. With no ice and no water, Bronstein tossed the liquid down his throat. "Ugg, that's horrible," he said.

Then he lowered the bottle and poured it directly on Goodlad's wounded palm. He winced with pain as the alcohol bit into the open flesh and dripped down his arm onto his pants.

"Bastard. That's a waste of good Irish whiskey," said Goodlad. He put his glass beneath his hand to catch the drippings.

"Shortstop eats dead birds and frozen rabbit shit. You might want to soak your hand in your glass."

"I'll bet you'd have a little more respect for the libation if you were pouring Manischewitz Concord Grape."

"Were it Manischewitz, I'd have said a blessing first."

"Get me a rag, damn it."

Bronstein got a rag.

"I trust that damned curr of yours has had its shots."

"I don't remember," said Bronstein nonchalantly.

The thought of having to endure rabies shots infuriated Goodlad. "He'll have to be quarantined and checked by a veterinarian."

"I suppose," said Bronstein with a chuckle. "But I wouldn't worry too much. You've been rabid for years."

Goodlad jumped to his feet. Shaking the index finger of his good hand, he let loose a verbal sally that began with, "You insolent bastard..." It went on for a good sixty seconds and was actually quite stunning in its passion.

It was just what Bronstein wanted. I could see this with my own eyes. No need to hold back now with the unblemished truth as both men saw it poised. He now listened to Goodlad's thrashing of him with a sense of satisfaction because now, with decorum by the wayside, both men were finally going to tell their truth.

Goodlad keened in upon him. When he took a breath, Bronstein brought his body in closer. He stared at him face to face, and for a moment I thought they might start throwing punches.

But Bronstein was older than that now. He had heard the cheerless rant spoken about him for years, and he moved past it. He poured Goodlad another drink.

Not about to be out-drunk by a member of the tribe that killed his savior, the Irishman gulped down the distillation, confident that his tirade had taken Bronstein down a notch. Let's not forget that there was nationalism involved too. For Goodlad, the idea of a Jew being able to stomach more of the Emerald Isle's own tincture than himself would be an insult to his ethnic manhood.

Each man, steely eyed and grimacing, focused on the other with all the strength their individual character could muster. Bronstein poured himself a large glassful and then another one for Goodlad, who accepted the drink as a sign of Bronstein's coming submission.

Of course, in my day, among Bolshevik circles, we Jews were famous for how well we held our liquor. Remembering that fact, I was giving Bronstein even odds. Bronstein had certainly drunk his share the day before. So for him, the Irish whiskey was the hair of the dog. As it raced through his veins, he was actually feeling better than he had felt all morning.

Soon the bottle was empty. For Bronstein, polishing off his half of the bottle was all in a day's work. Of course, Goodlad was no pushover. An accomplished tippler himself, twice in the past fifteen years I'd seen him with a gin blossom.

Thus far Goodlad had more than held his own, drink for drink, and he did so with confidence because he knew that splitting a half empty bottle with Bronstein required only a medium effort. Of course, personally, I'd be asleep by now. But there was still so much anger running through their veins that both were still relatively sober.

But Goodlad hadn't reckoned with bottle number two. When Bronstein returned to the cupboard and pulled down a second bottle, this one unopened, the priest realized the game was just beginning.

Now any Irishman will tell you that shooting down a bottle of Red Breast at the pace those two were setting is disrespectful to the spirit. Actually, if asked individually, they might even agree that it's comparable to premature ejaculation.

It dawned on Goodlad that Bronstein was baiting him. If he didn't get Bronstein talking and hence slow down the pace, he might soon be too shit-faced to talk at all. Plus, he feared embarrassing himself in front of Greta by mumbling and stumbling at this early morning hour while holding his wounded palm.

Something else concerned Goodlad. He had already used up some of his fiercest insults, and should Bronstein get snippy with him, he might be forced to repeat the same lines again. Bronstein, who had already heard them once might, at the second hearing, be prepared with a snappy comeback to one-up Goodlad rhetorically and hence gain verbal hegemony.

Lost in reverie, his brain starting to pickle, Goodlad sat pondering which scenario would be more humiliating—the shame of being caught at the home of a known Wiccan crone or being drunk under the table by a Jew. Neither scenario bode well.

He let his imagination run wild with the consequences of each and realized that it wasn't a choice presenting itself. Should the latter prevail, the former would follow in its wake. Thus he called on his God to give him all the strength necessary to beat back the infidel.

The men were now sitting at the kitchen table. Bronstein poured out two doses from the new bottle. Goodlad, realizing, like it or not, that he was in a contest, prepared for the end game. The seething stares were still in place. Going gulp for gulp in silence, each man hoped the other might throw up or fall over. It was 8:55 in the morning.

Now both faces were red from the firewater. All four of their eyes were glassy. Bronstein made ready to talk.

"I'm going to keep your secret, Terrence, but not out of respect, only out of contempt. Every time I hear your voice from now on, with its Irish blarney, I'm going to laugh inside."

"Bronstein, Bronstein, Bronstein. Why do you remain in our midst? Haven't you caused us all enough trouble? Haven't we suffered from your ill acts enough without having to watch you lurk around with riff-raff, stalk your son's grave, and remind us how deeply you fell from grace? Why don't you go back to your family in California or your reporter's job in Washington? Why do you remain here and make us feel the pain of our loss day after day after day?"

"Why do I remain?" He let out a laugh, and suddenly his expression softened. His eyes welled up. "Where am I going to go? Move to San Francisco? Move to Washington? Christ, I can barely keep my head in the game here. In a big city I'd become a street person and probably end up bludgeoned to death by someone equally pathetic."

"You brought it all on yourself, Bronstein. You'll get no sympathy from me."

"Now I know why the Jew wanders," Bronstein continued. "He reminds the Catholic of his shadow. You project all the darkness on us. Then you give us the bum's rush and cast us out into the wilderness with all your sins so you can retain your sense of sanctity."

"If you were any man at all, you'd do a moral inventory of your life and realize how much you've sinned," said Goodlad.

"Sin is indispensable to any society run by priests," Bronstein answered.

"Perhaps if you accepted the ways of the Roman Catholic faith your healing might come. I suspect that if all the Jews would repent and accept the sacrament and Jesus Christ as the messiah, a better life would be theirs."

"Jews are in no hurry for the messiah. We already have a covenant with God. We don't need his reappearance to prove it."

Goodlad snickered.

"The only thing we offend is Catholic narrow-mindedness," added Bronstein.

"There's nothing narrow-minded about it," said Goodlad. He picked up the bottle and poured Bronstein a dose and then one for himself. "This conversation illustrates for me the whole problem with Judaism. It is big on ethics and short on revelation."

"We only care about our covenant with God," Bronstein said. "We're not responsible for the rest of humanity."

"Do you really believe that Jews play no part in the tragedy that's befallen them for centuries? I assure you Bronstein, that

even if the whole of humanity achieves the level of consciousness that you hold in such high regard, anti-Semitism would not
go away."

"Oh yeah?" said Bronstein sarcastically.

"Yeah," answered Goodlad.

Having run out of things to say, Bronstein paused and
poured two fingers worth. Then he stared at Goodlad, daring
him to refuse. Goodlad hesitated only for a moment and then
pushed his glass forward. He got the same dose. Both men drank
it down.

"I can't believe I'm listening to you lecture me about integ-
rity, Joshua. You, who drove off into a lake and drowned your
son!"

Bronstein knew the debate would return to this. It was his
Achilles' heel. He knew it and so did Goodlad. Even though
he was waiting for it, Bronstein had no adequate response. He
poured himself another drink.

"And what was the man's excuse when he was interrogated
by the police? 'I ran off the road to avoid a moose that was praying to the moon in the roadway.' It was in the police report. Ha,
ha, ha, Bronstein. You claimed you swerved off the road to avoid
hitting a moose that was praying to the moon. You must have
been high on something else besides booze."

Bronstein gave a sigh of resignation. I saw the tide turning
in Goodlad's favor. But standing beside me, Himmelman was
smiling and I did not know why.

"Was it a full moon, a crescent moon, a quarter moon, or a
half moon, Joshua? Was the moose wearing a yarmulke and a
prayer shawl? Why did you later switch your story? Was it on
the advice of that shyster you hired? I suppose it was, wasn't
it? You recanted your story like Judas recanted his association
with Jesus. What did your lawyer tell you? 'Lose the moose story
kid or it's three to five in Stillwater Prison.' Talk about adding
insult to injury. The O'Shea family loses a beautiful little boy to
the wild hallucinations of the token member of the family. And

the mother, poor Victoria O'Shea... you ruined her life. Lucky for you, you only got sixty days in jail."

"I had a concussion," said Bronstein. "The policeman asked what happened. I wanted to tell the truth. I don't know why I said that thing about the moose. I must have been out of my head."

Goodlad realized that he had found the winning combination. So he shut up because he feared that if he changed the subject some of the moral high ground might be lost. After a minute, he added a little jab because he could. "What kind of alcohol were you drinking?"

The bump that Bronstein received from the windshield that night was at the top of his forehead. It was on the opposite side of yesterday's gash. Though now healed, the area suddenly began to throb. Bronstein forgot about the new stitches and covered the older wound with his left hand to make the pain go away. In truth however, it was Himmelman tapping Bronstein's skull with his index finger.

"I don't know what happened that night. Things were not going good in my marriage and the whole family was getting involved. I don't even know how to talk about it."

"Stop gushing... it's pathetic."

"I know."

"It's too late to fix it now. You're going to have to learn to live with it."

Bronstein stared into his glass. "I'm not sure I want to," he whispered.

Now there was only silence from the younger man. And his self-contempt was such that it even made me, the iron willed Kalinsky, feel pity.

Bronstein made a good show of it but now the debate seemed over. Perhaps if he had drunk Slivovitz instead of Irish whiskey he might have had a fighting chance. Who knows?

Goodlad turned his attention to his hand. It ached and was so swollen that he couldn't move his fingers.

"Now that we've settled this argument, it's time to take care of my hand. I need you to take me to the hospital on your snowmobile."

But Bronstein's mind was far away.

"Did you hear what I said? I need you to take me to the hospital."

"I'm not taking you anywhere," he said softly.

"Snap out of it, son. Your dog bit me. You have a moral obligation to take me to the hospital. That snow machine is the only thing that can make it out of here. You are going to take me."

"I'm not turning my snowmobile into a paddy-wagon. I don't care if your hand falls off."

"Before it falls off it's going to punch you in the face," Goodlad said. But Bronstein wasn't listening. He changed the subject.

"There's one good thing about being a drunk," said Bronstein, who was now slurring every third word. "You get to think a lot. They call you father even though you've never sired a child. I was a real father. I could have been a great father, better than you."

"I don't want to debate anymore. I need to go to the hospital... now."

"Call Tim O'Shea. Have him come out in his four-wheel-drive truck. He could be here in an hour."

"I can't have him come here to this house. You know that."

"Sounds like you're in a tough spot."

Goodlad was beginning to slur his words too. Though he had won back the verbal high ground, he still needed Bronstein to submit. He was scheming for a way to get to the hospital. What he finally said surprised even me. And it reminded me of that old Jewish proverb: when wine enters, secrets emerge.

"Okay, I suppose it's time to cut the deal, isn't it? We both knew it would come to this. So I'll trade you. In return for the ride to the hospital I'll give you something of equal value."

"You don't have anything I want."

"Oh, but I do. And the only reason I would tell you this is because I am drunk, and momentarily, my contempt for you has abated."

"And what might it be?"

"Absolution."

"No words from your mouth could ever absolve me."

"But what I could tell you, the information I know, maybe it could."

"So tell me then," said Bronstein.

"Do we have a deal then?"

"No, we don't have a deal."

"You're making a big mistake, Joshua."

"Why?"

"Because you are... trust me."

Bronstein let out a loud peel of laughter. "Trust you?"

"This is a good deal."

"No promises. You tell me what you know and then I'll decide if I take you or not."

The priest tried to find some other hook. While Bronstein was daydreaming, Goodlad poured himself another drink and bit his lip. Finally, the lips parted and down went another shot of whiskey. He played his card.

"Okay, here's what I have to say. While driving around Side Lake last winter at dusk I drove into a snow bank because there was a moose kneeling on the snowy roadway. He wasn't praying to the moon. The tow truck driver who pulled me out of the ditch told me that they sometimes kneel down to lick the salt off the roadway. I suspect the same thing happened to you the night your boy died."

Bronstein suddenly seemed to sober up. His anger returned.

"You beat me up over that confession," he said. "You told everybody it was proof of my lack of morality, my irresponsibility. Everybody in town scorned me. Now you have the nerve to tell me this big confession when not ten minutes ago you beat me up with it all over again? How long have you known?"

"What are you, drunk? I already told you… it was last winter. You should know that after witnessing the moose myself, I never spoke ill of you again."

"But you could have told me."

"I was too busy to give it much thought."

"You're lying," said Bronstein. "The reason you didn't tell me is because you didn't want to lose face."

"I've had it with you!"

Bronstein sat motionless for several seconds. "You priests are all the same," he said. "You'll say anything, do anything, lie, bear false witness, violate the truth… anything to stay in control."

Then he stood up and grabbed the whiskey bottle. It was half full. He stumbled to the sink and poured it down the drain. When it was empty, he dropped it in the garbage pail on top of the coffee grounds and bacon grease. He turned to Goodlad and shouted, "I'll never bow down to Pharaoh again."

He marched out of the kitchen to the front door and slipped on his boots. He went face to face with Greta's framed bronze statue of Jesus Christ, hanging piteously from the cross.

With inhibition cast aside, furious with anger, wanting to do damage, he shouted at the icon. "Why is it always about you? Three days on the cross. That's a piece of cake. I've had three years, you little bitch."

Himmelman, who had been a passive observer, felt the need to get involved. Bronstein rolled his right hand into a fist and threw it at the bronze wall hanging. Himmelman parried his blow away from it. It went right through the sheetrock wall, creating a hole and a cloud of dust.

I must admit I was disappointed by Himmelman's interference, and I told him so. For I was interested to see if the crucifix would be shattered by Bronstein's blow, or if the bones in Bronstein's hand would be shattered. Now I'll never know.

Furious at missing the target, Bronstein locked his fingers behind his head. He ground his teeth and every muscle in his face went taut. He took a deep breath and let out a giant howl of defiance that every person in the house heard.

But the dust from the punctured wall went up his nose. He sneezed. Then he sneezed again. Then he sneezed once more. In search of fresh air, he walked onto the cold front porch. The door shut behind him. He was locked out.

"So this confrontation is what you and Singer have been working toward all this time?"

"Yes, Kalinsky, this is what it was all about."

"And my Greta helped set this whole thing up?"

"Yes, she helped set the whole thing up," said Himmelman.

"It's a good thing she's done for our boy, hey Himmelman?"

"Kalinsky, she didn't do it for Bronstein. She did it for Goodlad."

CHAPTER NINE

Standing alone on the porch, Bronstein thought to call out Debra's name and ask her to unlock the door. But he was so drunk and angry that he didn't want to face anybody. He turned and gazed at the deep snow blanketing the meadow. "Oh fuck it," he muttered.

Himmelman and I watched him march off the front porch and wade into the deep drifts. Though the sun poked in and out of the cloudy sky, the morning temperature was well below freezing, and all he had on were boots, long underwear under his jeans, and a T–shirt covered by a long-sleeved flannel shirt.

For walking outside so unprepared you could blame his drunken state. Yet, he should have known better. For Minnesotans, Jack the Ripper is not so scary as Jack Frost.

How many times have I heard the story? Mumbling and stumbling on his way home after a big night at the bar, a man passes out in the freezing cold only to wake up in the hospital the next morning with his frostbitten fingers and toes amputated. Such things happen up here.

But knowing Bronstein, I'd have to say his motivation was more about self-hatred than it was that Irish whiskey. He had no faith. When forced to defend his Semitic heritage before judgmental Catholics he always got scared. And why is that, you might ask.

Because deep down, Bronstein feared that God loved anti-Semites more than he loved Jews.

He made a good showing, asserting himself with eloquence and that stiff-necked umbrage our people are so famous for. But ultimately, it was futile because deep down the priest really believed the negative stereotypes he hurled at him. In addition, the facts surrounding his dead son were something he could never transcend.

An impotent rage was the best Bronstein could do. He was too civilized to resort to violence. He could never bring himself to fight. That right hook he threw at Greta's Jesus icon was out of character. Sunday punching was not his style. He saw his reluctance to violence as a weakness that thousands of years of martyrdom tattooed upon his psyche. As compensation, it might be why Israel is so brazen in the Middle East.

Deep down he longed to be a Bolshevik—to be the kind of man who in the name of revolution is not afraid to stand up to mainstream pedantry; the kind of man who embraces his shadow and is actually proud of it; the kind of man with enough confidence to take a punch and throw a punch. Joshua would have loved to be such a man. But the truth was different. He was an American, middle-class dropout.

Where was the revolution when Bronstein needed it? Nowhere to be found.

He was now on a beeline for the igloo. Though the freshly fallen snow was as high as his knees, he trudged into the snowy field with vigor.

Their snowmobile tracks led directly back to the burial ground. The wind had not yet covered them. But do you think he would retrace them? Get on the well-worn path less difficult to walk? Give himself a break from the mounting drifts and make speed? He preferred to blaze a new trail.

Maybe deep down he figured that by taking the difficult path, by being so hard on himself, he could somehow expiate his sins for his infanticide, for his alienation, for his alcoholism.

Or maybe he thought that with enough masochistic behavior, God would get bored of fucking with him. Who knows? The fool had no clue of how things work in the realm of shades.

Father Goodlad, also drunk, now preening because he had won, stood at the front door watching Joshua's boots cut across the field. He called to him. "Joshua, where are your gloves, your hat, your scarf, and your jacket? Are you nuts or something? Come back inside right now. You'll freeze to death."

Joshua refused to obey. "Fine," shouted the priest. "Stay out in the cold, you stupid idiot. It'll teach you a lesson. When you end up with frostbite you'll wish you had taken my advice."

Goodlad closed the door and locked it. Then he walked to the kitchen and locked the back door too. He was happiest when he was in control. And now he was. The image of Joshua knocking on the locked door, humbling himself before the priest's moral authority, made him feel the way he liked to feel. Except for his hand, of course, which throbbed like a son of a bitch.

How much groveling would be required before he was persuaded to turn the latch and let Bronstein back inside? Watching him accept Catholic penalties, in order to find shelter in the warm home, which still smelled of hot coffee and cooked bacon, amused the priest. Then he whispered, "God, I hope Greta doesn't come back downstairs and spoil all this."

When the priest tripped over his own two feet and accidentally bumped the end table, he sent a plant hurtling down. Its orange clay pot shattered into a dozen pieces. Dirt and leaves spilled across the floor. He was mortified that he had done such damage. But what do you expect from so much drinking so early in the morning? Dropping to his knees, he gathered up the shards of the pot along with the purple leaved plant.

Singer, Himmelman, and I were alarmed. For what kind of plant do you suppose he knocked over? Greta's wandering Jew.

We rushed out into the cold day in hot pursuit. It took us a minute to catch up. We assumed our positions. I took the point and Himmelman became the sweep. Singer draped his gabardine coat over Bronstein's shoulders and hovered above him. He marched in the middle of us like salami between two pieces of pumpernickel. So close did we stand to him that no mustard-covered knife could pass between us.

We marched in a perfect line, together, in Semitic solidarity, shielding the coatless man from winter's sting. For though it's true that we were shades without corporeal form, our souls insulated Bronstein's own human body heat. Singer, hovering over the man like a yarmulke, breathed warm air down upon him so that his ears and his nose should not get cold. It was like this that the four Yiddish souls traipsed out of the field and into the forest.

Bronstein was suddenly as warm as toast. Perhaps he thought it was the Irish whiskey permitting him to battle the elements so deftly; or the athletic effort required to march back to the igloo through such deep snow. Or perhaps he believed it was the self-righteous umbrage beating from his breast that made him so stalwart. But no, it was the aegis of dead Jews shielding him from the elements. We wanted to tell him what was happening, but he couldn't hear us.

We marched along, all of us with perfectly timed steps. It reminded me of marching into battle back in the old days when Bolsheviks were ascendant, and the knees of capitalists around the world were knocking so fearfully that the kopecks in their pockets jingled.

And those memories excited me so. I began to long for the hour when I would actualize my poetic destiny and march through the pearly gates. There will be a retinue of fellow travelers to meet me. And my first act will be to once more lead a column of Bolsheviks—just like a May Day parade. I'll be at the head of the line, honored by my peers as the very last member of the Communist cadre alive on earth. They want to thank me for my diligence. But not, of course, until I find a way to make Bronstein a grave robber. Himmelman spoke.

"What do you think is the moral significance of the confrontation we just witnessed?"

"I don't know," I answered. "Given my choice, I'd prefer that it be Goodlad walking into the winter weather with Bronstein standing at the kitchen door imploring him to return and, of course, not really meaning it."

"But this was a good thing," Singer said. "Bronstein's outrage was caused by real flesh and blood, not by old ghosts like Fritz and Hans. The drama unfolded against a real live antagonist."

"I wondered what it must have felt like for Bronstein to finally speak to Goodlad again," Himmelman said.

"It's been three years since the crash," I said. "It was disappointing to see how his former antagonist still had the capability to hurt him."

"Look at him now… he's smiling," said Singer.

We were puzzled. Why was he smiling? The Jews may be known for diligence but the Irish are known for jest. Maybe the Harpy happy juice inseminated him with a quick dose of cheer. Who knows?

All I do know is that when their campsite came into view Bronstein actually began whistling a tune that none of us recognized. When he finally burst out the chorus, the song turned out to be "Amazing Grace." It was the very song Goodlad led his tone-deaf congregation through every Sunday morning at the close of Mass.

Back at the campsite Bronstein relit the fire. The flames were dancing in no time. But without the protection of his winter gear he was too cold to stay outside. He crawled into the igloo and picked up a sleeping bag. He draped it around his shoulders as he sat in the snow chair.

That goofy smile remained upon his drunken face. The higher the flames rose the more cheerful Bronstein became.

But the sleeping bag and the fire were not enough to protect him from the wind. He decided he would wait outside for Debra as long as he could. But soon he'd eventually have to retreat inside the igloo.

His eyes fixed upon the snow shack he had built with his own hands. He decided that though it was functional, what he had built was a squalid shelter. He hated the door. Yes, he hated that igloo he crawled in and out of. Overall, it looked like a big fat butt and the portal, a sphincter.

"Yes, that's it," he said out loud. "It looks like an asshole."

Suddenly, the image of him crawling in and out of it like some recycled stool specimen hit home. He decided to brave the cold a little longer rather than shove himself back into that colon. For in truth, Joshua Bronstein was sick of feeling like shit. That metaphor crept into his life relentlessly. But what was he going to do about it?

"There's got to be something better for me than this life," he called.

I don't think he was even aware of it, but he must have been speaking to us.

In disgust, he packed a snowball with his bare hands and hurled it at the snow house hoping to somehow knock it down. The ball hit the lip of the entrance twelve o'clock high and stuck fast to the structure. He packed another snowball and, standing up, threw a fastball. He was aiming for the hole again, hoping for a bull's-eye. He missed by inches. When it stuck to the side of the entrance, his shoulders slumped. But then he had a brainstorm. He marched to the igloo and began sculpting a new entrance.

He worked with great concentration. The cheeks that reminded him of a fat butt were slimmed until they took the form of a fine pair of hips. He extended the structure to include some luscious thighs and around the hole he created a beautiful rendition of Debra Crow's own fine vagina.

When it was done his heart was glad because now coming in and out of the snow house, stiff and straight so as not to knock down the walls, he was no longer a stool, but instead, an erect tool.

The remade entrance made Joshua's heart glad. His creative energy spent, sweet sleep weighed down upon him. He crawled into his structure like a man in love, zipped himself into his sleeping bag, and passed out.

The sound of Debra's snowmobile engine awakened him. How delightful it was going to be to have Debra snuggling beside him. The very image of her skin touching his was enough to warm his cockles. He crawled to the entrance and stuck out his head. But who was that on the back of her snowmobile? Who else?—Father Goodlad.

The priest needed a ride to Holy Ghost Hospital. Only Debra's snowmobile could get down the road. Still, she had Joshua's warm clothes with her, which she was delivering before heading off to town.

Jumping off the snowmobile, Debra got down on all fours to enter their domain. But before crawling through, she startled and noticed his artistic handiwork. "When did you find the time to do that?"

"Debra, come in."

"Joshua, you must be freezing. Here put your gloves and hat on," she said, crawling into the igloo. Then she began to cough. Bronstein's whiskey breath was overwhelming in that small space. It was like falling into a bottle of eighty proof. She fanned her face to circulate some air so she could breathe better.

"I'm cold as hell, honey. Get in this sleeping bag and warm me up."

"I can't," she said.

"Why not?"

"Greta asked me to take Father Goodlad to the emergency room. I'll be back in a few hours. Are you going to be all right?"

"I'll be fine."

She didn't believe him.

"Joshua, I know what happened at Greta's."

Then he began to giggle. "Oh God, it was great… wasn't it?"

"Great? What was so great about it?"

His two hands grabbed her two hands and he looked into her eyes. "Honey, there was a moose. Goodlad saw it himself. It was licking salt off the roadway. He admitted it. There *was* a moose. I'm not crazy. Isn't that great? I'm not crazy. There *was* a moose. It was no hallucination."

She was skeptical. "Are you sure?"

"I've never been better." There was such a glow coming from him that she almost believed him. But she dismissed it. Must be the whiskey, she thought.

"I feel like fifty pounds have come off my shoulders," he said. "Somehow, I always hoped that if I got drunk enough I might be able to see that moose again—to look at it closely, maybe scream at it, or take a gun and shoot it. I needed to know the truth about the moose."

"It was just bad luck, Joshua. It could have happened to anybody."

"Yeah, but it happened to me. Maybe I can deal with it now."

Well, this was somewhat of a relief given what she expected. Now she was searching around the igloo. Debra wanted a little bracer for the ride to town, so she grabbed the Johnny Walker Red and swallowed some down. She passed the bottle to Bronstein thinking he would want to toast his newfound confidence.

"No thanks. I've had enough for one morning."

"Goodlad's waiting. I've got to get going."

"Debra, don't go. Make the prick walk to town."

"I can't Joshua… it's too far. I have to take him."

"Let him take the snowmobile. He can bring it back when he's done."

"Shortstop did a number on that hand. I don't think he can drive. But, honey, I promise to come back soon. I'll even stop off and get some Chinese food at Wong's. We'll party when I get back."

"Don't rush off… stay a while," he said as he wrinkled his brow and placed his stitched forehead against hers. They were motionless in this position.

Now I happen to know that there are very few nerve endings in the forehead. So why were they sitting skull to skull, breathing deeply in and breathing deeply out as if lost in a trance with their eyes on each other's smiles?

I have no idea. All I know is that they were having fun.

Beside the snowmobile, not more than thirty feet away, Goodlad's umbrage waxed. He tapped the gloved fingers of his good hand against the gas tank of the machine. On his wounded hand he wore an oven mitt from Greta's kitchen that was large enough to fit over the makeshift bandage she had made for him.

"Debra, are you okay in there?"

"She's coming," Bronstein called back.

The priest winced. Was she preparing to return to the snowmobile where he stood, or was she close to orgasm? There was no way to be sure. The only thing left for Goodlad to do was wait. That's when he noticed the female anatomy that covered the igloo entrance. "Certainly not the usual mezuzah on a Jewish doorway," he muttered. "My God, that reprobate's gone positively Greek."

He waited for five minutes and still Debra failed to appear. He thought to go in and get her. But the idea of getting down on his knees and passing through that vagina stopped him cold.

"Debra. I'm waiting. We need to go now."

Now their locked foreheads were rocking slowly back and forth, back and forth, with their arms round each other. It was a great mood and Bronstein called out loudly, "We're not done yet."

"This is just great," Goodlad muttered sarcastically. "I'm sitting here in the cold with a bitten hand while Bronstein's inside having sex. How those Jews fuck so well with such small dicks is beyond me."

Looking around the snow-filled forest, he wondered what he should do next. He considered stealing the vehicle. Unfortunately, the keys were in Debra's pocket. And then he looked up into the sky, and with an incredulous expression said, "Ahhh, Father, it's not easy doing your work."

Goodlad resigned himself to the fact that he probably wasn't going anywhere until Bronstein was satisfied. Christ, he thought, with all that whiskey in him, it might take all day.

Needing help with his nerves, the priest fumbled around in his pockets for a cigarette. He attempted several matches, but the strong wind extinguished the flame before it reached the tip of his Marlboro.

In frustration he threw the matches down and, gazing hatefully at the igloo, mimicked in falsetto what he thought Debra might be moaning. "Oh, Joshua, what comes over me when I am in your arms? I'm born again. Yes, it's true. Oh, Joshua... fuck me, suck me, touch my ass..."

A rumbling in his bowel was heard. He walked away from the snow machine and let out a loud fart. Realizing that he hadn't taken his morning crap, he said a silent prayer to his God that the whiskey shits that plague so many morning drunks might stay away until he reached the men's room at Holy Ghost Hospital.

With nothing left to do, Goodlad paced the compound if only to stay warm. The fire was out and his earlier bad luck with matches convinced him that heat from his own blood circulation was his best bet.

"I want to know the name of your veterinarian, Bronstein," shouted the priest at the igloo. "I'll need proof that your dog has had its shots."

"I'm not telling you," returned a voice muffled by snow.

But the lovers had made him wait long enough. As Debra crawled out of the igloo she promised Bronstein a Dr. Pepper along with the Chinese food. He followed her out.

Jumping on the front of the machine, she started the engine. When Joshua walked close, Goodlad tensed up. But there was no violence. Bronstein just wanted to kiss his baby good-bye. When he stepped back, Goodlad put his hands around Debra's waist.

"Keep your hands off my girl's tits and don't rub your dick against her ass during the ride," Bronstein commanded. After all, wasn't that the main reason he let her drive?

"Your overactive sex glands are getting the better of you. Always thinking the worst."

"Always the worst," said Bronstein. "And I hate it when I'm right."

Goodlad glared some more. Bronstein glared some more too.

"Take him to the hospital, and be careful," he whispered to Debra.

"I promise," she answered.

"Then come right back."

He turned toward the snow house and crawled back inside.

"The man's a degenerate," grumbled Goodlad.

Debra ignored his comment. She pulled a wool hat onto her head.

But Goodlad, not to be ignored said, "Why do you stay with him?"

"You wouldn't understand," she answered.

"Oh really, and what is it that I wouldn't understand?"

"I love him."

Goodlad grimaced and in a voice of resignation said, "I should have figured that out."

Debra cranked the engine and they took off for town.

Joshua Bronstein had another delicious nap. So deeply did he fall asleep that when I whispered in his ear, I hoped that on some somnambulist level he'd hear me.

"Open up the casket, Bronstein. Peer inside. Take that cross from my claw."

But then I sighed. What a ridiculous predicament. Okay, so maybe it is only about my own vanity. The man I was counting on to redress my grievances had no idea I was present. I was but a shade. And even if he did receive my call, would he agree?

Mortal men have no idea how important they are to those of us living in the realm of shades.

The morning went by and now it was afternoon. A voice was calling to Bronstein from outside. I was sitting beside the sleeping man. At first I thought Debra had returned. But no, it was Greta.

She stood by the fire ring with such poise. She had come from her house on cross-country skis. She looked pretty good in those black Lycra pants. Just the sight of those red lips made me hot. I was reminded of passionate nights in her bed when I was alive and impetuous.

Himmelman was mooning over her, but Singer, that nudnik, had only caustic things to say. "You call that beauty. In my day, back in Warsaw, the women were a wonder. This female is no comparison. She's too skinny. No fun saddling up to a woman like that on a cold night. Give me a woman with big hips every time. That's sexy. Let me say another thing about that nose of hers. Pointy noses make all Christian women look like witches in old age, psychic or not. Such things don't happen with Jewish noses. That's why, for my money, I'll take a Teckla or a Miriam over a Greta every time."

"Suddenly you're an expert on women? Singer, I thought you died a virgin," Himmelman said.

"Does that mean I can't have opinions?"

"Witch nose or not, to me the woman is a goddess," I said with a sigh.

"I hear that calling a Catholic woman goddess is against their religion," said Himmelman.

"She's not Catholic—she's Lutheran," I answered.

"Lutheran schmutheran. What's the difference?" asked Singer.

"A Lutheran woman is a Catholic who's better in bed." And I said it with such authority that neither shade doubted me.

"Kalinsky, why is it you never married this Greta?" Himmelman asked.

"That is one of the great disappointments of my life," I answered. "Hilda was Catholic and wouldn't agree to a divorce."

Greta, unaware of us, was calling for Bronstein again. He finally awoke. He crawled out of his sleeping bag and stuck his head out of the igloo. She stood ten feet away. He watched her from his knees.

"Father Goodlad called on the phone. They've been delayed. It's going to be a while before Debra gets back."

"Thanks for telling me."

"Are you hungry, Joshua?"

"Yeah, a little."

"Meet me back at the house. I'll make lunch. Then," she said sternly, "you can clean up the mess you made of my wall."

CHAPTER TEN

Greta Niemi, having offered her hospitality to our boy Bronstein, nodded her head in his direction when he accepted her invitation. She mouthed a quiet good-bye to him and prepared for a graceful exit.

Let me just say that her idea of a graceful exit was not your usual fare. Certainly, it was no hasty retreat. She always seemed to drag it out a little bit. How many times have I seen her do it? Dozens.

She had this orchestrated action, which at one time I considered part of her vanity. It was as if she wanted you to moon over her a little bit before she moved on. Standing in your presence, she'd ignore you while fussing over some irrelevant trifle. Sometimes it was her makeup. She'd pull out a lipstick and cover her thick lips with red in preparation for her next encounter. Other times it was a focused search through her purse for sunglasses which, upon being found, never went over her eyes but upon her head. They held the hair out of her face.

Despite the fact that she was in her early seventies, she was still a flirt. She'd strike poses for male spectators, perfectly aware that their eyes were fixed upon her. At this time, you'd get to stare at her unabashedly while she acted like you weren't even there.

On this particular afternoon, standing in the winter wood with no one around but her and Bronstein, she spent time adjusting the hand straps of her cross country ski poles and positioning her warm woolen hat for the right effect. Then she put her head down and skied off into the sunset.

How gentle was the sound of her skis shooshing through the snowy forest. All of us, Bronstein, Himmelman, Singer, and I watched her purple jacket glide away. And when her figure was so small that it no longer was worth watching, I felt the kind of loss a child feels when a merry-go-round ride is over.

"That's a pretty face," said Himmelman. "I'd like to have met her when she was young."

I wanted to brag to my compatriots about the old days when I pummeled this woman with sexual abandon and afterward, with cigarette in hand, lay lazily in her arms like a piece of lox.

She liked to be submissive and let me tie her up. I'd do to her whatever I pleased, the naughtier the better. Afterward, I'd go out for a sandwich. And God help me if I returned to untie her without a Reuben from Buich's deli.

Were I still in my body, I might have howled after her like some lovelorn wolf. But, unfortunately, I'm dead.

Given my situation, perhaps it's best. Should Himmelman or Singer see such behavior they might have denounced me for 'shiksa love,' which is a kind of emotional love fever Jews contract for females not of their own kind. So discretion ruled. Yet, by the way those two stared, I could tell she provoked a longing in them too.

As I said, that little preconceived fussing before she departed was something I'd seen her do many times before. Yet I never grew tired of it. Perhaps it was because it reminded me of that old world graciousness, which today is lost in this bourgeois, philistine, Adam Smith–inspired America.

For me, here's what was best about doing Greta Niemi: she commended my Jewish manhood. Finding both Jewish and Christian women willing to take my seed was so very Communist. You all take it for granted today, but in earlier times such multi-culturalism was avant-garde.

In truth, it was partially responsible for the Jewish predominance in the Red Army ranks. For what our membership allowed us was the opportunity to leave the world of our rabbis and our mothers and fool around with bad girls. And if bad guys should be shooting bullets at us in the meantime, well, that was a small price to pay.

Now, why is this true, you might ask?

Because it just so happens that we get tired of being Jewish. Amazing, but true. There's a relentlessness to it that causes crow's-feet to appear beside our eyes and hemorrhoids beside our sphincters. Yes, it just so happens that we get tired of being Jewish. Why should this sound surprising?

Is it that hard to imagine that our stiff-necked umbrage should at times also be an albatross around our necks? Is it so hard to imagine that promoting Semitic *weltanshauung* might be a difficult job? It's one of the main reasons Jews pine so hard for heaven. Sometimes we get tired of being mortals and we just want to get the hell out of here.

We don't talk about it much because there's nothing we can do. It's like perpetually being *it* in a child's game of tag. The relentlessness of it is enervating. Did we ask to be born as Jews?

I don't remember exactly. But I think I signed a release form before beginning my incarnation.

Regardless, we're stuck with it, and the only way to forget our predicament is to avoid our own visage in the mirror and remain mute so our opinions don't offend gentile sensibilities.

But at night, asleep, don't we all dream of smaller noses? How about hair that doesn't curl like a dollar sign? What about sitting around on sofas in dirty underwear, drinking beer on Wednesday afternoons, watching soap operas in our living rooms with the shades wide open because we don't care who sees? Or writing bad checks to furniture stores and beating guys up just because we feel like it? How about confessing a secret love of pork?

For me and my Communist brethren, it was what we all pined for—a carefree life of Christian sloth. Unfortunately, inlaid Jewish guilt inhibits such indulgence. As a result, being Jewish gets lonely—even in the company of our own kind. But it's one of our big secrets so don't tell anybody.

Like Bronstein, I spent a lifetime trying to step outside of my shadow. Of course, lucky man, I had an advantage. I was born a Russian at the advent of the twentieth century. I found an outlet for my angst—international class struggle. The very words make me strong. I had cast off the shackles of my small world to embrace a worldwide movement bent on eliminating the barriers that alienate men from each other.

Have I told you that most of its great practitioners from Marx to Lenin to Trotsky to Zinoviev to Sverdlov to Kamenev were Jews? Probably. But I like to brag about it anyway. The subtext of this passion was the opportunity to escape from our narrow childhoods and be big men with big responsibility in the big world.

But poor Himmelman and Singer were Hasidic. They repudiated the real world and hid like turtles in their hard shells. Their task was to hold the light and wait for the messiah. Do you know how ridiculous it is to repudiate self-determination and adamantly believe that the proper response to challenges of this life is to pray harder and wait more patiently?

They ignored the Book of Esther. It's an Old Testament chapter that talks about the plot of Haman and his henchmen to destroy Jews in Persia. The self-reliance of Mordecai and Queen Esther in thwarting the evil plan is praised. For Communists, the Book of Esther was the only morally instructive chapter of the Bible because there is no mention of God.

But let's get back to Bronstein.

I knew that he was grateful for Greta's hospitality, not to mention the fact that she came all this way to offer it. He took in a cold lungful of air and rubbed his hands together. About sixteen degrees, he estimated. When night came, the temperature would dip. So such an invitation made him feel lucky. Given his fate, it wasn't very often that he felt lucky.

He had four hours of sleep in the igloo before Greta woke him. So, physically he felt better. He sweated out much of the whiskey while in his warm sleeping bag. As a result, a thin film coated his body and made him itchy. Poison ivy would have felt worse. Yet the sensation upon his skin was like a rash, especially since he hadn't washed since he cut his eye in the shower thirty hours ago.

So he gathered some personal belongings in a small back-pack and followed the cross-country ski tracks to Greta's house. This time he was protected by a warm hat, gloves, and a down coat. The sun sat in a blue western sky and as he walked right into its glaring rays, we walked too.

"What's with all this walking?" complained Singer. "He was just at her house. If he was going to end up there in the after-noon why did he even bother to leave it this morning?"

"If I were you, I wouldn't want to miss this," I said.

"Miss what? Something great is going to happen? With you Kalinsky, something great is always going to happen," Singer said. "I can do without your notion of hoopla. It's not unlike those other bullshit lines... Next year in Jerusalem... Your check's in the mail... Of course it's kosher."

"Look at him walking into the sun," said Himmelman, shielding his eyes. "It's indicative of the plight of twentieth century Jewry. They were not content with their good lives in the shtetls, so they migrated westward. Always westward into this same sun that's blinding us now. To Germany they went for culture, to France for debauchery, to England to become gentlemen, to New York City to make money, to Hollywood to make movies. Westward, why is it always westward? In the process, and along the way, they became blind to the sight of their own souls.

"Everybody knows that it's the eastern wall that is most sa-cred in the synagogue," he continued, "the one that faces Jerusalem. But do they honor this? Do they say that this is where light originates and we should focus our attention in that direction? No, they face west and turn their back on the sunrise. Is it any wonder they're lost? They're all going in the wrong direction."

Now, as we shades came to a standstill in order to argue, so too did Bronstein come to a standstill. He, who stepped so boldly to Greta's house, stopped in his tracks when her house came into view. And what do you suppose he was intimidated by now, alone in the boondocks on this sunny, cold afternoon? Who else?

Greta Niemi.

He was about to enter her home. He didn't have Debra to run interference for him. They were going to be alone and it made him nervous. But what choice did he have? He had to accept her hospitality. The sun was descending. It was going to get cold and he was sick of the cold. He considered what he was going to tell Greta.

In the igloo, Debra Crow had confessed that she and Greta eavesdropped on his argument with Goodlad. So he couldn't get away with evasions. He was stuck with the truth and he wondered what the truth coming out of his own mouth might sound like.

Furthermore, what if the rumors were true and she could speak to the dead? He uttered the name "Adam," out loud and a chill shot up his spine. It might be within her ability to conjure up his infant son.

What if she could raise Adam? What would the dead boy say? He remembered that Adam was so young that even if Greta was able to raise him, a conversation might produce nothing but baby talk.

So what? Even such gibberish would be great fortune.

Would Greta do it? Is it presumptuous to ask? Maybe she couldn't do it. Maybe she could do it but wouldn't do it for him.

All he had to cling to was a tombstone with his son's name inscribed upon it with his birth date and death date. Those dates were milestones in Bronstein's life. He needed something more.

Now let me just remind you that while Bronstein was conjuring the possibilities of communication with Adam, I was conjuring the possibilities of communicating with Bronstein. I got so excited I gave Bronstein a little shove in the direction of Greta's house.

"Get going, kid," I shouted out to his unhearing ears. He paused, took a deep breath, and walked to the house.

Greta greeted him at the front door and welcomed him inside. A late lunch of tuna fish on toast, potato chips, and a Coca-Cola from a clear, eight-ounce bottle waited for him at the kitchen table. But this time his antagonist was gone. Greta's presence was a step up.

We watched them eat. I never cared for tuna fish. For me, it was just a vehicle for mayonnaise. But that Coca-Cola might have been refreshing. I was feeling pretty good, glad that I had Bronstein right where I wanted him.

The radio was tuned to National Public Radio news. A reporter from Minnesota was describing the snowstorm that blanketed the upper midwest. The two of them listened carefully to the accounts of the killer storm while chewing their sandwiches. The reporter talked to a truck driver stranded at a motel along the interstate. A special interview from a National Weather Service representative followed.

The report was getting really dramatic when Greta and Joshua made eye contact. They both burst into laughter because the killer storm, which was promoting so much fear and chaos in radio land, was responsible for the two strangers sitting across the table from each other. Recognizing the absurdity of what they were listening to, Greta stood, walked to the radio, and turned it off.

"That was quite a fight I overheard between you and Terrence," said Greta, when she sat back down.

"He doesn't like me much."

"Why is that?"

"I was once a member of his parish. We had a falling out."

"I thought you were Jewish."

"I am. But I don't know any Jews around here. I've always tried to be open minded. I attended his church occasionally because we were once friends and it pleased my ex-wife and her family."

"What do you think of it?"

"You know that spot where Christ got stuck with the sword? I felt a jab in that exact same spot every time I attended Mass. I would moan under my breath during his sermon, and my wife would jab me there with her elbow."

"Then of course there was the death of my son and the divorce," continued Bronstein. "I think Goodlad figured I'd leave town in shame so he railed to his congregation about the evils of alcohol and bad parenting, knowing full well I was in the audience."

"I can see where that would be humiliating," Greta said.

"He stared at me the whole time he was speaking."

She considered his point while chewing on the inside of her cheek.

"When I didn't leave town I think he began to fear that I was some agent provocateur. I used to be a reporter. I think he got scared about what I might write about him and his congregation."

"Was there any basis to his fear?" she asked.

"Absolutely," he said, taking a big bite of tuna. Mayonnaise appeared at the corner of his mouth. "Did you know Catholics eat their young?"

She looked at him as if he were warped.

"It's their collective, authoritarian, beat-your-child-into-submission attitude. It's just downright wrong."

"I'm not really comfortable with that part of their culture either," she confessed.

He smirked and then nodded his head.

"I've learned more about life from Debra in these past months than I ever did during the years I hung out with Goodlad," Bronstein said. "You know that in the grand scheme of things, all religions are backward. I think that's why Goodlad is here with you, Greta."

"You're condemning a world-wide religious creed," she said. "Isn't that kind of a prejudice as bad as those who profess anti-Semitism?"

"I want to give as good as I get."

"Is that the only insight you've gleaned from your experience... an eye for an eye? Haven't you learned anything else?"

"I learned that everybody wants to be chosen."

"Is that all?" There was legitimate disappointment in her voice.

"That 'imitatio Christi' stuff offends Jewish sensibilities. That whole concept is contrary to our religion. Hero worship is a graven image—that's not allowed. Our allegiance is to Yahweh, not Jesus."

"Well, there's more to it than that. Jesus and his disciples had revelations that the Jewish establishment repudiated."

"So what?"

She thought about his 'so what' for a moment and decided it was an adequate response. She let it pass.

"Your life here seems difficult, Joshua."

"I drink too much. It's a terrible thing to admit. When I was growing up I never knew any Jewish drunks. After my son died in the car wreck, I drank to beat back the hate. But lately, something's happened. I've been hearing new voices, encouraging voices. I only hear them when I'm loaded. Sometimes I have to drink a lot to hear them. And the next morning I'm not sure which voice to believe, the encouraging voice or the damning one."

"You know there are really only two choices in life—love or fear."

"Those are some lousy choices," he said.

"I think you're torn between the two."

"Maybe."

"What is your greatest fear?" Greta asked.

He thought for a moment. A mischievous smile appeared. "My greatest fear is that the Nazis were right. The Jews are nothing but vermin who are unfit to live... that we are dirty, alienated Christ-killers."

"You don't really believe that, do you?"

"No, but you asked what my greatest fear was and I told you. When I was growing up nobody liked Jews. The Holocaust was a shameful topic. My parents didn't know how to talk about it. That was the hardest thing. But I was fascinated by it. Could the Jews take no responsibility for it? Were they just innocent victims? The Catholic kids in my neighborhood believed that God punished the Jews for their sins. They never let me forget it."

"Is that what you believe?"

"All I know is the facts, which are these. At the middle part of the twentieth century it was open season on Jews. And it wasn't only Hitler and Stalin. Some of our most creative men, Israel Joshua Singer, Franz Kafka, George Gershwin, and Hart Crane were all creative men who died abruptly. I'd have to say that God really punished the Jews back then."

"You really think so?"

"Yes."

"Now tell me what you love."

"The Jews. The pathetic, alienated, bourgeois lives of the Jews. I'm going to work for them."

"What do you want to do?"

"I want to absolve the Jews of their neurosis."

She laughed.

"It's not funny," he scolded.

"Of course it's funny. It's also impressive."

"Then you don't think I'm ridiculous?"

"No, not at all." Now I could tell she found some common ground. "I wonder if I can help you. How does one do this, absolve the Jews of their neurosis?"

"I'm not sure. For me, stating the problem is all I've been able to come up with."

"If you want to absolve the Jews of their neurosis you'll have to heal their wounds," she said.

"Which wounds are you speaking about? There are more than one."

"Which wound do you think Jews suffer from most? Is it the shame of being the victims of the Holocaust? Is it the relentless Christian propaganda against them? Is it that they're just a bunch of momma's boys who can't stand up to neighborhood bullies? Is it the alienation of being Jews in a Christian land? What about their materialism? Is it that they killed Christ?"

"It might be all of those things."

"When you can answer that question you'll know where to start," she said.

"What if it's the shame of the Holocaust?"

"Well, in my circle we believe that everything is on purpose, and the life we choose is agreed to by contract before we're incarnated into this life."

"Are you saying that the Jews agreed to be victims of the Holocaust before they were born?"

"It's as good an explanation as any other, don't you think? Ask yourself, what was the result of their martyrdom?"

Joshua thought about it for a while. "Well, they did get a homeland in Israel."

"No, I was thinking more about what it meant for the rest of mankind."

"Well," he said, "it brought down Fascism, which, according to my political science professors, was just a twisted version of nationalism. So in one sense it was a catalyst for what historians might say is the herald of the twentieth century—the advance of multi-culturalism and Democracy."

"That's good from a socio-economic aspect, but I can tell you some things from a spiritual level."

"Like what?"

"That through the Holocaust the Jews provoked an awful patriarchal shadow. The brutality was harrowing. Yet, it fostered the whole recovery movement and promoted talk about human rights, women's rights, civil rights, religious tolerance, gay rights, ecology, alcohol abuse, child abuse, drug abuse, sexual abuse, and a dozen other bad behaviors that no one ever talked about before. Following the Holocaust, it was impossible and irresponsible not to talk about it. And it might have never happened if the Jews weren't the martyrs of the new age.

"Your biggest fear is not true, Joshua," she said. "Jews did God a big favor... believe me. The universe does not judge. Jews have been around for 5,700 years. They needed to grow and they have. The world needed to grow and Jews have helped it do so. All your self-laceration has been a foolish error. As for the anti-Semites, ignore them."

"Like Goodlad? Yeah, he can go to hell."

She laughed softly. "Can you keep a secret?"

"Yes."

"There is no hell."

"No hell?"

"No hell," she repeated.

"Not even for Nazis?"

"Not even for Nazis."

"Get outta here."

"Sorry, it's true," she said.

"How do you know?" he asked.

"I know."

Then, after a pause, he changed the subject.

"What should I make of Father Goodlad's visit out here with you?"

Suddenly, she changed her expression. "Whether or not I fuck Terrence Goodlad is none of your business."

Bronstein blushed at the sound of the word *fuck* coming from Greta's mouth. He felt embarrassed. "Sorry," he said.

A few seconds passed.

"Since we're being frank," said Bronstein, "why did you reach out to me?"

"Debra asked me to look after you. I knew it was cold and you were low on food, so I offered to give you shelter."

"No, I mean the first time, last night." And now he puffed out his chest because the conversation was about to get interesting. "That blue hand that tried to pull me through the igloo wall. I recognize that hand—it was yours."

"It was."

"Where were you taking me?"

"Out for some conversation."

"It was nine degrees."

"Something is going on, Joshua, and you're involved. I had a dream about you and I had to find out more."

"What kind of dream?"

"It was an old friend of mine calling out your name. It was very powerful. I woke up in the middle of the night, and when I got back to sleep the dream began again. This old friend wants your help. It's Kalinsky."

A big smile broke onto Bronstein's face. "He went by Joe Vuckovich when I knew him."

"I only ever called him Kalinsky," said Greta softly.

"I know. I saw a book in your library that proves he was telling me the truth about his Communist past. I felt sorry for the old fart. He seemed caught between two worlds—the old world obliterated by lunatics like Stalin and Hitler and a new world of international capitalism that doesn't give a damn for the workingman. I don't think he ever grasped the fact that the Communist revolution predicted by Marx was not going to happen."

"I think he was a lot smarter than you give him credit for," she answered.

"Well, he's dead now. What does he want?"

"I'm not sure, but he thinks he can get it from you."

"From me? What could he possibly want from me?"

"I don't know," said Greta. "Maybe we should try and contact him."

"Do we have to?"

"There's been a disturbance in this house ever since last night. I think we need to deal with it."

"How do we do that?"

"I'll go into a trance and see if we can raise him."

"To tell you the truth, it's not that old goat I'm interested in raising. It's my son Adam," said Bronstein. "Spiritually, that's the issue that interests me. Talking to a dead Communist with delusions of grandeur sounds less interesting than Goodlad's Sunday sermons."

"I'm not sure who we'll be able to raise once I go into the trance."

"Can you really do that?"

"Maybe. It's up to the spirits. If they're interested they'll speak through me. But it's exhausting. I'll need to rest. There's a bedroom on the second floor you can have. It has its own bathroom."

"Good. I need a shower," he said.

"Before that happens, I'd like you to attend to that hole you punched in my wall. There's a broom and dust pan beside the refrigerator. We'll patch the hole tomorrow."

"Okay."

"Meet me in my study on the third floor at nine o'clock. We'll see what we see."

CHAPTER ELEVEN

When Greta Niemi's house finally came in sight, Debra Crow stopped the snowmobile. She let out a deep sigh. At long last her journey with Goodlad was over. The snowmobile had just come over the hill, and she idled her machine to admire the big white house enveloped in snow with its red trim all lit up by lunar light.

I could see what both were feeling by the looks on their faces—relief. Yes, the long, dark trip was all but over now. Debra couldn't wait to get Goodlad off the back of her snowmobile and a friendlier pair of hands around her waist. Goodlad's expression was one of longing. How he loved Greta's big strong house. He gazed at it in a dreamy state and fantasized about forgetting all the obligations of running a parish and retiring right here with her.

"Let's get going, Debra. I've got an appointment with a claw-foot bathtub. I'm going to fill it with hot water, drop some of Greta's special chakra oils inside, and finish reading my Andrew Greeley novel. Then a cup of hot tea and some good conversation with Greta before a roaring fire."

"Wow, you sure know how to have a good time, don't you?" Debra said sarcastically.

"I imagine you and Bronstein will be leaving immediately, yes?"

"A ball and chain couldn't make us stay."

Ironically, there was one person disappointed by the journey's end. Neither mortal had any idea that Singer was pancaked between the two of them. The Hasid, with his ambiguous notions of sexuality, had the best of both worlds—his hands firmly upon Debra's breasts and Goodlad's organ poking him from behind.

Debra startled when Greta appeared at the third floor window. She pulled back the curtains and put a three-pronged candelabra on the sill. The flames glowed through the window pane. Debra knew what it meant. It was Greta's supernatural invitation to all hovering spirits. Yes, a séance was about to start.

Debra grew excited by the sight of the candles because she suspected that the séance was with Joshua. Who knew what kind of insight he might glean? A message from Adam? Maybe a prophetic revelation? Perhaps Greta could heal him and improve their relationship.

But Goodlad's presence troubled her. To a papist like him, the candelabra might easily be mistaken for the devil's pitchfork. She didn't know how much Goodlad knew about Greta's relationship with the spirit world. But one thing she felt was true—in romantic relationships, everybody lies.

So imagine her alarm when she realized she was delivering the county's biggest party-pooper to the séance. The last thing Debra wanted was to throw Greta under the bus.

"Let's move on now. I'm freezing," said Goodlad who hadn't noticed the candelabra.

"No."

"What do you mean, no? I've been riding shotgun on this rice burner for almost an hour. Get me to Greta's."

"I can't."

"Why can't you?"

"She's got the spook candles in the window."

"The spook candles? What on earth are you talking about?"

"Greta is having a séance."

"How do you know?"

"My mother gave her that candelabra. It's disrespectful to interfere. We have to wait."

"You expect me to wait out in the cold while Greta conducts a séance?" Suddenly, it dawned on Goodlad that Greta was probably with Bronstein. A smack of betrayal came across his face. "I'll put a stop to this."

Debra hit the throttle. Snow tore out from beneath the tread. She was going to haul out of there and lead Goodlad far away. But when he slid off the back, she found herself alone on the machine. He immediately set out on foot through the knee-deep snow, heading for the house.

"You're supposed to be her friend. Haven't you ever seen her do this before?"

"No."

"You can't go in until the candles come out of the window."

"Oh yes I can."

"No, you can't," repeated Debra. She turned her machine around and blocked his path. But his icy stare intimidated her. He sidestepped the snowmobile and marched on.

Debra's eyes trailed after him and she muttered, "How could Greta ever fall for a guy whose head is so far up his ass?"

With the long cold ride at its end, she took stock of what Goodlad had put her through. The trip to the emergency room that morning had begun quite innocently with Debra taking the wounded priest to town.

Speeding along snow-covered county roads, the spider came out in her. She began weaving a web whereby she might snare him. She actually mumbled the contents of her plot out loud. Of course with the roar of the engine, Goodlad did not hear her. But we did.

"I am going to humiliate him at the hospital the same way Joshua was humiliated there yesterday," said Debra.

This was her plan: drop Goodlad off at the hospital, buy a bottle of cheap whiskey, chug it down, and remove her sweater and her bra so only a tee-shirt covered her top. Showing off her tattoos and breasts, she'd return to the hospital and hang around the emergency room with Goodlad as if she were his mistress.

From Joshua's experience, Debra figured there was going to be a long emergency room wait. Once inside she might put her hands on Goodlad's ass and initiate some seductive drama. Perhaps she'd even request a pregnancy test? *That might get him*, she thought.

But when the wounded Hibbing holy man burst through the emergency room doors, the nurses and the doctors made such a fuss over him that he was whisked right into the operating room in front of several others. Goodlad snatched the snowmobile keys from her hand. "And don't you leave this room," he commanded. The hospital staff ignored the stink on Goodlad's breath.

Attending the wound didn't take very long. In less than an hour, Goodlad was ready to go. He took Debra to the rectory where Mrs. Donovan, his widowed housekeeper, fed them a tasty meal of chicken and potatoes. They ate in silence. When dinner was over, Goodlad spoke. "I'd like you to come with me to the high school tonight. There is something I need to see before I return to Greta's. And there's someone I'd like you to meet."

"I have to get back to Joshua before the sun goes down."

"Call Greta and ask her to take him in," said Goodlad.

"What if she won't? I'm supposed to ask Joshua to wait by himself while I hang out with you at the high school?"

"Make an excuse. This is important," Goodlad commanded. "Tell him I have a meeting to go to and that you are going to wait for me. It will only be a few hours."

He was standing close to her, hoping that his physical presence might intimidate her. She refused to be bullied. But she accepted the situation when the priest himself went to the phone and delivered the message. Greta promised to get Bronstein and bring him in from the cold.

★ ★ ★

Goodlad and Debra arrived at the Hibbing High School gymnasium at seven p.m. It was the first time Debra had set foot in the place in fifteen years. She had attended it for two years when she was a teenager but dropped out.

There were two hundred people attending a candidate forum featuring Victoria Bronstein O'Shea and her opponent, incumbent State Senator James Anderson, a handsome Swedish steelworker from Nashwauk. The competitors were vying for the Democratic Farmer Labor Party's local state senate seat endorsement. Local television stations were covering it and WHAT AM 690 was broadcasting live.

It was a given that whoever won the DFL primary was assured victory in the November election since, traditionally, Republicans were as welcome in this part of the state as mosquitoes.

Victoria, a rising star in Iron Range politics, was the talk of the town. She had always been active in the community even before she had become the childless mom and victimized divorcée. When Adam was killed she became a media martyr, the local equivalent of the Virgin Mary, whose son was lost because her reprobate ex-husband didn't obey drunk driving laws.

As a state senate candidate, she appealed to the man-hating feminist wing of the party. Brought into her coalition was the formidable Mothers Against Drunk Driving. She was their righteous champion, and, of course, pro-life groups, which Victoria spoke out for lest her mother, Mona, disown her.

Many of the area bluestockings had reservations about her pro-life stand. But when she held up a picture of her dead darling and explained the reason for her pro-life stand, no one questioned her further. Her political mentor was Father Terrence Goodlad.

Goodlad had convinced her to run for office. It was he who advised her to keep Bronstein's name in all her campaign literature so that it should be a reminder of what she stood against— the wanton morals of non-Christians.

Victoria's extroversion helped her recover from the twin crises of her divorce and her dead child. She sublimated her angst into her campaign. She was so rooted in the Iron Range soil that it actually helped heal her.

But Bronstein, the introvert, the writer who wasn't writing, father without a son, alienated member of Iron Range society, whose soul never found a home in this rocky, frozen soil, had no opportunity to heal. So he drank. And you'd drink too if you became the poster child of patriarchal abuse for the region's most promising new politician.

Small town editors, AM radio talk show hosts, church groups, the League of Women Voters, the ladies at the beauty parlor, and every motorist who could read repeated the story of Victoria Bronstein O'Shea's tragic fate. Many felt that electing her would heal their own wounds too.

One time, as a joke, someone put an "O'Shea for Senate," bumper sticker on the back fender of Bronstein's powder blue Cadillac as it sat in the parking lot of the Homer. The humiliation ruined him for days.

He felt so violated that he drove the car into the woods and meticulously scraped the sticker off with a razor blade. But no matter how hard he polished the chrome, the scratches from the sharp-edged razor blade remained.

Was Victoria's portrayal of him fair?

Who knows from fair? A child was dead, and someone had to be blamed. It was good political capital. And how lucky was she that no direct blame could be laid at her feet.

* * *

The reason Goodlad commanded Debra to come to hear the woman who was once Bronstein's lawful wedded wife, was not only because he needed a ride back to Greta's house, but also to make Debra understand what he had done.

She had no idea what she was getting into until she saw the large campaign posters hanging on the wall behind the stage.

Joshua never spoke of his ex-wife but it wasn't hard for her to put two and two together. Though the urge to flee came, she took a deep breath and steadied herself.

Victoria was on the gym floor in front of the stage surrounded by supporters when Goodlad entered with Debra. The two of them waited a few yards away while Victoria finished her conversation. Debra had never seen Victoria before and studied her carefully.

Victoria's one-inch Ferragomo heels and Chanel suit were more expensive than most of the women in the audience could afford. Her short styled haircut, parted to the side, looked nothing like Debra. It surprised Debra that Joshua had married someone like Victoria, so opposite of herself.

When Victoria spotted Goodlad, she beckoned him. Debra marched beside him. As they approached the candidate, the crowd parted.

Victoria smiled and shook Debra's hand when they were introduced. But when Goodlad leaned in and whispered in her ear that this was the trash her ex-husband was now running around with, her Irish temper flared. She took two steps back. "Oh, it's you," said Victoria, reneging her welcome.

Mrs. Donovan, Goodlad's housekeeper, was standing close by. She knew what Goodlad whispered in Victoria's ear. When Donovan cleared her throat and winked at the group, several women followed her to a corner of the room where she revealed Debra's identity.

Goodlad found two seats in the front row. Debra actually felt the penetrating eyes of the bourgeois house ladies sitting behind her from the heat upon the back of her neck. Even Maureen O'Shaunessy, my sister-in-law who had given Hilda the cross, gave Debra the evil eye.

Mona O'Shea and six of her daughters were in the front row to offer Victoria moral support. Little Sammy Nord was there with his father, Mel, a union politico who was also the evening's moderator. Another two dozen members of the O'Shea clan sat in the back rows.

Senator Anderson was a shallow, pretty-boy. When he first ran for office twelve years ago he had the good sense to pay his respects to me and ask for my blessing. So I gave it to him. Later in the campaign, several other old cocks and I lobbied the rank and file on his behalf.

The incumbent was not without his friends and family either. Though outnumbered by O'Shea's supporters, he had a union goon squad at his disposal to intimidate the opposition. They were seven tough bullies with big muscles wearing cloth jackets with black leather sleeves and their local union insignias on the back.

But as the evening wore on it became obvious that it was the goon squad itself that was intimidated—not only by the boisterous women, who in some cases were their own aunts and mothers, there to show support for Victoria, but from the fact that her father, Tim O'Shea, the retired local mortician, and her brother, Tim Junior, the current local mortician, might be the last pair of hands to ever touch their mortal bodies. So they comported themselves politely to avoid any future indignities.

Debra gazed around at the red, white, and blue balloons, the streamers, and the campaign posters decorating the gym. She stared longingly at the table set with homemade cookies and boxes of Chablis for afterward, and she wondered if there was a discreet way to sneak a glass or two before the debate.

Why she remained sitting beside Goodlad was beyond me. The snowmobile keys were now tightly in her grasp. But even though part of her wanted to run, a stronger part of her wanted to stay.

While the crowd clapped politely for Anderson, they forgot their prissiness when Victoria rose and hailed their support for her. Though Debra was a stranger to Iron Range politics, not even she could miss the manipulation. The O'Shea clan, strategically seated, was making the most noise. Half were in the front rows where they would urge Victoria on. The rest sat in the last rows shouting affirmations, knowing that polite Minnesotans won't turn around to see who's raising the ruckus. To the radio listening audience at home, one would have thought that the whole place was pro-O'Shea.

Victoria's speech was forceful. As her manager, Goodlad felt he had done a good job stoking her passion by bringing along her ex-husband's paramour.

Now, I must admit that ever since 1948 I've never liked Minnesota Democrats. Hubert H. Humphrey kicked the Communists out of the state party that year. He then went on to the Democratic national convention to champion the cause of Blacks instead. Communists in his own backyard, which numbered over 50,000, he would not tolerate. But the Black man, which numbered no more than a few thousand and none on the Iron Range, he went to bat for. So I was hoping Humphrey's ghost might show up at the rally so I could give him a piece of my mind.

Politics was the mother's milk of my life and I was enjoying the debate between the two candidates. The back and forth was spirited. Both of them were making points. But somehow the rhetoric offended Debra Crow. "This is all a crock of shit," she muttered.

Goodlad jabbed his elbow lightly into her arm in reproof. But it did little to calm her, especially after Victoria made a reference to irresponsible husbands and lost children.

Quietly, she began humming an Ojibwe folk song to drown out the political rhetoric. Goodlad heard it and considered another elbow jab but he was afraid to make a scene. Every so often she would stop chanting and repeat a sarcastic mantra into Goodlad's ear. "White people are monkeys. White people are monkeys. White people are monkeys."

The debate between Anderson and Bronstein O'Shea was heating up. The gloves had come off and they were getting mean and personal. Truth is, the only reason people come to these debates is to see if someone will be humiliated. The audience was getting their money's worth. So was the radio audience at home.

"Blah, blah, blah," Debra muttered, "Joshua was right. The bigger the group the lower the IQ. Who is that a quote from again? I can't remember. But I finally understand what he means. I've got to get out of here. I think I'm going to puke."

Debra reached for her bag which was at her feet. But Goodlad grabbed her arm before she could rise. "Not yet," he commanded. "It's not over."

"I think I'm going to be sick."

"No, you're not," whispered Goodlad. "Vomit on your own time, not mine."

"What the hell am I doing here?" she whispered to herself. "How could Joshua ever have loved someone like that? No wonder he drinks."

When Mel Nord asked for questions from the audience, Debra raised her hand immediately and jumped to her feet before Mel even recognized her. She shouted out.

"I heard you mean-mouth your ex-husband. But isn't it true that on the first date you drank five gin and tonics and looking in his face with drunken eyes said, 'Oh Joshua you're so hot I'd even take it up the ass for you.' To which he replied, 'no thanks, I think that promotes the spread of AIDS'?"

I swear I heard a collective gasp.

Were Debra's words true?

Who knows? Bronstein never said much about Victoria, but politics is politics and everything is fair game. The crowd hooted and hollered. Mona O'Shea, sitting fifteen seats away and intent on pulling Debra's hair out, had to be restrained by three of her daughters. The Anderson people were delighted. Victoria, so glib on stage, was suddenly speechless.

When Goodlad pulled Debra into the hallway by her elbow, the Anderson supporters applauded. Once outside, Goodlad put his face into hers, "How dare you?"

"Asshole," she replied.

Debra walked out of the building to her snowmobile. She jumped on the machine and cranked it up. When Goodlad jumped on the back no more words were spoken. They rode off in silence until Debra stopped at the top of the ridge and saw the spook candles burning in Greta Niemi's third floor window.

* * *

When Bronstein looked at the lighted dial of his watch it was almost nine. He put down the book he had taken from Greta's shelf, jumped out of bed, and put on his shoes. Hugging the handrail in the dark, he walked up the stairs to the attic and knocked on the door. Greta opened it.

The candlelit room had been an attic before she remodeled it. The vents cranked out so much heat that the snow covering the skylight melted away. The clear panes highlighted the Milky Way.

The smell of eucalyptus incense was the first thing Bronstein noticed as he entered. The red Oriental rugs looked new. They complemented the pale blue walls. He noticed the artwork, especially a Maxfield Parrish print featuring women with pretty faces enthralled by an Arcadian setting. Himmelman and I hid behind the long black drapes flanking the window. A few minutes later, Singer joined us.

Bronstein was surprised by her get-up. She looked like a swami. A purple turban with a silver dollar sized amethyst in the front, sat on her head. The black shawl around her shoulders covered a long, purple, silk gown. She was barefoot. She moved to a comfortable chair and invited Bronstein to sit across from her.

"How was your shower?" Greta asked.

"Fine."

"Do you feel refreshed?"

"Yes."

"Are you ready for this?"

"Yes."

"Real good then. Let me tell you what's going to happen. I'll need a few minutes to get comfortably in a trance. Then I will leave my body in search of the spirits who are haunting this house. It may be Kalinsky. It may be your son Adam or it may be someone else. It's my belief that someone is trying to contact us. During this time, you'll be able to talk to me and me to you, but technically I won't be in my body. I'll be on the astral plane seeking information."

She went still. From behind the curtains I could see that she was hunkering down. Her breathing became very deep and then suddenly stopped entirely. She was ready.

"State your full name please," said Greta with closed eyes.

"Joshua Milton Bronstein."

"What is your date of birth?"

"June fifth, 1982."

"And you wish to have this reading?"

"I do."

Greta Niemi sat motionless for a minute and then she was in our world. I could see her spirit hovering above her body, though to Bronstein she seemed just as she had been.

"I am now out of my body and am looking at your aura. An aura is kind of a light field that surrounds you. You can learn a lot about people by the shape of their auras."

"What can you tell from mine?" asked Bronstein.

"You are what we affectionately like to call a space cadet." She laughed. "You're not very grounded."

"Can you tell me something about my son, Adam?"

"He is no longer in the spirit world… he's on his way back."

"Where?"

"I'm not sure."

"What do you mean that he is on his way back?"

"It often happens that when someone dies young they are reincarnated soon thereafter."

"So he will be born again?"

"Yes."

"Of different parents?"

"Yes."

"Then he is not really mine anymore."

"I'm sorry," said Greta sadly.

"So he's really gone forever."

"Yes," answered Greta.

Bronstein stared at his hands. The realization that the child's soul might no longer be part of his, hit him hard.

Meanwhile I, the great Kalinsky, soon to be a Bolshevik celebrity, stepped out from behind the curtain in plain view. I stood tall and puffed out my chest. I called Greta's name. She turned to face me. I appeared to her as when we met so many years ago, a sturdy man of fifty. We stared into each other's eyes. She recognized me instantly. Our emotional attachment reignited and it was love all over again.

"I was hoping it was you," she said.

"I couldn't go off without saying good-bye."

Of course Bronstein heard none of this, but Singer, seeing that Greta's body was vacant, suddenly leapt out from behind the curtains and jumped right into her. That fucker... I was just about to kiss her too.

Jumping into Greta's body caused her to jolt. Up from the chair she popped and then back down again. Her arms and legs flailed in a most undignified way. Her robe parted and Bronstein blanched when he saw that she was naked beneath the robe.

The feeling of being inside a woman filled Singer with glee. A strange look contorted Greta's facial features, her shoulders stooped, her legs spread open wide, and she began to giggle with a Yiddish accent. There was a glass of water next to the chair and the hand brought it to her lips.

"This feels so great," said Singer, now inside Greta's body. "I've wanted to be a woman for so long. By some cosmic mistake I've been a woman stuck in a man's body. But wheeeee! Now I feel fabulous."

Bronstein leaned back in his chair with a frightened look on his face.

"Hello boychik, good to see you."

"Who are you?" asked Bronstein.

"My name is Singer," he said and then howled with laughter. "I've got to tell you, Bronstein, the other night with Debra Crow in the igloo was about the best—"

Greta, horrified that the Hasid had hijacked her, screamed, "Get out, get out of my body!"

She confronted the Hasid inside her. But Singer had no intention of leaving. He spotted the door and bolted in that lovely, size three robe. I jumped on his back, wrestled him to the ground, grabbed him by his side locks and started yanking. Greta had him by the left ear and pulled so hard that Singer's wild screams of pain were audible to Bronstein, as he watched the body of Greta wrestling with itself on the floor.

When her gown opened and Brownstein saw her pubic hair, he put his hand over his eyes. But he only hid his eyes for a minute because the spectacle was too remarkable to miss.

The sight of the woman he thought so dignified, now pulled this way, now pulled that way, the turban flying off her head and rolling along the floor, scared the shit out of him.

He shot straight up and seemed ready to bolt. "Himmelman," I called, "the door."

The chub-a-chub ran to the door and locked it.

Singer was wily enough to throw me off. But Greta, who had wrestled spirits before, got a sensitive part of his ear and pulled the man right out of her skin. Now the two of them were wrestling on the floor trying to scramble back into her mortal shell.

The candles in the window were like the vacancy sign at the Kahler Hotel because other spooks began to arrive. I was afraid that if I didn't jump in right now I'd have to wrestle ten more for the chance.

Breathless from the struggle, I jumped into Greta's body. In thirty seconds she and Singer would be mauling me. So I took a deep breath and hollered at the top of my lungs, "Bronstein. It's me, Kalinsky. Get that rotten cross out of my casket, you fuck."

"Kalinsky? Is it really you?"

"Of course, it's me. Who were you expecting, the Prophet Elijah? A terrible wrong has been done to me. I will not move on to the afterlife until it is settled."

"How can I help?"

"Dig up my casket. Take the cross that has been put in my hands and throw it away. Then bury me facing east."

Bronstein, wide-eyed at the disheveled female figure with the Russian accent, said, "Sorry buddy, I only bury bodies. I don't dig them up."

"But it's at your cemetery. You could do it tonight and no one would ever know. I cannot go to heaven with that cross in my claw. I'll be a laughingstock."

"So what? I've been the laughingstock for years," answered Bronstein. "I'll be happy to let you carry the ball for a while."

"Joshua, you have to do this. That cross, it's sticking so deeply in my sternum that I can hardly breathe. Take it out."

"No," said Bronstein adamantly.

There was a banging on the door. "Greta, Greta, what's going on in there," shouted Goodlad. He banged on it some more. When no one opened it, he put his shoulder down and rammed it. He broke the door open. For self-defense, he held the framed crucifix, the one from Greta's wall. Using it as a shield against all evil, he stood there shocked at the sight of Greta. Debra entered, five steps behind him.

"What have you done to Greta? Be gone Satan," Goodlad commanded. "Leave this woman's body and go back to hell where you belong."

When Goodlad heard my voice issuing out of Greta's mouth, he shuddered with fear. This is what I said to him.

"You big Irish butthead. Were it not for you, I'd have been on my way to heaven days ago. But no, you had to be a dope, didn't you? You let Hilda put that crucifix in my hands even though Tim O'Shea told you not to. But did you listen? No!"

Bronstein rose from the chair. "Wait a minute. Goodlad's to blame?" he asked, pointing his finger at the priest. He changed his mind. "Oh yeah, I want a piece of this action. Where are you buried?"

"In Nashwauk. Where else? You work there for God's sake. You're the only man who can help."

Bronstein had heard enough. He brushed by Goodlad and grabbed the keys out of Debra's hands. Downstairs, he put on his warm clothes with purpose. He walked to the snowmobile and turned it on. Debra came out with him.

"There's something I've got to do tonight," Bronstein said. "Go inside and stay warm."

She pointed up at Goodlad, who was watching him from the third floor window. "Stay here with him? The hell I will."

She jumped on the back of the snow machine. "I'm coming with you."

As she put her arms around him, Joshua looked up and yelled, "Fuck you and the moose you rode in on, Goodlad!"

CHAPTER TWELVE

God is motion. Aristotle said that. And while I never considered what it meant before, I gleaned insight into that sentiment watching Bronstein's hasty snowmobile retreat.

He went seeking divine motion to get as far from Greta's house and Goodlad as possible, and with it escape the bizarre events that accosted his sensibilities beneath her roof.

The séance, which culminated with me entering Greta's body shouting commands, the drinking bout with Goodlad, and the priest's confession that he too saw the moose, was a lot for Bronstein to take in all in the same day.

The emotional energy surging through his veins mirrored the snowmobile's mad dash in the moonlight. He was one with the machine, steering it over hills and down slopes, sidestepping trees and stumps, never changing speed. When he got to the two-lane, homebound, snow-covered highway, he drove straight down the middle.

Lunar light reflected by the snow was so bright he barely needed his headlights. His inner light glowed as brightly, inspired by Debra's left hand, which was around his waist with her right hand cradling his balls.

Though his eyes paid keen attention to the road ahead, his mouth expressed an incredulous feeling of bewilderment. I heard him mutter, "That shit was weird."

But then I heard him say, "That damn Goodlad. If he hadn't

barged in with that ridiculous cross in his paw and ruined the whole thing, Greta might have found out more about Adam."

He tried to figure out how he would write about this day if, as a reporter, an editor sent him to cover it as a feature story. He was undecided.

Now he was eager to get back to the safety of his own little home where he could shut out the rest of the world and process everything with Debra. She knew about such things. They arrived home with cheeks red as borscht. It was then that she broke the news.

"Joshua, we forgot Shortstop."

"Oh hell. I can't go back there. You go."

"I'm not going."

"Come on. You have to. I can't face those people again."

"I've been on that snowmobile all day," she said. "I'm not going tonight."

"What about Shortstop?"

"What about him?"

"I don't like the idea of leaving him in the same house with Goodlad. What if Shortstop bites him again? What if Goodlad kicks the hell out of him?"

"He'll be fine."

"How do you know?"

"Because he was asleep on Greta's bed last time I saw him."

"Are you crazy? Do you really think Goodlad's going to give up his side of Greta's bed to my dog? He'll never settle for the couch. And you know how hard it is to get Shortstop off a bed."

"Relax, Joshua, your dog will be fine."

"He better be."

"I'll get the dog tomorrow," she said.

"I need a drink."

"I thought you were going to the graveyard."

"Are you kidding me?"

"But you promised the spook in Greta's body that you'd dig him up. I heard you."

"Debra, the ghost of Kalinsky, together with the body of Goodlad, was the double whammy. I would have said anything to get out of that room. I'm home now. It's ten-thirty and I'm in for the night."

"But you promised."

"What if I changed my mind?"

"I don't know what that ghost will do but I can tell you this, I won't be having sex with you."

"You'd cut me off?"

"Yes."

"You're kidding, right?"

"I never kid about this stuff."

Bronstein went silent. He stared at her, waiting to see if it was a bluff. She held her ground. He considered what his life would be like without all the fucking and sucking she did to him. Her love made this his best Minnesota winter ever.

"All right, I'll go," said Bronstein. "If I leave now I can be back before dawn."

"I'm coming with you."

"No, you're not."

"Yes, I am," Debra said.

"No, you're not."

"Why?"

"Because."

"Because why?"

"A maximum of fifteen years in prison and a two-hundred-fifty-thousand-dollar fine—that's why."

"What are you talking about?" she asked.

"Grave robbing. It's against the law."

"Oh yeah, I forgot."

"It's a hell of a thing you're making me do for a blow job."

"Joshua, I heard the voice. I'd recognize that accent anywhere. Even though he said his name was really Kalinsky, you know as well as me it was Joe Vukovich. He said get the cross out of his casket or else."

"Or else what?" Joshua asked.

"I don't want to know."

"Is it the same spirit that's been hovering around us for the past three days?"

"It would make sense," she said.

"Can I trust him?"

"He's going to bug the hell out of us until you do. Let's go."

"No way."

"But you'll get lonely," she said. "It's dark out there at the cemetery. You'll need someone to watch out for the cops."

"You can't come."

"Whatever happens to you, I want it to happen to me too."

"Even if it means jail?"

"Are you sure about the penalty for grave robbing?"

"Of course I'm sure. I'm in the business."

"Joshua, I'm afraid..."

"Then stay the fuck home."

"I'm sorry," she said hurriedly. "I'll shut up."

"If we're going to do this, let's go now. I don't even want to go inside the trailer. Once inside I may change my mind again."

They retraced their fresh snowmobile tracks from his trailer back to the highway where Bronstein kept his car in winter. There, a few yards from the road, underneath a large black drop cloth, was Bronstein's magnificent powder blue Cadillac. He gently pulled the covering off his car. The windows and mirrors were ice free. Just then the county snowplow came through. The road was clear.

No need to look in the trunk. Everything necessary for the mission was inside. For even though Bronstein let many aspects of his life fall by the wayside, he kept the car's rear compartment in remarkable order.

When Debra jumped in the passenger seat, he put the pedal to the floor and the Cadillac slid down the road.

Bronstein stopped at the SuperAmerica store and bought a package of hot dogs and a big bottle of Coca-Cola. Mustard was already in the trunk. So was a can of sauerkraut.

There at the convenience store counter the cashier called out the total. Bronstein remembered seeing the guy last night. The television was still on CNN. This time they didn't speak.

Highway 169 took them right to the graveyard. It was twenty minutes away. Bronstein gingerly drove down the road.

But this time he didn't have to worry. With his trunk loaded down with equipment, not to mention me, Singer, and Himmelman, nothing was going to derail him.

"Grave robbing," said Debra softly, "wow."

"Yes," Bronstein whispered.

He proceeded to tell Debra about the séance in Greta's study. He recounted how she had left her body and two spooks tussled for its possession.

"One of the ghosts was Kalinsky," Bronstein said. "What's even weirder is that what he really wanted was me and my shovel."

"I told you the spirits around the trailer were there for you," Debra declared. And a look of satisfaction came over her face because she got it right. "Who was the other one?"

"I don't know. He said his name was Singer. He had a Yiddish accent and talked about how much he enjoyed watching me and you have sex."

"Yuck," said Debra. "I've got to buy more sage."

"I wonder what Greta will make of all this."

"Greta won't remember any of it," Debra said. "Mediums rarely remember anything that happens while they're in a trance."

"We have to get this digging done quickly. Goodlad heard what we heard. He might call the cops."

"Aren't you even a little afraid?"

"No," said Bronstein. "It reinforces something I've suspected for years. Men don't need spirits… spirits need men to help them resolve their own unresolved issues."

"Don't you think we need each other?"

"I never needed those bastards. I'll never bow down to any of them either. No, not after Adam. But no one ever spoke so directly to me before. Kalinsky, Vuckovich, whatever that ghost's name is... he got my attention."

There was only one other car on the road. They pulled up behind it at a stop sign. It was a black Ford pickup with an "O'Shea for Senate" bumper sticker on it. It struck them both as a bad omen.

When the Cadillac pulled up to the front gate of the Nashwauk Cemetery, Bronstein took the car out of gear, pulled his work keys from the glove compartment, and unlocked the padlock that secured the iron chain around the gate's metal bars. When Debra drove the car through, he locked it behind them.

The cemetery office was a one-story, white stone building with large windows of leaded glass. It contained a small chapel and an office with green carpet and mahogany furniture. It was where the boss conducted business.

Bronstein went to a pile of papers on the desk and found the manifest sheet. He had hoped that the body might still be in storage and that all he'd have to do was unlock the casket and retrieve the cross. But there it was right on the list—a rush job because of the coming snowstorm.

"Shit," said Bronstein, "he's in the grave. And I would have buried him myself if I hadn't gashed my forehead."

"Kalinsky, you blockhead, you missed your own funeral," said Singer, trying to stifle his giggling. "But I must admit, I'm interested in seeing what you looked like in the flesh."

Fortunately for me, Tim O'Shea was a master mortician. I happened to know that I looked great against the red velvet lining of the mahogany casket in my sharkskin suit. With O'Shea's Hollywood makeup and my hair slicked back, I looked like such a wag.

Bronstein and Debra got back into the car. The graveyard road had been plowed earlier that day and the site lay just a hundred yards away. They drove to it with the lights off. The location was a good one because it lay behind a hill and nobody driving down Highway 169 could see it.

In the cemetery there wasn't much to look at... just long rows of vertical stones whose inscriptions were hidden by snowdrifts. The exposed names were hard to see in the moonlight. But, oh boy, just wait three months and what a place. Not only was it immaculately kept, but in the warm season this earth, fertilized with humanity, gave the grass and the trees an aroma that not only filled mortal nostrils with pleasure but kept mosquitoes away.

My plot, 1917-A, and 1917-B, Hilda's plot, were situated with the huddled masses in the low part of the graveyard where the land was cheap. Bronstein got out of the car and looked around for my grave. He quickly found it. As for me, I held my breath. My goal since entering the realm of shades, was to get that cross out my casket, and now that goal was within reach. I walked to my own grave slowly, treading closer to this resting place, my own hallowed ground.

The graveyard was hallowed ground for Bronstein too. It contained the issue of his loins. The baby's marker was only fifty yards away. It was inscribed with both the cross and the Star of David.

He had lunch with his son twice a week—a camping chair, a sandwich pulled from a brown bag, chips, and stories for the boy about his day. The marker got plenty of attention when Bronstein stroked it when lunch was over, or when Victoria O'Shea came to cry.

Emotionally, he felt his best here, especially since he got to putter around. There was always work to do. It might be plowing the road in winter, mowing the grass in summer, or painting the black wrought iron fence surrounding it.

The plot beside Adam's grave was in Bronstein's name. He had paid for it, and nothing could change the fact that it was legally his. Victoria might own the political rights to her boy's memory but Bronstein was haughty in the knowledge that in death he would be next to Adam in the ground. Not even Victoria O'Shea was mean enough to dig up her son.

Adam's grave was on a hilltop. When Bronstein was there he could see people coming through the gate. When Victoria or a member of her family came to the cemetery, he always had time to slip away. That quick exit proved important the afternoon Victoria had called a press conference at Adam's grave. A parade came through the gate led by a white car.

She stood beside Adam's headstone while cameras flashed. She talked about the need for tougher drunk driving laws so the tragedy that befell her might never devastate another mother.

Bronstein, who was digging that day, saw the TV cameras, the reporters, and the photographers hovering around the burial plot while Victoria held forth.

He realized that a temper tantrum directed at those violating the sanctity of his son's grave would be captured by cameras and microphones. Making himself look ridiculous in front of Victoria and the media was something he wanted no part of. So he watched from a distance. After they all left, he picked up a gum wrapper and a cigarette butt. Then he raked the trampled grass.

Debra asked, "Are you sure you're digging up the right body, Joshua?"

"If not, it will be a grave mistake, won't it? Put out your arms."

Debra carried two shovels, a broom, a spade, and a bucket to my gravesite. She dropped it all a few yards away. He carried a small Weber grill, charcoal, fire starter, an iron stake, and the bag of food.

Bronstein went right to work. The first thing he did was sweep the snow aside with a push broom. He examined the gravesite carefully. He was happy to find that beneath the snow was a green canopy that the wind had knocked down on top of the grave following the graveside ceremony. It acted like a blanket protecting the soil from frost.

Still, moving so much weight was going to be difficult. He pounded iron stakes into the ground with a ball peen hammer to loosen up the dirt in four spots. The sound of the hammer against the iron stake echoed off the tombstones.

Joshua stripped down to a sweater and laid out a large drop cloth next to the grave to hold the dirt. It was his plan to make it so neat a job that nobody would have the slightest idea what he'd done. Every ounce of dirt was going to be replaced just like it was. Picking up his sharpest shovel, he put on his work gloves and began cutting the earth.

I got excited to see myself one last time. What a relief! I felt like an idiot for missing my own funeral.

While Bronstein worked, Debra made a fire in the grill. She took out a camping chair and warmed herself beside the fire while her man dug. The lantern needed a new mantle and she fiddled with that next. Soon it glowed brightly.

The fire in the grill died down to hot coals. Out from the convenience store bag came a package of hot dogs and a package of buns that she laid out on the metal grate. Bronstein continued digging.

"I met your wife today," said Debra. His digging motion went uninterrupted.

"She's not my wife anymore."

There was a long pause.

"Don't you want to hear how I met her?"

"Hasn't this day been crazy enough?"

"But..."

"No," he interrupted and now the digging stopped. "This conversation is more than I can stand right now."

"But..."

"Do you still love me?"

"Yes. Why?"

"I just want to make sure she didn't change your mind."

There was another long pause.

"Goodlad took me to hear her speak at the high school."

"Did she talk about Adam?"

"Yes."

"Then she also talked about me."

"Indirectly."

"Damn."

"Joshua, relax. I'd never side with white people against you."

"Do we have to have this conversation again? I'm white, Debra. Really, I'm white."

"Then why don't you fit it?"

"Because I don't believe what they believe."

"No. It's because you're not white. Now if you want to pretend you're white, I'll play along. But maybe we should agree to disagree."

Debra felt better because she'd confessed. Perhaps she was right to leave out the event's graphic details since it has always been my opinion that truth is best doled out in small doses.

While listening to their conversation, it came to me. "Himmelman," I said, "Debra might have a point. Take a close look at Bronstein's aura. I noticed it yesterday. It's not the same color as Goodlad's or Greta's. Do you see it?"

"Now that you mention it, I do," Himmelman said.

"It's got a little green in it too," I said. "Think there's any significance to that?"

"Don't know," said Himmelman.

"It's the color of the Lamed Vav," said Singer. "I see it as plain as day."

Joshua hit the casket with his shovel. "Shit," he said. "Look at this, they didn't even go down six feet. Damn, if you want something done right around here, you've got to do it yourself."

It was a good time to stop. The hot dogs were ready. He pulled another chair from the trunk and put on his heavy jacket. He ate a hot dog with mustard and sauerkraut, which Debra had heated up in the can. No words passed between them.

They ate two hot dogs each. Then he went back to work. Done with the shovel, Bronstein jumped onto my casket on his hands and knees, took out a whiskbroom, and proceeded to brush the dirt from the top. "Look at the horse-shit casket they buried him in."

It was true. It was an old pine box slap-dashed together. The mahogany job at my wake must have been a rental.

When Bronstein finished brushing the dirt from the top of the pine box, he walked to his trunk and returned with a small spade. He dug out both sides of the grave. Then he and Debra stood shoulder to shoulder staring at the casket.

"Okay," he said, "you lift one side and I'll lift the other. We'll pull the casket out of the ground." They flanked it, got down on their knees, and prepared to lift.

"Ready?"

"Ready," she answered. They groaned as they lifted the heavy box.

It was almost out of the grave when the handle in Debra's hand snapped off. She let out a shriek. Bronstein was not strong enough to shoulder the entire weight, and the casket fell back down in the hole at a forty-five-degree angle.

"You okay, Debra?"

"That was scary."

"No matter. Let's just leave him in the hole."

Bronstein took his spade and cleared the dirt near the clasp.

"What's going to happen when you open the lid?" she asked.

"Hopefully, all we'll find is a corpse and a cross."

"I remember this story from Greek mythology about Pandora's Box. When it was opened all the evil things in the world were let loose."

"I don't think that will happen," said Bronstein.

"Is he going to smell bad?"

"I doubt it. Tim O'Shea Krazy-Glued all his orifices so all that bad stuff is sealed inside. Are you ready for this?"

Debra cast her eyes around the cemetery looking for the police and hovering spooks. "I think so," she said.

"Okay, then let's open it up."

He knelt over the casket and pulled at the latch. But it was frozen fast. He grabbed the butt of the shovel and knocked it three times until the latch came loose. This was the moment of truth.

All five of us—Bronstein, Debra, Singer, Himmelman, and I, were shoulder to shoulder, on our knees in anticipation. Bronstein pulled the lid and the casket opened.

I was not as handsome as I was at the wake. When the casket fell, my body must have flipped over onto my side. My hair was a mess. My nose, so prominent, so masculine, was bashed into the casket. When Bronstein rolled me over, it had a cleft creased into it and was bent to the right.

"So that's Kalinsky?"

"Yep, that's him," he said. "Poor guy."

"Damn, we really messed him up."

"Yeah, I know."

"Don't they usually close your eyes when you die?" she asked.

"Yeah, that is strange. His eyes are wide open."

"Look at the nose."

"Yeah, it must have happened when we dropped him."

"Where's the cross?" Debra asked.

"I don't know. It's not in his palms the way Greta described it."

"Search his pockets," she said.

Bronstein rummaged around the sharkskin suit. All he found was Sammy Nord's cherry Dum-Dum lollipop.

Then he put his hands around my neck to see if it had been placed around my neck. When that failed, he lifted up my body to see if it was underneath me. It wasn't there either.

"Is that it, stuck in his chest?"

"Yeah, there it is," Bronstein said.

"It seems like the sharp part of it pierced his skin when we dropped him."

She reached for it and seeing that it was stuck, gave it a tug. Nothing happened. Bronstein squinted. "Wait, I wouldn't do that if I were you," he said.

Too late. Debra gave the cross a good pull and it came out of my body. Along with it, we heard the sound of a high-pitched whistle, like air escaping from a pinched balloon.

When Bronstein and Debra saw the emerging gray cloud gathering above the corpse and got a whiff of it, they panicked. In their haste to get inside the Cadillac, Debra dropped the cross on my chest, and Bronstein dropped the shovel on my face.

"Phew! That smells terrible," cried Debra from the front seat.

"I told you not to pull that."

"How was I to know?"

"God, I hate that smell," shouted Bronstein.

A cloud of fetid gas rising from my body lingered in the air like some vapory kinetic sculpture. It took a strong wind from my own two lips to blow it away.

"So, finally we get to see what Kalinsky is like on the inside," laughed Singer. "Years and years of un-farted wind."

Minutes passed. Nobody moved.

"Is it safe to get out of the car?" asked Debra.

"I think so."

"I can still smell it. Did any of that stink get on me?"

"I don't know," said Bronstein, "let me smell you."

He sniffed her all over. She was all right. But when she sniffed his clothes, it was discovered that a small stain, not unlike a skunk's, tainted his jacket sleeve. Fortunately, he had a black plastic trash bag in his trunk. He stashed the jacket in the bag, sealed it with a wire tie, and placed it in the wheel well. But he couldn't decide what he was going to tell Mrs. Manson at the Hibbing Deluxe Laundromat.

Traces of embalming fluid dripped off the end of the cross when Debra held it in her hand. She opened my suit coat and wiped it on the white shirt. "So this is the cross he wanted taken away, huh? Look at it. It's got four stones in it."

"Well, we did our part," said Bronstein. "The cross is out of the casket. Now what are we going to do with it?"

"I don't know? It looks expensive."

"No way, it's just pewter."

"Maybe we should give it back to Father Goodlad."

He looked at her in disbelief. "Are you nuts?"

"Yeah, I guess we can't do that, can we?"

"No."

"We can't keep it?" she said.

"Why not?"

"That's grave robbing."

"The corpse asked us to do it," Bronstein said. "We heard it with our own ears."

"I guess you're right. You keep it."

"Me? I don't want it. I'm a Jew. What use could I have for a cross? You take it."

"Get out of here. I don't want it. It was stuck in the belly of a dead guy."

"It doesn't have cooties."

"How do you know?"

A cautious look came over Bronstein's face when he realized that holding the cross might be bad ju-ju.

Debra brought it closer to the lantern. She examined the stones carefully against the light. "Do you think the red stones are rubies?"

"They look more like garnets," he answered. "But they might be glass beads. It's hard to tell in this light."

Debra stared at the cross for several seconds and then noticed the expression of the man on it. She studied the details. The flowing hair, long straight nose, high forehead with the little scar. You know, she thought to herself, *it looks a lot like Joshua. Holy shit, it even has his thick neck*. She cast her glance to her lover's face and then the likeness on the cross. It gave her pause. Then she lowered the cross from the lantern light because she didn't want him to see what she saw.

"They might be worth something," he said. With his knife he tried to pry the stones out. They wouldn't budge. "Get me an M-80 from the trunk."

Debra brought the firecracker to Bronstein as he continued in vain to pry the stones from their setting. He laid the cross on the snow, slipped the firecracker underneath it, lit the match, covered it with the grill top, and stepped aside.

Boom! The explosion sent the grill lid five feet in the air. It came straight down with a clang against the earth. Beneath the lid, four red gems lay on white snow. Collecting them, Bronstein rolled them around in his palm like a pair of dice. They made a scraping noise that he liked. Then he put them in the breast pocket of his shirt. "I'll keep these in memory of Kalinsky," he said.

Debra found the cross a few yards away.

"Wow," she said. "We really fucked it up."

She ran her fingers along the rough edges of it. Then she handed it to Bronstein. He got an idea.

Walking to his trunk, he found a pair of needle-nose pliers. He worked the battered pewter cross for a few minutes beside the car. When he returned to the gravesite, he held it up against the moonlight. "I think Kalinsky would like this."

It was no longer a cross. Now it was a bruised and battered hammer and sickle.

They leaned over my casket. Bronstein grabbed my body by the shoulders and straightened me out. Debra pulled a comb from her purse and ran it carefully through my hair, making the part straight again. Then she put on her gloves and with a strong tug, straightened my nose. With a little makeup, she covered the spots that rubbed off against the casket when the handle broke.

Bronstein refolded my hands on my chest and in place of the cross he put the hammer and sickle. Then the couple admired their good work.

"Hopefully, he can move on now to the afterlife, instead of hovering around us," said Bronstein.

"Let's hope so," Debra said. "He was a lot of work."

"So long, Kalinsky. Good luck in the next world."

A car horn broke the silence. Debra and Joshua stiffened.

He blew out the lantern. The horn sounded again. Then came the sound of a barking dog.

Bronstein crept to the crest of the hill and looked down at the cemetery gate. Goodlad's car lights were on with the motor running. He turned to Debra and called back. "Damn, it's Assy-Wassy, and he's got my dog."

"Are the police with him?"

"No. There's just one car."

"Is he alone?" asked Debra.

"There's something smoking a cigarette in his front seat."

"That's probably Greta."

The barking was endless.

"Why is Shortstop barking like that?"

"He's on the other side of the fence."

"Does your dog have a thing for graveyards?"

"So many tombstones, so small a bladder," he answered.

Bronstein considered his options. There weren't any. He walked down to the locked gate and went face to face with Goodlad.

"I know what you're doing Bronstein. If you know what's good for you, you'll stop it now."

"Too late. I already dug him up."

Bronstein saw Greta Niemi in the front seat. "Is she okay?"

"She's got a migraine."

"I'm not surprised," said Bronstein.

"I was there, you know. I heard everything. I still don't know what to make of it," said the priest.

"Are you telling me that a Catholic priest is having trouble believing in spirits?"

"No. I just never imagined that they'd speak with Jewish accents."

"All this certainly broadens one's notion of sin, salvation, and the spirit world, doesn't it?"

"I suppose it does," Goodlad said.

Bronstein unlocked the gate. Shortstop ran inside.

"Joshua," Greta called.

Bronstein walked over to the passenger side window. "You feeling okay, lady?"

"I'll be fine."

"He's up there, you know, your Kalinsky. Would you like to see the body before I rebury it?"

"I think I would," she answered. "And here, I brought you something."

She put an old, black Hebrew prayer book in his hand.

Greta and Goodlad drove his Pontiac through the gate and parked next to the Cadillac. Bronstein locked the gate again and joined them.

When Greta came to my grave, a warm smile creased her lips. She saw me in my suit, hair slicked just so, nose straight, eyes open, with the hammer and sickle between my fingers. It was a damn good look. "Good-bye old friend, I'll never forget you."

"Debra, bring the lantern over," said Bronstein.

Bronstein opened the prayer book to the right page and there in the midnight stillness of a northern Minnesota winter, with not even a minyan present, he read Kaddish over my body while Debra held the lantern.

He sang it as beautifully as any cantor I've ever heard. And he was in no rush. He chanted slowly, as if there was a musical delicacy to the words that he wanted to savor.

Not only was I moved, but so were Singer and Himmelman. For them, Bronstein's recitation of Kaddish was the culmination of their work.

Prayer said, Bronstein closed the casket, picked up the shovel, and began throwing dirt over the pine box. After four shovelfuls, he stopped, looked up, and tossed the shovel to Goodlad, who caught it in his good hand.

"Accomplice!" Bronstein smirked. Goodlad blushed. Then Bronstein, reaching for the sharper shovel, continued the work of covering up my casket.

I can't tell for sure whether it was out of solidarity with Bronstein or from the fact that Goodlad wanted to get the hell out of there before the cops came. Regardless, the priest took the shovel and with both hands, one of them bandaged, helped rebury me.

The thud of dirt against the wood grew softer and softer with the piling of soil and soon all traces of me were covered.

Goodlad picked up the prayer book and led Bronstein up the hill to his own son's grave. Greta and Debra followed. There, Bronstein read the Kaddish again, this time for Adam. Goodlad held the lantern. When Bronstein broke down and started sobbing midway through it, Goodlad put his hand on his shoulder for support. Joshua regained his composure and finished saying Kaddish for his son.

"Well, Herman," said Singer. "We've done our job."

"What exactly was your job?" I asked them.

"To retie Bronstein to his religious roots," answered Singer.

"And you've done that?"

"Yes."

Bronstein held Debra's hand while they walked from Adam's gravesite back to mine. The priest followed with Greta. Bronstein loaded up the shovels and other tools and repacked them neatly in the trunk.

The priest looked Bronstein in the eye. "I suppose we don't need to ever mention this again, right?"

"That's fine with me," answered Bronstein.

I walked to my mortal friend and put my hands on his shoulders. I looked him in the face. "For this mitzvah, Bronstein, I shall be eternally grateful."

Bronstein was oblivious to my gratitude. He looked at Debra instead with a smile of relief. "Come on Peanut, let's go home."

Goodlad and Greta climbed into the Pontiac, Bronstein and Debra into the Cadillac, and they drove the cars through the gate. Bronstein got out and reconnected the padlock and chain. Goodlad waited for him to finish. Then the two car caravan drove off toward Highway 169 and away. This time they remembered Shortstop.

And so it was done. There was no sound except the rustle of branches in the soft night breeze. Yes, at long last, it was done. The closure I ached for was at long last granted. My mortal incarnation was complete. It was love I was feeling and I began to sniffle.

"Quell the kvell, Kalinsky," said Singer. "You're embarrassing yourself. We did what we had to do. You did what you had to do and Bronstein was the beneficiary."

He was right. I suddenly felt lonely and out of place here in this American Siberia. A reunion was at hand. No need to get sentimental. The time had come.

"Do you think he'll get called for the Lamed Vav?" I asked.

"It's not up to us," Singer said. "But I feel confident that we held up our end."

"You know, I have to say," said Himmelman, "you two are a pretty good team. Singer's hypnosis of your sister-in-law and your Hilda seemed a little drastic, but look how well it worked out."

Singer and I faced each other.

"Kalinsky, we could have never pulled this off were it not for you getting rid of Hans and Fritz," Singer said. "And I have to admit that while I was skeptical of the way you made Bronstein step in the dog's bowel movement, it set a chain of events in motion that worked out pretty well for everybody."

"It did, didn't it?" I said.

"I'm just glad you got to do something positive before you left this earth," he said. "We turned you into a regular Bodhisattva."

"It's true, Singer," I said. "But it was your negotiations with Greta last night that gave me that opportunity to say good-bye. She was the great love of my life. I wouldn't have felt content moving on without that."

Himmelman smiled. "So what happens now, Kalinsky?"

"I'm off to heaven where a great party in my honor awaits me. All my Communist brethren are waiting for me. Trotsky, Zinoviev, Kaminev, Lenin, Bonk, Rubey, Babel, and a bevy of pretty girls."

"Why are they all turning out for an old dog like you, Kalinsky?"

"Because, Singer, I am the very last man. That's right, the very last Bolshevik from the class of 1917. And they'll sing my praise when I arrive. Speeches will be made. Vodka will be consumed. And merriment? Like you've never seen."

Singer raised his eyebrows skeptically.

"No, landsman, on this one, give me the benefit of the doubt," I said. "This reception is a reward for my diligence after so many decades of loneliness and isolation. I was a big-hearted Bolshevik with a soft spot for the working classes. It didn't matter what their religion, education, class, ethnicity, or their country of origin was. We respected them all."

"True, but you Russian Communists have blood on your hands," Singer said.

"You'd be hard pressed to show me a mortal nation without blood on its hands. Perhaps that's what mortality consists of. But that precious light I held so long was just like Chanuka light."

"How so?" Himmelman asked.

"It's the light of globalization and multi-culturalism," I said. "It's now a force in the world that no one can stem. And we Communists, and the Americans, sometimes working at cross purposes, were the only two nations in the world who could pull it off. It's also why we never went to war. We had the same goal in sight. I did my part holding that energy during that dark night of the soul. And for that dedication, my brethren are going to honor me."

"So now go do what you have to do," said Himmelman. "And don't let the door hit you in the ass on the way out."

"You guys want to come along?" I asked.

Singer laughed. "You're going to go to a party full of Russian Communists dressed in a sharkskin suit designed by an Italian homosexual?"

"Now that you mention it, that might not be appropriate."

"We could probably find you something in gabardine," Himmelman said.

"Okay, I'll need a forty-eight short."

ABOUT THE AUTHOR

Bob Gilbert was raised in Jackson Township, New Jersey. He attended American University and after several years in the nation's capitol moved to Minneapolis where he worked as a reporter and a waiter while raising a family. He returned to Washington D.C. in 2011, where he writes and waits tables at upscale restaurants, eavesdropping on ripe political discourse. His dining room experiences inspired his first novel, *Mintwood Place*.

www.ingramcontent.com/pod-product-compliance
Lightning Source LLC
Chambersburg PA
CBHW031101020726
47495CB00007B/1991